TENDER
Is the
BITE

A CHET & BERNIE MYSTERY

Spencer Quinn

FORGE A TOM DOHERTY ASSOCIATES BOOK
New York

TENDER IS THE BITE

Copyright © 2021 by Pas de Deux

A Forge Book
Published by Tom Doherty Associates
120 Broadway
New York, NY 10271

www.tor-forge.com

Forge® is a registered trademark of Macmillan Publishing Group, LLC.

The Library of Congress has cataloged the hardcover edition as follows:

Names: Quinn, Spencer, author.
Title: Tender is the bite / Spencer Quinn.
Description: First Edition. | New York : Forge, a Tom Doherty Associates
    Book, 2021. | Identifiers: LCCN 2021009120 (print) | LCCN 2021009121
    (ebook) | ISBN 9781250770240 (hardcover) | ISBN 9781250770257 (ebook)
Subjects: GSAFD: Mystery fiction.
Classification: LCC PS3617.U584 T46 2021 (print) | LCC PS3617.U584
    (ebook) | DDC 813/.6—dc23
LC record available at https://lccn.loc.gov/2021009120
LC ebook record available at https://lccn.loc.gov/2021009121

ISBN 978-1-250-77026-4 (trade paperback)

Our books may be purchased in bulk for promotional, educational, or
business use. Please contact your local bookseller or the Macmillan Corporate
and Premium Sales Department at 1-800-221-7945, extension 5442, or by
email at MacmillanSpecialMarkets@macmillan.com.

First Forge Paperback Edition: 2022

Printed in the United States of America

10 9 8 7 6 5 4 3

For Isaac

TENDER IS THE BITE

One

"I think we're being followed," Bernie said.

That had to be one of Bernie's jokes. Have I mentioned that he can be quite the jokester? Probably not, since we're just getting started, but who else except Bernie would even think of saying that? We were creeping along at walking speed on the East Canyon Freeway at rush hour, stuck in an endless river of traffic. Of course we were being followed, followed by too many cars to count! Not only too many for me to count—I don't go past two—but also for Bernie. And Bernie's always the smartest human in the room, one of the reasons the Little Detective Agency is so successful, leaving out the finances part. It's called that on account of Bernie's last name being Little. I'm Chet, pure and simple, not the smartest human in the room, in fact, not human. I bring other things to the table.

Bernie glanced at the rearview mirror. Our ride's a Porsche, not the old one that went off a cliff, or the older one that got blown up, but the new one—which happens to be the very oldest—with the martini glasses paint job on the fenders. We used to have a top and also a very cool chain hanging from the rearview mirror, a chain we'd taken off a biker after . . . what would you call it? A dispute? Good enough. But recently, we'd had to use it to temporarily cuff—wow! Another biker! How amazing was that? I came close to finding some sort of deep meaning, but before I could get there, Bernie said, "Three lanes over, six cars back, in front of the Amazon truck—see the maroon Kia?"

I checked the rearview mirror myself. Three? Six? Amazon? Maroon? Kia? Every single one of them not easy for me. But I've always been lucky in life, so all I saw in the rearview mirror was Bernie. My Bernie. He has the best face in the world, especially if you like strong noses and eyebrows with a language all their own, and I do. He has plans to get that slightly crooked angle in his nose straightened out after he's sure it won't be broken again. But that would mean game over for his uppercut, that sweet, sweet uppercut guaranteed to put perps to sleep, so I hope his nose stays just how it is forever.

"Can't make out the driver," he said, "but that Kia was in the back corner of the Donut Heaven lot, meaning whoever it is has been with us for ten miles on a real complicated route." He turned to me and smiled. "Dollars to doughnuts, Chet."

That was a puzzler. Bernie'd had a cruller, and I'd gone with the sausage croissant, doughnuts not even mentioned. Just to make sure, I licked my muzzle, picking up the unmistakable—and wonderful—taste of sausage. But in our business, you have to be sure, so I did it again and again and again and—

"Something the matter, big guy?"

Nothing. We were good. I stopped whatever I'd been doing, sat up straight in the shotgun seat, alert and ready for action, a total pro.

"Let's run a little test," Bernie said, suddenly crossing several lanes and taking an exit. There was some honking, but I'd heard worse. The point was we were taking charge and naming names! Chet! Bernie! Those are all the names you need to know for now.

We've been followed by bad guys more than once, the last time down in a little village south of the border, an incident involving an army-type tank packed with unfriendly cartel dudes and a dead-end alley. That had turned into an exciting adventure, full of all sorts of fancy driving on Bernie's part—and even for a fun moment or two on mine!—but nothing like that was happening now. Instead, we rolled along nice and easy, turning onto one street, then another, and a bunch more, and finally ending up in a shady part of Old Town, with small wooden houses on one side and a park on the other, not one of those green, grassy parks that Bernie hates but the rocky, cactusy kind he likes. He didn't check the rearview, not even once. We pulled over and stopped on the park side and just sat there. A car went slowly by. Was that what maroon looked like? So nice to be learning new things! Meanwhile, I caught a glimpse of the driver: a young woman, eyes on the road, baseball cap on her head, ponytail sticking out the back. Ponies are horses, and I've had lots of experience with horses, none good. They're prima donnas, each and every one. So how come some humans want to look like them? A complete mystery. But solving mysteries is what we do, me and Bernie. Life was good. I felt tip-top.

Meanwhile, the maroon car kept going, made a turn at the next block, and vanished from sight. Right away, I got the picture. She'd been following us. Now we were going to follow her! That's called *turning the tables* in our business. Here's a secret: you don't always need a table to do it, although once we did use an actual table, turning it upside down on the Boccerino brothers and perhaps also on some unlucky folks sitting nearby. That was at the Ritz, where we haven't been back.

But forget all that, because Bernie wasn't turning the key, jamming the car into gear, stomping on the gas, burning rubber. He was just sitting there, gazing peacefully ahead, possibly even falling asleep. Bernie? I laid a paw on his shoulder in the friendliest way.

"Ooof!" said Bernie, possibly crashing into—well, not crashing into, more like leaning against his door, most likely what he wanted to do anyway. He gave me a look that could have meant anything. I gave him the same look back. Bernie laughed. Laughter's the best human sound, and Bernie's is the best of the best, even when it's a quiet laugh like this one.

"No worries," he said. "We're not dealing with a pro."

Good to know. Were we dealing with anything? Anybody? When was the last time we got paid? I was wondering about all that when the maroon car came by again, this time slowing down, pulling over, and parking in front of us.

"The most amateur kind of amateur," Bernie said.

We sat. The ponytail woman sat, not once checking her mirror or glancing back at us.

"An amateur and scared," Bernie said. He made a little click

click noise, meaning, *Let's roll, big guy.* We hopped out, me actually hopping right over my closed door and Bernie just getting out in the normal human way, which was our usual MO. But I'd seen him hop out—for example, the time with that whole cluster of sidewinders under the driver's seat—so he had it in him.

We walked up to the maroon car. The way we do this, amateur—whatever that happens to be—or not, is Bernie on the driver's side and me on the other. How many perps have taken one look at Bernie and then dived out the passenger-side door, only to get a real big surprise—namely, me? But that didn't happen with the ponytail woman. Instead, she went on sitting there, hands holding the wheel tight.

Bernie leaned down and spoke through her open window. "We've got to stop meeting like this," he said.

Whoa. We'd met this woman before? One thing about my nose: it remembers the smell of everyone I've ever met, and it did not remember this woman. She had an interesting smell, a bit piney, that made me think of New Mexico, which we'd visited on several cases, picking up a speeding ticket every time. Through the open passenger-side window, I was getting my first clear look at her face. A young face, but not quite as young as the face of a college kid. In the faces of college kids, you can still see a bit of the little kid face that was. There was no little kid left in the ponytail woman's face, which was turning pink. Her eyes were big and the brightest blue I'd ever seen, actually the color of this morning's sky, like the sky was shining inside her.

"Sorry," Bernie said. "Bad joke."

I'm sure it was a very good joke, although it's true the woman hadn't laughed. But I was glad to hear it was a joke and we hadn't met before, because now I didn't need to choose between my nose and Bernie's word, which would have been the hardest choice of my life. Stay away from hard choices if you want to be happy.

The woman looked up at Bernie. Something about her face, turned up like that, made an impression on him. I can feel those impressions happening in Bernie, but what they are exactly is something I find out later or not at all.

"No, it was a good joke," she said, agreeing with me. I was already liking her, and now I liked her more. "I feel so stupid."

"Why?" said Bernie.

The woman's eyes shifted the way human eyes sometimes do when the mind is delivering news. "Because I thought I was in control of the situation and I wasn't," she said. "The usual story."

"Not your fault," he said. "We're professionals when it comes to following and being followed."

She shot me a quick glance. "You meaning you and Chet?" she said.

Bernie smiled. "That's us," he said. "Chet and Bernie, in that order." He handed her our card, the one with the flowers. Instead of flowers, why not the .38 Special? But the card was designed by Suzie, back when she and Bernie were together, so that was that. As the ponytail woman took the card, sunlight flashed on a diamond ring on one of her fingers. I knew diamond rings from an unfortunate incident where a former client's diamond ring had gotten buried somewhere in her garden, the precise location proving a bit elusive. Buried things have a way of changing positions underground, one of those things you learn in this business. But the point was that the ponytail woman's ring was bigger than the one I'd—the one that had somehow gone missing, I hoped not forever. Meanwhile, Bernie, too, noticed the ring, and the ponytail woman noticed him noticing it and quickly withdrew her hand and laid it in her lap.

"And your name, if you don't mind me asking?" Bernie said.

"I—I'm not ready," she said. She glanced around. "Is there somewhere we can talk?"

Bernie gestured toward the park. There were some benches nearby, all empty. Bench-sitters often chowed down on snacks—or even a whole meal!—meaning under benches is good territory if scraps are an interest of yours. I was already leaning that way when the woman shook her head.

"Somewhere private," she said.

"We could go to our place," said Bernie.

"Oh no," the woman said. "Isn't there somewhere where no one . . ." She went silent.

"Who are you afraid of?" Bernie said.

"I didn't say I was afraid of anyone."

Bernie nodded. He has many nods, meaning all sorts of things. This particular nod—just a tiny movement, eyes with an inward look—meant he wasn't buying it.

"How about you come with us?" he said. "We can just drive around and talk."

She glanced back at the Porsche. "Where will I sit?"

"In front, of course," Bernie said. "Chet'll be happy on the shelf in back."

Was . . . was there some other Chet suddenly in the picture? What a strange thought! There was only one Chet, and that one Chet, I knew for a fact, would not be happy on the shelf, not now, not yesterday, not tomorrow or whatever other days were out there.

The woman got out of her car and turned toward the Porsche. By that time, I was around to her side—to greet her, you might say. She sort of bumped into me, a gentle bump. How anxious she was! I nuzzled against her. Don't ask me why.

She looked down at me, her eyes big and oh so blue. Then she touched my head, her hand a little unsteady.

"Hop in, um, ah . . . ," Bernie said.

"Mavis." She climbed in, only to find that I was already in the shotgun seat myself! How the hell had that happened? I had no memory whatsoever of getting in the car. Life was full of surprises, most of them very nice. And here was another: Mavis squeezed past and took her rightful place on the little shelf without a word of complaint. I was liking her more and more, and gave her one of my friendliest looks, showing pretty much all my teeth.

Bernie sat in the driver's seat. "Mavis what?" he said.

At that moment, Mavis noticed something on the floor. She picked it up: a small rectangle—about the size of a bumper sticker—with writing on it. We already had a Max's Memphis

Ribs bumper sticker on the car, and this one on the floor didn't look nearly as interesting, lacking a picture of ribs glistening on a hot grill. But this new bumper sticker was a big problem. How had it gotten into the car? I'm in charge of security, and that means I track every single thing in the car, coming and going, and I had no memory of this new bumper sticker.

Mavis didn't look happy about it either. Her eyes narrowed and then filled with fear. The smell of her fear filled the car, and very quickly. She gazed—almost in horror—at the back of Bernie's head.

"Meaning, what's your last name?" Bernie said, not turning around.

"Oh my god!" Mavis said. "What the hell am I doing?" She dropped the bumper sticker back on the floor, rose, and jumped out of the car.

"Mavis?"

She ran to the Kia, an unsteady kind of run, almost losing her balance. What was going on? Was she a client? This wasn't normal client behavior—maybe later in a case, yes, but not at the very start. She got in her car and slammed the door.

"Wait!" Bernie called.

Mavis took off, pulling into the street and speeding down the block. Bernie! Let's go! On the stick!

But Bernie just sat there. "What happened?" he said. He watched until Mavis was out of sight. "Any point in chasing after her?"

Any point in chasing after somebody? I didn't understand the question.

"We'll only scare her more," Bernie said. "Easy there, Chet."

Uh-oh. I seemed to be up on my hind legs, my front paws on Bernie's shoulder, my face kind of in his. I got that straightened out, and pronto.

"She'll get in touch when she's ready." He winked at me. I love the human wink—one of their very best moves—and Bernie's is off the charts. "And if not, we've got her plate number."

We did? Wow. He took out a pen and wrote on the base of his

thumb. That was Bernie. Just when you think he's done amazing you, he amazes you again.

"Did you notice that diamond ring?" he said as we drove off.

For sure! Am I a pro or not?

"Looked like an engagement ring, but not worn on the ring finger. What's that about?"

Ring finger? The ring had been on one of her fingers, no doubt in my mind. How else could she have worn it? I gave Bernie a long look, which he missed, his eyes on the road. No one could be amazing 24-7. I decided we were in a little dip between amazements.

Home is our place on Mesquite Road, the best street in the Valley, which may be in Arizona, but don't count on that. On either side live the nicest neighbors anyone could ask for, except for our neighbor on the fence side, old man Heydrich. He's not a fan of the nation within the nation—which is what Bernie calls me and my kind—and spends a lot of time watering his bright green lawn even though Bernie has mentioned the aquifer problem on more than one occasion. On the other side, the driveway side, live Mr. and Mrs. Parsons—a couple even older than old man Heydrich and maybe not doing too well—and Iggy. Iggy's my best pal. The fun we used to have, in the days before the electric-fence salesman paid them a visit! Their lawn is like ours, the desert kind, or even more so. If you didn't know better, you might think it's nothing but dirt and rocks, but we know better, me and Bernie. The reason I'm possibly going on a bit about their yards is that both Mr. Heydrich and Mr. Parsons were standing outside as we drove up, a very unusual situation in the late summer heat.

We turned in to the driveway and got out of the car. Mr. Heydrich and Mr. Parsons were both hammering signs into their yards, one red, one blue—or possibly one orange and one green, since I can't always be trusted when it comes to colors, according to Bernie—and as they hammered, they exchanged glares and hammered even harder.

"Oh, god," Bernie said in a low voice. We went into the house.

Normally after a hard day's work or even not a hard one, like to-day, we'd grab a drink first thing, bourbon or a beer for Bernie and water for me, but now we lingered by the window, me because he was doing it, and Bernie for reasons of his own. Outside, old man Heydrich and Mr. Parsons hammered and glared, hammered and glared. Then from the Parsonses' house came Iggy's amazingly high-pitched yip-yip-yip. I trotted over to the side window, and there was Iggy, front paws against the glass of his side window, yipping in fury. I knew exactly what Iggy wanted to do—namely, burst out of there and show old man Heydrich what was what—but the Parsonses could never get the electric fence working right, so these days, Iggy stayed inside. Was it up to me as a friend to take care of the old man Heydrich problem? All I had to do was go to the door and Bernie would let me out. I could actually let myself out. Bernie and I had done a lot of work on door opening and I'd finally mastered the round-type knob just the other night while Bernie was sleeping. So he didn't know! Only I knew! What an exciting feeling! I started forming plans for old man Heydrich, but before they took shape, Bernie backed away from the window, shook his head, and said, "Politics, Chet. And the election's not for a whole year."

Politics? A new one on me. Was politics the glaring and hammering or the yip-yip-yipping? Or possibly all at once? Glaring, hammering, yip-yip-yipping? Politics sounded alarm-ing. I hurried into the kitchen and lapped up all the water in my bowl. Bernie refilled it and cracked open a beer. He sat down and put his feet up. I lay down and stretched my feet out. We spend a lot of very happy time like that.

The phone rang. The phone at our place is usually on speaker, but I can hear the other end perfectly well even if it's not. My hearing's not like yours, no offense.

"Hello, Bernie," said Mr. Parsons. "Hope I'm not disturbing you."

"Not at all. How are you and Mrs. Parsons doing?"

"Neither hospitalized at the moment," said Mr. Parsons. "Doesn't get much better than that."

Mr. Parsons laughed. So did Bernie. I missed the funny part, but I don't worry about things like that.

"Anything I can do for you?" Bernie said.

"In a way," said Mr. Parsons. "And no pressure, but you may have noticed our sign. It's for Les Erlanger. He's running for Senate, and Mrs. Parsons and I are supporting him. We happen to have an extra sign."

The look on Bernie's face—a lovely after-laughing look—changed to no expression at all. "I'll bear that in mind," Bernie said.

"Much obliged," said Mr. Parsons.

They said goodbye. Right away, the phone rang again.

"Mr. Little? Heydrich, here. Your neighbor."

"Yes?"

"Do you have any political affiliation, Mr. Little?"

"Not that I discuss at random."

Silence. Bernie looked at me. His face changed again, started to look like it did when fun was in the air. I popped right up.

"I'm supporting Senator Wray in the election," Heydrich said. "I have an extra sign you can have for free."

"Is Wray charging for his signs?"

"Only the special three-color ones. Which happens to be what I want to give you for no cost."

"The election's a year away."

"In one sense, possibly. But you may have noticed that in a big-picture sense we are in a permanent state of election."

"That's depressing."

"Even more depressing is the prospect of an Erlanger victory in the coming battle."

"We'll be the DMZ," Bernie told him.

"That does not exist," said old man Heydrich. "If the sign is too . . . too vivid, perhaps you'd care to display the bumper sticker I left you."

"Bumper sticker?"

"I happened to have one with me on my walk yesterday. I took the liberty of dropping it into your car."

"Thanks," Bernie said. "I'll take the liberty of returning it to you."

"Not necessary," said Heydrich. "I have a big supply."

Click.

We went out to the car. Bernie leaned in, fished around in the back, found the bumper sticker where Mavis had dropped it. Bernie read what was on it: "'Wray's OK!'" Back inside, he tossed it in the trash and downed a big slug of beer. "Is monarchy better?"

I couldn't help him with that. The sun set at last, and things cooled down a bit. We went out to the back patio and sat by the swan fountain, all that Leda left behind after the divorce. We hardly ever ran the water anymore on account of the evaporation issue, whatever that was, but now Bernie turned it on, and we listened to the beautiful sounds, a sort of music with water as the instrument. Bernie had another beer. He kept the phone in his lap, kind of unusual, and glanced at it once or twice.

"I thought she'd be in touch."

Oh? Who would that be? Leda? Not likely. We were more likely to hear from Charlie, Bernie and Leda's kid, now with us only on some weekends and holidays, or even Malcolm, Leda's new husband with the very long toes, who'd become sort of a pal. Then there was Suzie, at one time Bernie's girlfriend and a likely caller, but now married to Jacques Smallian, busy with some start-up they were working on, and now unlikely. So who?

Bernie gazed at the writing on the base of his thumb, sipped his beer, gazed, sipped. At last, he picked up the phone.

"Rick?" he said.

"Gone for the day," said Lieutenant Rick Torres, our buddy in Missing Persons.

"I'm a taxpayer," Bernie said. "I pay your salary."

"Now you tell me. All this time, I had no idea why the wolf was at the door."

Oh no! Rick was a buddy. We had to do something and fast!

"Can you run a plate for me?" Bernie read the writing on his thumb.

Running a plate? On a wolf case? I was lost.

A short silence on Rick's end and then: "Maroon Kia registered to Johnnie Lee Goetz, 1429E Aztec Creek Road, Agua Negra."

"I owe you," Bernie said.

"The tab is getting long," said Rick.

"I can get you a three-color Senator Wray sign."

"You know him?"

"Nope. You?"

"Not exactly."

"What does that mean?"

"Buy me a drink some time."

"You got it."

Bernie hung up. "Not exactly" meant buying Rick a drink? But how would he get outside, what with the wolf? Before I could even start on any of that, Bernie rose in the quick way that meant we were on the move, which is when I'm at my best. Who's luckier than me? There was some confusion at the door, but I ended up being first.

Two

"Johnnie Lee Goetz," Bernie said. "But the name we have is Mavis. So therefore . . ."

We followed the last of the daylight on the Crosstown Freeway, housing developments going on and on, each one darkening as we passed by, like . . . like we were bringing the night. What a thought, although perhaps a little scary, so I hoped it wouldn't come again. Meanwhile, I waited for Bernie to continue with the so-therefore, so-therefores being his department and me bringing other things to the table.

"None of this was here when I was a kid," Bernie said.

Was that part of the so-therefore? So-therefores were pretty much always unpredictable in my experience.

We took an exit and soon went over a bridge. Down below was a dry riverbed. "Agua Negra," Bernie said. "We used to come out and water-ski on weekends." He pointed. "Where that strip mall is now was the boathouse. Gone. And so is the water."

Uh-oh. The so-therefore was about water? I should have known. Water was a big problem in these parts. What could I do about it? I searched my mind and came up with only one idea, involving peeing out the window, something I'd actually never tried and might prove kind of tricky, what with the car moving and all. But I still wanted to help out, so I laid my paw on Bernie's knee, just letting him know everything would be fine. At the same time, we happened to speed up—and big-time!—just surging like the message about things being fine had gotten through to the car. Wow! The car is a machine, of course—machine smells being some of the most obvious ones out there—but isn't it sort of alive in a way that—

"Chet!"

Speed always gets Bernie excited. I'm the same way. He steered us back onto our side of the road and gave me a quick look. Hard to read, but at least it wasn't gloomy anymore. Hey! Was speed the solution to the water problem? Well, well. Bringing the night and solving the water problem. I was on top of my game.

We turned onto a street lined on both sides with clusters of low, sand-colored buildings with tile roofs. "Condos, Chet. One day there'll be condos nonstop from here to LA." Was that good or bad? Maybe it would help if I knew what LA was, but I did not. The problem vanished from my mind. We pulled into a circular drive and parked at the end of one of the sand-colored clusters.

"1429E Aztec Creek Road," Bernie said, "although there's no Aztec Creek and never was."

We went to the door and knocked, Bernie doing the actual knocking and me standing beside him, nice and tall. Aside from the nice and tall part, you might have thought I was doing zip, but you would have been wrong. I don't blame you because there was no seeing what I was up to—namely, sniffing up all the smells that came from the other side of the door. Not much in the way of cooking or food aromas of any kind, except for yogurt, always a disappointment, and lots of the usual cleaning product smells you always get in these situations, including dry cleaning smells, which never make me want to stick around. Mixed into that—and quickly unmixed by my nose into separate streams—was lots of the scent of two different women, one of whom I knew—Mavis, the ponytailed driver of the maroon Kia, the woman with the piney smell and the big blue eyes. When you get lots of someone's scent at the door, you can be pretty sure they live there. But we haven't even come to the main smell yet, overwhelming all the others, a certain strong musky-plus-pee odor that meant a male ferret was in the house. I've had some experience with ferrets, both the indoor kind and the outdoor kind, and every single one of them had to be taught a lesson. The fur on the back of my neck stood up, all on its own. I was good to go.

Bernie raised his hand to knock again. Was it possible he

didn't hear someone coming to open it—a woman, actually, not big, barefoot? I glanced at Bernie's ears: not tiny for a human, not at all—and very nice looking, in my opinion—but was that all they were for? Just stuck on his head for beauty? I liked almost every human I'd ever met—even the perps and gangbangers—but I'd never want to trade places with any of them. Well, maybe Bernie. Because . . . because then I'd have me to hang out with! A rather confusing thought. I was still lost in it when the door opened.

A young woman looked out. Not Mavis, a fact I noticed only in passing. What caught my attention was the ferret on her shoulder. And I'd caught his attention, no doubt about that. He showed me his teeth first thing, just like every ferret I'd ever met. I showed him mine. You'd have done the same. His tiny eyes burned hot. Would playing a game of some sort get us off to a better start? For example, how about the grabbing-the-little-fella-by-his-collar—a velvet collar, by the way, velvet being a material I knew well from an incident with a tapestry, best forgotten—and-flipping-him-up-to-the-ceiling game? Who doesn't like being flipped up to the ceiling? Although I don't know personally on account of who could flip the likes of me that high, or anywhere at all? Ah, the likes of me! A hundred-plus pounder, by the way. Once, I'd flipped a bunny rabbit name of Ursula—true, not a ferret—so high that I'd had time to run over and catch her in midair and flip her up again! The look on her face! So when would be a good time to get things under way with my new ferret buddy? Now, maybe, like right away, this very—

I felt Bernie's hand on my back, not heavy, just there. Perhaps a slight wait before the gaming portion of our visit was the way to go. The joy is in the anticipation, as a safecracker name of Sneaky Keats, now sporting an orange jumpsuit, had once explained to us.

"Hello?" said the young woman.

This young woman might have been a bit older than Mavis, or perhaps she just seemed that way because her face was harder. It was also tanned, as were her arms, strong arms, and her hands looked strong, too. She smelled of the desert, a smell I like very

much. Her hair was long on one side and shaved on the other. You
see that kind of look plenty in these parts, but Bernie's still not
used to it. He didn't say or show anything, but I could feel a little
shift inside him, like he missed a step. Don't be surprised. We're
partners, after all.

"Uh, hi," he said. "We're looking for Johnnie Lee Goetz."

The woman peered past us to the street, where nothing was
going on. Then her gaze went to me and finally to Bernie. He
smiled, just a quick, small, friendly smile.

"That's me," the woman said, her voice not unfriendly but not
friendly either.

"Nice to meet you. I'm Bernie Little, and this is Chet."

I happened to be watching her eyes—sort of greenish. Sometimes when perps have heard of us, their eyes shift when they
realize we're right there in front of them and the end is near.
Johnnie Lee Goetz's eyes did not shift, although I thought I felt
something inside her go still. Before I could even try to make
sense of that, the ferret, who'd been lying flat on her shoulder, sat
up suddenly and squeaked. Did that mean the ferret was a perp
and Johnnie Lee was not? Any reason that didn't make sense?
Not that I could see. In my mind, I got ready to do what had to
be done.

"Griffie's not comfortable around dogs," the woman said. "Especially aggressive ones."

"The cute little guy's got nothing to worry about," said Bernie.
"Chet's not aggressive, are you, big guy?"

"Then why is his mouth open like that? His teeth are huge."

"That's just his smile. Maybe ease up on it a bit, Chet."

Ease up? On what exactly? Before I could figure that out, I
realized I'd snagged my lip on one of my teeth. I got everything
squared away and pronto. You've got to look the part in a job like
mine.

"Better, Ms. Goetz?" Bernie said.

"Not really."

Bernie laughed like Ms. Goetz had made a joke. She wasn't
joining in. "Okay to call you Johnnie Lee?" Bernie said.

Ms. Goetz shrugged.

"Well, Johnnie Lee—a great name, by the way," Bernie said, "I was wondering if your car's around. The maroon Kia."

Despite how—what would you call it? Charming? Close enough. Despite how charming Bernie was being, Johnnie Lee was looking less friendly by the moment.

"I don't have—" she began, then took another look at us and started over. "Who are you?"

"I told you that already."

"Those were just names."

Bernie handed her our card. She gave it a close look, actually seemed to spend quite a long time on it.

"You're a private detective?"

Bernie nodded.

"Working for who?"

"We keep that between our clients and ourselves."

What great news! That meant we had a client, exactly what we needed, what with the state of our finances. Don't get me started on our warehouse packed with unsold Hawaiian pants, or our tin futures play, which came close to making us rich, except for a last-minute earthquake in Bolivia, or possibly an earthquake we were counting on but didn't happen.

Johnnie Lee's face turned up in a way that showed she was actually a bit of a tough customer. "Is it someone I've heard of?"

"Like who?" Bernie said.

"I don't know," she said. "Maybe some household name?"

"Such as?" said Bernie.

"Fill in the blank."

"We'll try," Bernie said, his voice quiet.

That got Johnnie Lee angry. It didn't show, but I could smell it. Griffie was also getting angry—I could smell that, too. Johnnie Lee glanced down the street.

"Where's your car?" said Bernie.

"It was stolen. Nice meeting you." Johnnie Lee took a step back and slammed the door in our faces. Or almost. Bernie has very quick feet, which comes as a surprise to a lot of people, and he stuck his foot in the doorway just in time. But then—oh no—came a surprise on us. Griffie darted down and nipped Bernie's ankle.

"Ow," said Bernie, withdrawing his foot. The door closed all the way. Locks thunked into place.

And now I, Chet, was the angry one. A big part of my job was protecting Bernie from the Griffies of this world. I threw myself at the door, making the whole building shake in a very gratifying way, and was gathering myself to do it again when Bernie held up his hand. I didn't stop, exactly. Let's just call it a pause.

Bernie called through the door. "Open up. We're not going to hurt you."

No answer. Possibly Johnnie Lee knew that while there were no plans for hurting her—we'd never hurt a woman, me and Bernie—Griffie was a different story.

"When was it stolen?" Bernie called through the door. "Did you report it?"

No answer.

"Do you know a woman named Mavis?"

Silence.

"Is there any reason she'd be driving your car?"

More silence.

Bernie pulled up his pant leg, glanced down. There was a tiny drop or two of blood. Oh, what a disgrace! Biting ankles was what I did! Not Bernie's, of course, but that wasn't the point. This was the time to spring into—

Whoa. Bernie was turning away? We were leaving? At the very least, I had to bite Griffie's ankle—or better yet, all his ankles—before we left. Any job worth doing was worth doing well. You heard that all the time, or at least once in a while. Growling started up in the night.

Bernie touched the top of my head and spoke quietly. "Let's go, big guy."

The day had taken a very bad turn. Growling followed us back to the car and all the way home.

"What am I going to do with you?" Bernie said.

At first, I had no idea. Then I thought of fetch. Soon Bernie and I were playing fetch with a nappy new tennis ball and feeling a lot better. I glanced around before we went inside, security on pretty much all of Mesquite Road being part of my job. No unusual sights, with the exception of a small spotlight on old man Heydrich's lawn, aimed at his three-color sign.

Three

Bright and early the next morning—maybe a little too bright, a summertime thing in these parts—we drove down to Donut Heaven, the same Donut Heaven we'd been to yesterday. There are a number of Donut Heavens in the Valley, but this one, past the airport, was our favorite on account of Mrs. Borbon, the owner, who believed in doing things right, meaning that everything was better than at any of the other Donut Heavens, especially the sausage croissants. Normally, we order right away and start chowing down, but now we just sat in a back corner of the lot, Bernie checking out the comings and goings, and me being patient.

"All right, all right, knock it off," Bernie said after what seemed like a very long time, perhaps talking to himself. "Kind of a long shot that she'd show up anyway." I didn't even bother wondering who he meant. Your interests shrink down to just one when you're famished, as you probably know already.

Bernie got out and went inside to order. A black and white pulled into the lot and parked beside us cop-style, driver's-side door to driver's-side door. Rick Torres—our buddy in Missing Persons, as I may have mentioned already, and a particular buddy of mine since I'd lived at his place when Bernie was in the hospital, a terrible time that followed the terrible ending of the stolen saguaro case, a case I've tried and tried to forget but can't, even though I'm a champ at forgetting—leaned toward me. By that time, I'd shifted over to Bernie's seat.

"Morning, Chet," Rick said. "Finally canned him?"

Who could he have been talking about? I had no idea. But it was nice to see Rick. We had things in common—for example, a love of Slim Jims. He took one from his pocket, bit it in two, and tossed half to me. I snapped it out of the air and made quick work of it. More? Was there more?

Rick held up both hands, empty.

More? Was there more?

Rick laughed. He reached across and scratched between my ears, not quite as perfectly as Bernie, but close. His hand slowed and the expression on his face changed. "Tell you the truth," he said. "I love my job. It's not that. But I've got ambitions. Who wants to be a lieutenant forever?" He shook his head. "Sorry to whine at you, Chet. But the bastards made Ellis a captain! Can you believe that? I wanted—"

Bernie came back with a cardboard tray, stood between the cars, gave us a look and then a second one. He handed Rick coffee and a cruller, took a sausage croissant off the tray, and handed it to—but no. Instead, he flicked it right past my nose and onto the shotgun seat. We were playing fetch in the car? That was new. My Bernie. The next thing I knew I was sitting on the shotgun seat, happily chowing down on a sausage croissant that was even better than yesterday's, and Bernie was behind the wheel, sipping coffee.

Bernie has a real casual voice he sometimes uses for asking about things he doesn't seem to care much about. I'm not sure what that's all about, but it was the voice he was using now.

"What were you guys talking about?" he said.

"Cats," said Rick.

Cats? Had cats come up? When cats come up, I always get a bit . . . tense. Well, not tense, but more like . . . not quite tip-top. And I felt tip-top or even better. So therefore cats had not come up. Whoa! Had I just done a so-therefore? So-therefores were Bernie's department. I knew immediately that I wanted no part of them ever again. Why? Because if cats hadn't come up, why had Rick said they had? Rick was our buddy. This was confusing. Does a buddy bring up cats when there are no cats? I might have even started panting except for the fact of the sausage croissant in my mouth. I've been lucky pretty much my whole life, and for sure since we got together, me and Bernie. And—wait for it—a cat was involved that day! Life really is beyond belief, whatever that means, exactly.

Rick took a bite of his cruller. "Get what you wanted off that plate number?" he said, or something like that, hard to tell on account of his mouth being full.

Bernie shook his head. "Any chance that car's been reported stolen?"

"Search me."

Bernie glanced at him. "Having a bad day?"

Rick looked down. "Give me the plate number again."

Bernie told him the plate number. Rick got busy on his screen. "Nope," he said.

"Can you run the owner?"

Rick nodded and went back to the screen. He took another bite of the cruller. Bernie sipped his coffee. I polished off the sausage croissant and felt nice and full. But it didn't last.

"Johnnie Lee Goetz is down for two traffic violations, none moving. No criminal record." Rick tapped at his screen. "She did take out a restraining order last month."

"On who?"

Rick checked the screen, wrote on his coffee cup lid, and spun it over to Bernie.

Bernie caught the lid the way he catches everything, his hand folding softly around it. He glanced at the writing. "Mickey Rottoni, a PO box in South Pedroia. You're sending restraining orders to PO boxes?"

Rick raised his voice. That was a first. "Like I'm in charge of the whole stupid setup?"

Bernie looked surprised. His eyebrows usually take care of the surprised look, and they're great at it. "Whoa," he said. "You know I didn't mean you personally."

Rick glared at Bernie. Bernie glared right back. It hit me then that maybe they weren't getting along. That didn't make sense. Rick was a buddy. I barked a bark I use for letting people know in no uncertain terms.

They both turned my way real quick.

"Oh my god," Rick said, a hand to his chest. "What's with him?"

Bernie gave me a close look. "I think he wants another sausage croissant."

No! I did not. That was not at all what I wanted. And then . . . and then it was! And nothing else mattered. How do you like that?

Meanwhile, Rick was working at his screen. "The restraining order was served by Sergeant Weatherly Wauneka. Say thanks."

"Thanks," Bernie said.

"You should meet her."

"Why?"

Rick shrugged. "Just a feeling."

Not much later, Rick had driven away, and I was chowing down on a fresh sausage croissant, right out of the oven. Mrs. Borbon brought it over personally.

"Don't you just love someone who appreciates good food?" she said.

"*Appreciates* is an understatement," said Bernie.

Mrs. Borbon laughed. Laughing made her jiggle a bit. It was easy to like Mrs. Borbon, and I did.

"Can I ask you a question?" she said.

"As many as you like," said Bernie.

"You're a good customer," Mrs. Borbon said. "I look out for good customers." She took a quick scan of the parking lot. "Did anything unusual happen after you left yesterday?"

"Why do you ask?" Bernie said.

"Well, Mr. Bernie, I know what you do for a living."

"Oh?"

"Of course. In the kitchen, they call you el *cazador*."

"The hunter?"

"Yes, sir."

"What about Chet?"

"He's el *jefe*."

Sometimes Bernie has this real quick inner look, there and gone, which I saw now. I think it means he's seeing something in a new way, but don't take that to the bank, certainly not our bank, where there'd recently been an unpleasant discussion with Ms. Mendez, the manager.

"My question," Mrs. Borbon went on, "is what happens if the hunter is hunted. I don't know the answer. But a woman drove in first thing yesterday morning, parked over in that back corner, and just sat there. After a while, she came inside and ordered a macchiato with extra sugar. I served her myself, a pretty young woman—beautiful, really, with a ponytail. I'd never seen her before. And while I was serving her, I happened to notice—over her shoulder, if you understand . . . ?"

Bernie nodded.

"—an unusual thing. A van pulled up beside the woman's car, and a man jumped out. He unlocked her trunk, dropped something inside, and drove away. I thought, should I speak up to the woman? But maybe he was her husband and she'd forgotten her phone, something simple like that?"

"Then why the trunk?" Bernie said.

Mrs. Borbon hung her head slightly, a human thing when they disappoint themselves. I didn't like to see that from such a nice person as Mrs. Borbon, and neither did Bernie. He touched her arm and said, "But you might be right. Are you sure it was a phone?"

"Or some sort of gadget, from the size and shape," Mrs. Borbon said. "Then the woman went back to her car. You and Chet came soon after that, and she watched you the whole time you were here. When you left, she followed. It was no coincidence. I saw her face through the windshield. It had a sneaky look."

Was this a worrisome story? I was wondering about that when Bernie smiled, and I stopped worrying at once, even if I hadn't quite started. "You'd be a good investigator," he said.

"Is there any money in it?" said Mrs. Borbon.

Bernie laughed. What was funny? No humor that I could see, absolutely zip.

"I'm assuming you'd never seen the man before," Bernie said.

"That's right."

"Can you describe him?"

"Kind of big. Shaved head. I—I was more interested in what he was doing than in how he looked."

"I know that one," Bernie said. "What about his van?"

"White, like all those white vans you see."

"Any writing on it?"

Mrs. Borbon shook her head. "And if you're going to ask about my video system, when the temperature hits one ten it gets—what's the word?"

"Wonky?"

"Exactly. So there's no video since last Tuesday. I apologize."

"Nothing to apologize for—you've been very helpful."

"So there's meaning to all this? Maybe you know the woman?"

"We're getting to know her," Bernie said.

"And?" said Mrs. Borbon.

"Too soon to tell." Bernie handed her some money.

"What's this?"

"For the croissant."

"It's too much."

"Plus a tip."

"You don't tip the owner, Mr. Bernie."

"That's what my mother always said."

"Is she still alive?"

"Oh yes."

"She must be proud of you."

Bernie's mom—a piece of work—was suddenly in the conversation? She lived in Florida but had visited us last Christmas, bringing her new husband. He wore a white leather belt and said that bad times were the best times for making money. Bernie's mom had told Bernie to give that some thought. The subject of being proud of him hadn't come up.

Back on the road, Bernie was very quiet for a while, and then he said, "Do we find ourselves at the edge of the dark forest?"

Not from where I sat. We were actually in one of the most treeless parts of the Valley, where the Automile went on forever.

"So easy to lose the straightforward pathway," he went on.

I gave him a close look. The Automile was as straight as it comes, nice and wide, pretty much impossible to get lost on. Plus anyone traveling with me can never be lost. My nose will always get you home. Maybe Bernie was dehydrated. He had that problem in the heat. I leaned down and pawed at a water bottle on the floor.

"Thirsty, big guy?"

No. Not me. You. What was the best way to get him to drink? I still hadn't figured it out when he said, "How about we settle for the most obvious step? Let's look into that restraining order."

We walked up to the door at 1429E Aztec Creek Road. Before Bernie could knock, the door opened, and out came a round little dude carrying a mop and a bucket.

"Uh, yeah?" he said.

"Hi," said Bernie. "Is Johnnie Lee around?"

"Nope."

"When will she be back?"

"Never."

"I don't understand."

"She vacated the premises."

"You work for the landlord?"

The round little guy stood as tall as he could. "I am the landlord."

"Ah," said Bernie. "This must be a headache for you."

"Not really," the landlord said. "She was paid till the end of next month."

"Any idea why she left?"

"Nope. But it was in a hurry. That goddamn ferret got loose when she was packing the car, and she didn't even stick around to find him."

Interesting. I wandered off to the trash can enclosure at the side of the building. The plywood door was slightly open, and in the doorway stood Griffie, holding the remains of a pizza slice in his cute little paws. Random pizza slices found here and there are mine as a rule. First, I made sure that Griffie would be aware of that from here on in, and then I escorted him nice and gently around to the front.

"The name Mickey Rottoni mean anything to you?" Bernie was saying.

"Nope," said the landlord. "When it comes to the tenants, I keep my nose—"

Then they were both staring at me, so I never found out about where the landlord kept his nose, which actually seemed to be in the normal place.

"Chet?" said Bernie. "What you got there?"

Four

Have I mentioned the usual seating arrangement in the Porsche? Bernie's behind the wheel, I'm in the shotgun seat, and once in a while someone has to be on the little shelf in back. Suzie, for example, and Charlie after T-ball practice. I turned out to be quite talented at certain aspects of T-ball, but no time for that now. There's even been a perp or two on the shelf, including a former basketball player name of Stilts Wilton, who'd shaved points in arenas on every continent, wherever those were, and hadn't been at his happiest with our seating arrangement. The truth was that no one was happy on the shelf, not until now.

Bernie glanced back. "Looks mighty content back there, doesn't he, Chet?"

I did not glance back. I could smell Griffie perfectly well, and even hear his tiny breaths going in and out, and the even fainter sound of those tiny breezes ruffling his tiny whiskers. Why did we have Griffie? Where were we taking him? Someplace close by, I hoped, where he would be dropped off and never seen again. Meanwhile, he breathed his tiny breezes and ruffled his tiny whiskers. I knew he was doing it just to annoy me, and he knew that I knew, and I knew that he knew that—

"Chet!"

If any barking had been going on, a matter of doubt in my own mind, it stopped. Perhaps a member of the nation within was shut inside one of the houses we were passing and wanted out. I checked the neighborhood, not very good, and suddenly recognized Cooler Heads, a barbershop not far from our self-storage, where we keep the Hawaiian pants, meaning we were in South Pedroia. Bernie pulled over and parked between a rust bucket up on blocks and a pile of trash. A messy neighborhood, except for right in front of Cooler Heads, where a nice clean bench stood against the wall and the sidewalk was spotless.

We hopped out, me actually hopping, but Bernie not, on account of his leg wound from back in the war. Griffie's eyes snapped open, and he sat up straight on the shelf, looked like he might be forming some sort of plan.

"This is when a roof would come in handy."

A roof for the Porsche? I didn't see why. It hadn't rained in ages, and besides, what was better than the wind in your face? Meanwhile, Bernie was fishing around under the seats. He found an old bungee cord—left over from a case involving cave-dwelling arsonists that I never wanted to think about again—clipped one end to the gearshift and the other to Griffie's velvet collar.

"There's a good little fella," Bernie said.

Griffie looked at him with—what was this? Adoring eyes?—and lay back down like a team player. I knew with every little bit of me that Griffie was not a team player. For no particular reason, I wondered whether I could chew right through a bungee cord should the need arise.

"Chet? Something on your mind?"

No. Nothing at all. We walked into Cooler Heads, where we hadn't been in a while, Bernie currently getting his hair cut by the inmates in the job-training program at Central State Correctional on account of some bet he'd lost, the details not coming to me.

"Well, well, well," said our buddy Earl Adamokoh. "Look what the cat dragged in." He dropped what he was doing and hurried over, slipping me a rawhide chew on the fly.

Here's a good place to stop and back up a bit, maybe straighten things out. First, Earl didn't actually drop anything. That would have been a bad move, since what he had in his hand was a straight-edge razor. Earl's the best barber in town, and he was shaving a jowly-faced customer with a cigar in his mouth. Second—what the cat dragged in? You heard that from time to time, but what could it possibly mean? Where was the cat who could drag in me and Bernie? Plus I know first thing when people have a cat in their lives—that's basic—and Earl did not.

Back to the live action, as they say on TV. Live action is always best. There's no action whatsoever from the dead. That's the kind of unhappy thing you learn in a job like mine. For live action, we had Earl hugging Bernie and pounding him on the back, although not with the razor-holding hand.

"Sight for sore eyes," he said. He stepped away, gave Bernie a close look. "Except for your hair. When are you coming back to me?"

The jowly-faced man turned to watch, some of his jowls covered in shaving cream, some not, the cigar smoking between his lips. He was an interesting sight, and I was enjoying this visit very much. Then I thought, *Are we actually on a case? If so, who was paying?* And I began enjoying it a little less.

"Soon," Bernie said. "The program ends next month—budget cuts."

Earl turned to the jowly-faced man. "Hear that? State's falling apart. That's why I'm voting for Erlanger."

"Wray all the way," said the jowly-faced man. "Erlanger's a phony."

Or something like that, hard to tell what with the stogie in his mouth. Whatever it was, Earl didn't like it.

"That's a goddamn—what is it, Bernie? Bold-faced or bald-faced? I never get it right."

"Um, I think they're pretty close," Bernie said. "*Bold-faced* would be kind of brazen, whereas *bald—*"

Earl made an impatient gesture with the razor, somewhat alarming from my point of view. "Bold-faced and bald-faced lie," he told the jowly-faced man. By now, of course, I was completely lost. Bold-faced, bald-faced, and jowly-faced were all in play?

"Tell him, Bernie. Tell him Erlanger's no phony."

"Well," Bernie said, "I don't follow these things too closely and—"

"What's your excuse for that?" The jowly-faced dude waved his cigar at Bernie. "You don't care about this country?"

Sometimes—not often, and in fact I can remember every single occasion—Bernie can look dangerous. So dangerous he comes close to scaring me. The fur on the back of my neck stands straight up, and then I'm dangerous, too. We're a team, me and Bernie, a team you don't want to mess with—a truth that was starting to dawn on the jowly-faced dude. I could tell from the way he blinked and suddenly began looking smaller.

Earl put the razor down carefully on the shelf in front of the mirror, beside his scissors and combs, and then turned to the jowly-faced dude and spoke quietly. "Is that any kind of question to ask a war hero?"

When humans get alarmed, their features all move higher, not a good look on the jowly types. "Um, I had no idea that . . . uh, and of course it would change the way, er—"

"Saved my life." Earl's voice rose. "And I wasn't the only one, far from it. So there's a whole bunch of guys like me who wouldn't take kindly to Bernie here getting asked that type of question."

The jowly-face dude swiveled the barber chair in Bernie's direction. "Ah, Bernie—if you don't mind me calling you that—if I've given any offense, that wasn't my intention, and I'm a big supporter—thank you for your service, by the way!—of our wonderful mili—"

Bernie had already stopped looking dangerous. "We're good," he said. And then to Earl: "Can you spare a moment?"

Earl laid his hand on the jowly-faced dude's shoulder. "Mind taking a little break?"

"Love to!" The jowly-faced dude rose, hustled outside, and sat on the bench, still wearing his smock, patches of shaving cream on his face.

Bernie and Earl looked at each other. "Get in the chair," Earl said. "I'll take care of that rat's nest while we talk."

Bernie sat in the chair. Earl got busy with the scissors, clip-clip-clipping in rapid, no-nonsense style.

"The name Mickey Rottoni mean anything to you?" Bernie said.

"Not Mickey specifically," said Earl. "But I know some Rottonis. They run Rottoni Transport, trucking company over on Cain Boulevard. A tough bunch."

"Oh?" Bernie said.

And they went back and forth about the Rottonis. As for me, I was stuck at rat's nest. There was no rat's nest to be seen anywhere in Cooler Heads. Plus there wasn't the slightest suggestion of rat scent, of which there was usually plenty in South Pedroia and most parts of the Valley. Humans—no offense—are often in the dark about all the different critters they have for roommates. But there were no rat roomies here at Earl's. I waited for some rattish clue to pop up in the conversation. It never did, so I busied myself with the rawhide chew. It's a fine way of relaxing the mind, which you may not know, kind of like . . . like smoking a stogie, perhaps? Hey! What a thought! Was there a whole world of thoughts out there, just waiting to be found? Whoa! Another thought right there, and on the scary side. I shut the whole thing down.

I love riding in the Porsche, and nothing beats the shotgun seat, of course, but during our visit to Cooler Heads, I'd forgotten all about Griffie.

"Hey, there, little fella," said Bernie as we got in the car. "Thanks for being patient."

Excuse me? We were thanking Griffie? And Griffie was giving Bernie that adoring look again? This had to stop. I sat up tall in the shotgun seat and ignored them both. That was bound to get Bernie's attention, after which we'd dump Griffie wherever we were dumping him and get on with our lives. There was no need for Griffie in this operation, no need for anyone else, for that matter. But especially not Griffie. I hope I've made that point. About Griffie, I mean. No Griffie. That's all you need to know.

We drove into the old part of South Pedroia, the narrow streets lined with brick warehouses, lots of the windows boarded up. Bernie turned in to an alley lined with loading docks and parked behind a truck where a skinny, bare-chested man with a dolly was taking a cigarette break. Bernie and I got out. The sign on the brick wall showed a truck with a big grin on its face.

"You be good now," Bernie said. Well, of course I was going to be . . . and then I realized Bernie wasn't looking at me. He was looking at Griffie. This was intolerable. I barged—well, let's not say *barged,* more like advanced urgently—through an open doorway in the brick wall and into some sort of office. A gum-chewing woman behind the counter looked down at me. I looked up at her. She wore cat's-eye glasses. Do I have to even mention how I was in no mood for cat's-eye glasses at that moment? Why wouldn't the mere sight of cat's-eye glasses be more than enough to get me leaping over that counter and—

"Chet? Getting a little ahead of me, big guy."

And there was Bernie beside me. It's hard not to get ahead of humans sometimes. But I made up my mind to try harder, and calmed right down even though I hadn't realized I was un-calm. You can learn new things about yourself, maybe not necessarily a plus.

"Dog looks a mite aggressive," the woman said.

"Oh, not Chet," Bernie said, resting his hand on my back, not too hard, not too soft, just right. "He couldn't be friendlier."

"Uh-huh," said the woman, snapping her gum, a sound I love. Right away, this woman was fine in my book. If I had a book, which I don't, of course, but I knew quite a bit about books—their taste, for example. "Can I help you?"

"I hope so," Bernie said. "We're looking for Mickey Rottoni."

Her face, not the particularly open type, I now noticed, closed up a little more. Humans are brainy. Maybe not all of them, and maybe not brainy in every way, but braininess is their thing, when you compare them to say, snakes. Scariness is snakes' thing, if you see where I'm going with this, which I'm afraid I no longer do. I think it had something to do with how braininess shows in their eyes. Humans, I mean, not snakes. Yes, that was it—braininess in the eyes, and this woman had it big-time. Also, now that I was taking the time to actually look, there was some scariness, too, even—uh-oh—snakelike.

"No one here by that name," she said and snapped her gum again. This time it didn't have the same effect on me. I wandered over toward the window, not from fear—an impossibility as you'd know if you knew me—but just to make a little space between me and her.

Bernie smiled. "I was hoping someone here might help me reach out to him."

"Someone here?" said the woman.

"I believe he's a member of the family," Bernie said. "The Rottonis—the owners of this business. Is the boss around?"

"You're lookin' at her," the woman said. "I'm Sylvia Rottoni. And who are you?"

"Someone I'm sure Mickey would want to talk to," said Bernie, handing her our card.

Sylvia Rottoni's face, already closed, now hardened as well, but I'm a little unsure of what happened next, on account of getting distracted by events down in the alley. I had a very good view of the Porsche parked against the curb, with Griffie curled up on the shelf, the bungee cord clipped to his collar. An annoying sight, but not unexpected. The unexpected part was this big, shaved-headed dude who came strolling up like he was going to turn toward the office door, but instead noticed the car and stopped dead. He leaned closer, spotted Griffie, and sort of jolted, like he'd had one of those finger-in-light-socket incidents that follow light-bulbs-breaking-off incidents, which I'd witnessed perhaps too often.

The big, shaved-headed dude looked over at the skinny, bare-chested dude and said something. The skinny, bare-chested dude said something back and pointed at the door of the building. After that, the shaved-headed dude moved very quickly, whipping out a knife, slashing through the bungee cord, and grabbing Griffie. Then he jammed Griffie into his jacket pocket and hurried away, down the alley and out of sight. The skinny, bare-chested dude stood with his mouth open.

I . . . I was at a loss. At a loss? How strange! I'd never been at a loss, hadn't even known what that was, until right now. On the one hand, as humans say, I had no need for Griffie whatsoever in my life, so the shaved-headed dude had done me a solid and we were hunky-dory. On the other hand, the Porsche belonged to me and Bernie. Didn't anything inside it also belong to me and Bernie? And who was in charge of security for everything without exception belonging to me and Bernie?

There's a bark I have for getting everyone's attention in no uncertain terms. It's thrilling to have a sound like that come out of you—try it sometime. Sylvia Rottoni actually covered her ears, a very pleasing sight.

"Oh my god! Chet!" Bernie rushed over, began patting me here and there, like . . . like a vet in a hurry! As if . . . as if there was something wrong with me! Imagine my frustration! I rose up to my tallest height and placed my paws on the window, my breath clouding the glass.

Bernie glanced out. "I don't—" He took another look and saw what there was to see—namely, an absence of Griffie.

And then we were on our way. Sylvia Rottoni picked up a phone as we zoomed out the door.

Five

"So stupid of me," Bernie said, reaching into the Porsche, a remark that made no sense and therefore forgotten by me at once. "I should have assumed he could chew through anything, including . . ." Bernie unhooked what was left of the bungee cord from the gearshift and gave it a close look. "Hmm. Teeth didn't do this, Chet, not even a set like his. Straight cut like that? Had to be done with . . ." He started walking down the alley, in the wrong direction if following Griffie was the plan. I steered him gently around, and we headed the other way.

"Smell something, huh?" Bernie said.

Hard to know how to handle that one. *Always* was the answer, but perhaps not helpful. I concentrated on my work, following a powerful stream of Griffie scent mixed with a trickle of male human scent of no particular distinction, other than a faint garlic aroma. Rick has it, too, in his breath but also coming off his feet, which I took to sniffing practically every day when I was living at his place after the saguaro case. "What the heck's so interesting about my feet?" he'd said, completely baffled. There's fun to be had in small ways.

But back to Bernie and me in the alley, moving at a good pace now, what with the trail being so easy-peasy. "Onto something, aren't you, big guy?" he said. "I've heard that ferrets—especially the males—have a distinct odor, but I never picked it up from Griffie."

I paused for a moment, not my body, which was busy working, but my mind. Bernie hadn't picked up Griffie's smell? That was a stunner. It would be like me . . . I couldn't even think what. That's how bad it was. I made up my mind that very instant to stick by Bernie's side always and forever, and was just remembering that I had already made up my mind about that a long time ago when a powerful new smell entered the scent stream. This was a car smell, specifically the slightly smoky one they make when just starting up. Griffie, garlic man, and car-starting-up smells got mixed into a small sort of cone and then began flowing together down the alley. This car—with Griffie and the garlic guy in it, if you're following along—came to the end of the alley and turned onto a busy street. I kept on going to the point where the scent stream finally got swallowed up in the mighty river of traffic smells, and even a little farther, in case we got lucky. But we did not. I sat down on the sidewalk.

"Good job," Bernie said.

We turned around and went back down the alley. The skinny, bare-chested man with the dolly was taking another cigarette break, looking at us sideways. We stopped in front of him.

"Hi, there," Bernie said.

"Uh-huh."

Bernie pointed to the Porsche. "That's our car."

The man nodded.

"Did you happen to notice anyone taking an interest in it while we were gone?"

The man puffed a pretty little smoke ball into the air. I got a crazy urge to fetch it! Instead, I let it drift away and disappear. We were on the job, after all, and if you're a pro, you behave like a pro. Better to know what the job is, of course, but not necessary. That's what being a pro is all about. Hey! What a thought! All of a sudden, I understood my work like never before. When a breakthrough comes along, you want to move. Would jumping up on this bare-chested dude be good or bad? Perhaps bad, but it was real close.

The man's eyes shifted toward the window of Sylvia Rottoni's office. "Interest? Like—?"

"Like looking inside the car, for example. Reaching in, maybe. Possibly taking something."

"Nope," said the bare-chested man. "Don't know nothin' about any of that."

Bernie took out his money clip. I loved the money clip, a skull-and-bones money clip with two angry red eyes. It was kind of new, won by Bernie off a dude name of Bruiser in an arm wrestling contest we stumbled on by accident at a meeting of Civil War reenactors, whatever those were, the whole thing very confusing, but the point was that skull! Those angry red eyes! Good things keep happening to us, me and Bernie.

Meanwhile, Bernie was sliding a bill out of the money clip, the bill with the narrow-faced guy on it. "This helps some folks think harder," he said.

Did that mean eating it would help you think harder? Although there was nothing wrong with my own thinking, not that I knew of, I considered making a play for that bill myself. How could it hurt? But before I took the next step, the bare-chested dude's eyes shifted to the window again, and he said, "Let's go for a little walk."

We walked down the alley, me on one side of the bare-chested dude and Bernie on the other, which is how we handle walks with strangers, especially strangers we meet on a case. Was this a case? A case means someone is paying. I searched my mind for who that could be, came up with zip.

We stopped in the shadow of a big dumpster. "Yeah," said the bare-chested dude. "I saw, like, what you said."

"Meaning?" said Bernie.

The bare-chested dude pointed back down the alley. "Looking in the car, reaching in, taking something, all that."

"You saw someone do that?"

"Yup." The bare-chested dude held out his hand.

Bernie ignored it. "Man or woman?" he said.

"Man, of course."

"Why of course?" said Bernie.

"Huh? I don't get ya."

Sometimes in the middle of things, Bernie takes a deep breath. I've never been sure what it means, but he did it now. "Describe him."

The bare-chested dude squeezed his eyes shut, not a good

look on him. "Little black guy. Jeans and a T-shirt. Wore one of them do-rags. Red. Not the real bright kind, more like Alabama."

"Alabama?"

"The Crimson Tide." He opened his eyes. "Crimson. A crimson do-rag. That's all I can tell you. But not too shabby, huh?" He held out his hand again.

"You're sure it wasn't a big white guy with a shaved head?"

"Course I'm sure. Think I can't tell a big white guy from a little black guy?"

Bernie gazed down at him. "What's your name?"

Usually people come up with their names pretty quick, but not always, in our business. This was one of those not-always times. "Rico," said the bare-chested man.

"Any last name?"

Rico licked his lips. "Miller."

"Rico Miller?" Bernie said.

"That's right. Now I get my money or not?"

"First let's hear exactly what the little black guy did."

"Just like you said. He checked out the car. Then he took out a box cutter, I think it was, but it might have been a pocketknife, and he reached inside. I couldn't see his hands, like for what he was doing, but when he straightened up, he was holding this little critter. I thought it was one of them stuffed toys until it wriggled around. Couldn't tell you what it was, kind of like a giant squirrel. Then the guy walked thataway. All she wrote, man." Rico held out his hand again.

"Anything you want to add or change?"

"About what?"

"Your story."

Rico shook his head. "That's it, A to Z."

Bernie handed him the money. Paying meant we were on a case. That was the good news. But us doing the paying: that was new. Had Bernie tweaked our business plan? I came close to . . . to doubting Bernie! Oh, how bad of me! I got myself back with the program and pronto. If Bernie thought the business plan needed tweaking, then that was that. I realized something for the very first time: we were going to be rich. My tail got going like nobody's business. I almost missed the dude looking down from a rooftop across the alley, a broad-shouldered type in a tracksuit and one of those flat caps. Nothing interesting so far, but then a breeze blew his tracksuit jacket open, and I spotted a small holster on his belt. A bark came out of me, pretty much on its own.

"Chet? Some problem?"

Bernie glanced up at the rooftop. The broad-shouldered dude was gone. Packing iron and wearing a tracksuit didn't exactly go together, but it didn't not go together either. Not in these parts, amigo.

"Nothing in the universe," Bernie said as we drove through Spaghetti Junction, where all the freeways meet, up and around, over and down, then back up and almost out and finally around and around and out, always the part where I get pukey, "can go faster than the speed of light." He raised one finger. "But that doesn't apply to the universe itself, as whole, if you see what I mean."

I believed I came very close, might have reached full understanding had it not been for the pukeyness. Pukeyness can be a distraction, as you may or may not know. Meanwhile, Bernie tapped out something on his phone, and very soon came a ping. He glanced at the screen and popped the phone in the glove box. Sometimes there were Slim Jims in there, but not today. Would a Slim Jim make you more or less pukey? Had to be less, or otherwise life made no sense.

"So suppose," Bernie went on, "you'd somehow gotten a toehold in a fold of the universe where you'd be moving faster than the speed of light. Therefore when you gazed into it—the universe is what I'm talking about—you'd be gazing back in time. You could solve every crime that had ever been! We could see where Mavis went after she drove away in the Kia. We could go further back and find out what she's scared of. We could see where Griffie is. I wonder if a program could be designed that would simulate . . ." His voice faded away, a lucky break for me because something about the skin of the universe was about to make me barf all over the car. I stuck my head over the side, took some deep breaths, felt better. The next thing I knew, we were parking in front of Valley PD HQ, not the old one but the brand-new one we'd be paying for forever, Bernie said, meaning we'd have to ramp things up.

"We started in the wrong place," Bernie said as we walked into the building. "My fault, big guy."

Wrong place? Bernie's fault? That all zipped by like buzzing insects, and then we were at the counter. We know lots of folks at Valley PD, but not the uniformed counter guy. Some humans have helpful faces and some do not. This guy was the second kind.

"Here to see Sergeant Wauneka," Bernie said.

"Yeah?" Then came one of those long quiet spells, maybe called *awkward pauses.* We always win when it comes to pauses of any kind. Bernie's a master. "Got an appointment?" the guy said at last.

"Would we be here otherwise?" said Bernie.

Sometimes—although not often—you get to see an unhelpful face turn purple. How come that's such a fun sight? I have no idea, but I was having a good time and I knew that Bernie was, too. Don't forget we're a lot alike in some ways. As for exactly how the situation was going to . . . what's the word? Escalate? Something like that, and it reminds me of a scary story or two I could pass on regarding me and escalators—even worse than elevators—but we'll have to let that slide on account of a new development, the arrival of Captain Stine.

He came walking into the lobby, not a big guy, but strong and lean, wearing his perfectly fitting uniform with all the gold, a tall, silver-haired dude beside him, the two of them trailed by a well-dressed little group of what Bernie calls flunkies. You can tell flunkies from their eager faces. As for Captain Stine, Bernie once told me he was an *homme sérieux,* one of the strangest things he'd ever said. Was he talking about how Stine has a sharp-shaped kind of face and all his looks were dark? I had no idea, so never mind all that. The important thing was that he wouldn't have made captain if it hadn't been for us—us and possibly a cat named Brando, that whole case now very dim in my mind. My mind is on my side, maybe why I've been so lucky in life.

Stine saw us and came to a halt, the silver-haired dude and the flunkies all halting, too.

"Here's a nice surprise," he said. Stine has a harsh, hoarse sort of voice, like he partied every night, but in fact he and his wife—somewhat younger than him—had a new baby at home who wasn't sleeping much. That new baby's middle name was Bernard, by the way, sort of another name for Bernie, a somewhat confusing detail I'd learned around the time the baby was born. Life is full of little details. They'll get away with murder if you let them. Whoa! What was that? Little details getting away with murder? I'd just surprised myself, and not in a good way.

"Senator," Stine was saying, "I'd like you to meet the best crime fighter in the Valley."

"Well, I wouldn't—" Bernie began and then noticed that Stine seemed to be gesturing in my direction.

The silver-haired guy's eyebrows rose. "The dog?" he said. His voice was much more pleasant than Stine's—possibly the kind of voice known as folksy—and the lines on his face curved up, like a smile was coming any second. His eyes—the color of the ice cubes floating in a blue drink that Bernie's mom likes maybe too many of—were watchful and showed no signs of a smile in the works.

"His name's Chet," Stine said. "But forgive my little joke, Senator."

"A real thigh-slapper," said Bernie, quite softly, although Stine caught it and frowned just the slightest bit.

But he recovered real quick, smiled, and said, "I'm giving the senator a tour of the new building, only fair since he got the funding."

"I've been a big believer in law enforcement my whole career," the senator said.

"Much appreciated, Senator," Stine said. "Say hi to one of

our leading private investigators, Bernie Little. Bernie, Senator Wray."

Did those ice-blue eyes shift? Not that I could tell. But they did something, a sort of flicker perhaps, here and gone. Then Senator Wray and Bernie shook hands. The senator turned out to be one of those two-handed hand shakers, grabbing Bernie's in both of his. He gave Bernie a big grin. "Pleasure to meet you, sir," he said. "And this handsome pooch of yours. I'd appreciate both your votes in the upcoming election, but I'll forgive Chet here if he can't manage the lever."

"He probably could," Bernie said. "But to be safe, I'll just vote twice."

There was a pause. The flunkies all watched Senator Wray. Stine gave Bernie a sharp look. Then the senator started laughing. He laughed and laughed and patted Bernie on the back. The flunkies all laughed, too. "Hear that?" the senator said. "Just vote twice!" And he laughed all over again. The flunkies laughed harder. What was funny? I didn't know, but one thing for sure—Bernie had made a great impression. That didn't always happen, for reasons I'd never understood. The tour moved on, a female flunky at the end of the line giving me a nice pat without breaking stride.

Bernie turned back to the counter.

"Sergeant Wauneka, was it?" said the unhelpful uniformed dude, all of a sudden getting helpful. "Right this way. My name's Ernie, at your service."

Six

Could I manage a lever? First I'd have to find out what a lever was, but after that it would be a snap. As we went down a long hall at the new Valley PD HQ, I thought, *Lever?* And then again: *Lever?* And once more: *Lever?* Soon the answer would come to me! I started feeling pretty good about myself, so good I almost didn't notice a red-haired guy sitting at a desk in his office as we passed by the open doorway, red hair of the curly type and also receding. There was lots of gold decoration on his uniform, and he had his feet up on the desk. He wore cowboy boots—snakeskin in his case—which you sometimes saw on cops, but only on their days off. The red-haired cop glanced at us and then looked a lot more carefully. We passed by.

Farther down the hall, we came to another office, this one small and tidy with a window, filing cabinet, and a desk. Behind the desk sat a uniformed woman with glossy black hair tied up in a bun—always a good look, in my opinion, reminding me of poodles in a way—and very smooth skin.

"Sergeant?" said Ernie. "This here's, uh . . ."

"Bernie Little," said Bernie. "And Chet."

"Captain Stine said to show 'em up."

"Thanks, Ernie."

Ernie nodded, backed out, and went away.

The sergeant turned to us and smiled. "I've wondered whether this would happen."

"Oh?" said Bernie.

"Chet being pretty well known in this building," she said.

"Ah," said Bernie. "So you wondered if you would ever meet him?"

"For a special reason." The sergeant rose, took a framed photo off a shelf and brought it over. "Here's Trixie."

We all gazed at Trixie, a member of the nation within—and a particularly good-looking one. She was sitting up nice and tall, her mouth a bit open, revealing the tip of a fine pink tongue. The rest of her was jet-black, except . . . except for one white ear. All black but one white ear? That reminded me of . . . of something. And then it came to me. Me! It reminded me of me. This may surprise you, but sometimes humans discuss my appearance in my presence, and when they do, they always mention what they call the mismatched ears. Seeing those so-called mismatched ears now on someone else—namely, this Trixie character—I couldn't help but think, hey, not too shabby! Not too shabby at all! One more thing: I found myself wishing I could smell her, in fact wishing that quite strongly.

Bernie's eyes went to me, then back to the photo. Sergeant Wauneka watched him the whole time, so when he looked up at the sergeant, her eyes were waiting, if that makes any sense.

"This is kind of amazing," Bernie said.

"Agreed," said the sergeant.

"My god," Bernie said.

"Yes," said the sergeant.

"Is it possible they were littermates?" Bernie said. "Whoa! Did you actually see the litter, Sergeant?"

"I wish," said the sergeant. "Trixie was a rescue I got two years ago. So we'd need a DNA test to make sure. And call me Weatherly."

"Weatherly," said Bernie, kind of carefully, like he was trying something new.

"My father was in the merchant marine," said Weatherly, possibly a bit irritated.

"For the umpteenth time," Bernie said.

"Ha!" said Weatherly.

Bernie checked the photo again. "Might be fun to get the two of them together."

Weatherly got an odd look in her eyes, almost as though she'd
had a sudden pain inside. "That would have been nice."

"I don't understand," Bernie said.

Weatherly shook her head. "Trixie disappeared June 28."

She went silent, then slowly sat down in her chair. Bernie sat
in the chair on our side. I stood beside him. Bernie said nothing.
Sometimes we just wait, me and Bernie. That's something I learned
from him. He learned from me, too, by the way. He'd even told me
so. This was one time out in the desert when he'd had to pee very
badly—I know that one!—and he'd hit the brakes, hopped out,
and peed and peed and peed against a big red rock, looking over
his shoulder at me for a moment or two and saying, "Learned this
from you, big guy!" We're a team, don't forget, me and Bernie.

Weatherly took a deep breath. "I blame myself," she said.
"This was after Bob—this was after there was no one home to
watch her while I was at work. I kept her inside, of course, windows closed and AC on, but when I came home from the night
shift that morning, she was gone. I did all the usual things—
posted flyers, searched the neighborhood, checked the shelters—
but . . ." Weatherly raised her hands and let them slowly fall on
the desk.

"Sorry to hear that," Bernie said. "We'll keep an eye out." He
thought for a moment. "Have you got anything with her scent
on it?"

"Not here, but I could get you something."

"Here's the address." Bernie handed her our business card,
the business card with the flowers on it, designed by Suzie, which
I know I've already mentioned but want to mention again, especially the Suzie part, for some reason.

Weatherly glanced at the card, then took a closer look. How
often had I seen that, usually followed by a smirk or snicker? But
not from Weatherly. Instead, for an instant, she seemed about to
smile. Then she tucked our card in the chest pocket of her uniform shirt. "Much appreciated, Bernie," she said. "Now what can
I do for you?"

"On June 15, a woman named Johnnie Lee Goetz got a

restraining order on Mickey Rottoni of South Pedroia. Our in-formation has you as the serving officer, but his address is a PO box, so we wondered if—"

Weatherly interrupted. "If I actually bothered to stick the papers in his lousy hand?"

Hey! All at once she looked angry, the bones of her face some-how more prominent. What was that about?

"Something like that," Bernie said.

Weatherly came pretty close to glaring at him. And we'd been getting along so well! Human behavior had its ups and downs. I prefer the ups, which is maybe why I like to turn the downs into them. Whoa! Had I just realized something about myself? I got a very good feeling about this case, and it didn't go away even though all I understood about it was that no one was paying.

"I always stick the paper in their lousy hands," Weatherly said.

"Glad to hear it," Bernie said. "What can you tell us about Mickey?"

"Why do you want to know?"

Bernie got going on a long story that started with Mavis in the maroon Kia, parts of which seemed very familiar to me. Don't forget I'm a pro. And it's always nice to listen to Bernie tell a story. I could see from the way the anger faded from her face that Weatherly was feeling the very same thing.

Bernie wrapped it up. I'm afraid that toward the end—or maybe the slightest bit earlier—my mind had let me down a lit-tle and wandered off to think of other things, one of which was Trixie. Were there actually any others? Maybe not.

Meanwhile, there was silence. "Well?" Bernie said at last.

Weatherly put her fingertips together. "You had an inconclu-sive conversation with a woman driving a maroon Kia. Now you're looking for her. You had another inconclusive conversation with Johnnie Lee Goetz, owner of the Kia, who told you the car had been stolen. If so, she didn't report it. You found out about the restraining order and now you're looking to have what'll probably be another inconclusive conversation with Mickey Rottoni, if you find him."

"That's one way of putting it," Bernie said. "If you've got a better idea, let's hear it."

Weatherly leaned back in her chair in a way I'd seen men— especially of the boss type—lean back, but never a woman. "Who's the client?" she said.

"Prospectively," Bernie began, losing me right off the jump and on a very important point, "Mavis, the driver of the Kia."

"Your business plan allows for prospective clients?" said Weatherly.

Ah. Our business plan. Ms. Pernick, our accountant, had raised that subject on several occasions, with Bernie always saying he'd "clean it up a little" and "shoot it over," but while I'd witnessed him cleaning from time to time, no shooting involving Ms. Pernick ever happened.

Now Bernie sat back, too. "Sometimes we go on instinct."

Weatherly's gaze went to me, then to Bernie. "When you say 'we,' you refer to you and Chet?"

"Correct."

Weatherly rubbed her hands slowly together and then nodded. "Fair enough," she said. "In a PO box situation, I do some digging."

Aha! There comes a special moment when you make up your mind about someone, now and forever, and never have to think about it again. This was one of those special moments. Weatherly Wauneka did some digging, and so did I. There was nothing more to say.

That didn't mean things stopped getting said. Another long conversation started up between Bernie and Weatherly, possibly about how she'd tracked down Mickey Rottoni. An interesting story, even exciting in parts, with lots of twists and turns, although don't count on me for the details, since my mind was mostly occupied with organizing a digging expedition for me and Weatherly. I'd noticed a giant flower pot outside the entrance of the new Valley PD HQ. Always nice to know where to start. Now all I needed was when. Hey! Where and when! Was this how Bernie thought, 24-7? He really is beyond belief when it comes to brainpower. And everything else, of course. Goes without mentioning.

"Sylvia Rottoni?" Weatherly was saying. "Any luck with that?"

Bernie shook his head.

"The Rottonis are hard people," Weatherly said, "and look out for themselves first, last, and always, but they're not criminals. Mickey's the criminal, and they cut him out of the business. Doesn't mean they don't support him. Also doesn't mean they don't protect him from the law. I tried her anyway, of course. I'm a plodder."

Bernie's eyebrows, with a language all their own, have a way of showing that he's not buying it. Just one eyebrow does the actual talking, rising up quite sharply, although never too sharply. Meanwhile, the other eyebrow stays put. What amazing body control! But that's Bernie, world class all the way.

Weatherly seemed to give his eyebrows a quick, odd sort of glance, and went on. "Next, I tried Johnnie Lee, although I don't like involving the complainant."

"Why not?" said Bernie.

"Because," Weatherly said, "it takes a lot of strength to get that restraining order in the first place. Sometimes they're clean out of strength after that, and start having doubts, especially if their particular Mickey Rottoni is making nice."

"You're handling the decision for them?" Bernie said.

Weatherly's chin jutted out a bit. That was a look Bernie had, too. It means he's digging in his heels. So Weatherly was digging in her heels, although about what I didn't know. I happen to be an expert at digging in heels—I can make myself completely immovable, a fun thing to do from time to time, even for no reason—but I leave out the chin-jutting part. Bottom line: there was a lot to like about Weatherly.

"I would never do that," she said. "I help them keep the faith."

"Did Johnnie Lee need help with that?"

"I wouldn't have thought so, but when I drove out to her place on Aztec Creek Road, Johnnie Lee claimed to have no idea where

Rottoni lived, where he worked—no leads at all. I didn't believe her. Some folks are adept liars and others not, as I'm sure you know. Johnnie Lee's in the second group. I didn't press her." Weatherly gave Bernie a sharp look. "Pressing's what you do to bad guys."

This is where Bernie would usually nod one of his nods, but instead, he simply watched her.

"I just left," Weatherly went on. "But as I got into my car, a woman ran out the side door of Johnnie Lee's place. She didn't say a word, just handed me a piece of paper and ran back into the house." Weatherly opened a desk drawer, took out a sheet of paper, and paused. "A noticeably good-looking woman, by the way. Is Mavis, this prospective client of yours, noticeably good looking?"

"Well, I'm not one to—"

"Bernie? Are we going to play games?"

Bernie went the slightest bit pink, not an everyday sight. I was paying close attention. What sort of games was Weatherly talking about? We could play pretty much anything, me and Bernie.

"Yes," he said. "Mavis was noticeably good looking."

Weatherly grinned like some fun game was already happening. I wondered what it could be.

She handed Bernie the sheet of paper. "Mickey Rottoni," she said.

"So you served him?"

Weatherly nodded.

"What was his reaction?"

"Didn't say a word. Just took the papers. He watched me drive off. I had him in the rearview. The bastard kept watching." Weatherly's eyes, dark to begin with, darkened some more.

"Got a picture of him?" Bernie said.

"Nope. He's a big shaved-headed type like so many others."

Right then, the cop with the receding red hair strolled in. "Sounds interesting, Sergeant. Who are we discussing?"

Bernie turned to the red-haired guy. Their eyes met. The room got very still. Two facts—not merely one—came to me immediately. They knew each other. But were not buddies.

"Uh, Lieu—Captain Ellis," Weatherly said. "I didn't hear the knock. This is Bernie Little, a private—"

"Oh, I know Bernie," said Captain Ellis, waving his freckled hand. "We go way back, served together in our misbegotten youths. How are things, old buddy?"

"No complaints."

"That's what I hear, not since the dog came along." He glanced at me. "So this is the famous Chet."

A nice thing to say, you might think, but there was nothing nice about his voice. Some people have a constantly teasing voice that can land on the unpleasant side, especially if there's a grating sound mixed in, like in the voice of Captain Ellis.

Bernie nodded a very slight nod, hardly visible. "They actually made you a captain?" he said.

Ellis smiled a big smile, although his eyes, a dull golden color, seemed to get smaller. "I know you're happy for me," he said. "Deputy director of Missing Persons—a big responsibility. I'm humbled."

Bernie rose, pocketing Weatherly's note. Ellis's eyes followed his every movement. And I followed every movement of his.

Bernie turned to Weatherly. "Thank you."

"No problem," she said.

"You two know each other?" Ellis said.

"Getting to," Bernie said.

We walked out. I could feel Ellis's gaze on the back of my neck.

Seven

Captain Stine was climbing into a squad car, but he climbed back out when he saw us leaving HQ. The sun was in one of its real hottish moods, and sweat shone on Stine's lower lip.

"Productive visit?" he said.

"Not bad," Bernie said.

"See anyone in particular?"

"Weatherly Wauneka. And don't grill me."

"What did you think of her? Or would that be grilling?"

Grilling? Specifically grilling Bernie? I've been around many grills in my time, and here's one thing about them: they're hot. Stine was a friend. Why would Bernie think he'd want to do something so horrible? But did I need to know the reason? Never! I changed my position slightly, got Captain Stine into perfect striking distance.

"She's very good," Bernie said.

Stine nodded. "Potential chief in twenty years. In a world that's not upside down."

"What does that mean?"

I was with Bernie on that. Just imagine! We'd be lying on our backs in the sky! And the birds would be—well, I couldn't even picture what the birds would be doing, and actually don't care. Would I have such angry eyes if I could soar around on the breeze day after day? Birds!

Stine glanced around, maybe lowered his voice a little. "It's the goddamn building."

"I don't get it."

"You know what it cost?" Stine said. "I'm talking about the real cost?"

"No."

"Join the club. There's been so much maneuvering that no one will ever know. But that's not even the point. You don't get a building like this without some big quid pro quos."

Quid pro quos? You hear that from time to time in our business, but the meaning never comes, at least not to me. I don't worry about things like that. What I worry about is . . . for what seemed like ages I couldn't come up with any worries, and then I hit pay dirt. Food! Food is my only worry. When is the next meal? Will it be enough? Why not a treat? A treat right now! Suddenly, I was starving. But other than that, no worries.

"Such as?" Bernie saying.

"Figure it out," said Stine.

"Where do I start?" Bernie had a thought, one of those real powerful ones I can feel, although I can't see inside them. "With Ellis?" he said.

"Our Ellis? Why would you say that?"

"They made him a captain, Lou. Deputy director of Missing Persons means he's running it, day to day. How the hell did that happen?"

"I know the two of you had some issues back then, but—"

"Issues? He should've been locked up for what he did."

"Not gonna get into all that. It was the tail end of the Wild West days around here. We've got to move on."

"Maybe you," Bernie said. "Not me."

What was this? We were staying put in the Wild West? You can count on Bernie to make the right decision.

"Ellis," said Bernie as we drove away from HQ, "how is it—"

The phone buzzed.

"Hey," Bernie said.

"Hey," said Rick, his voice coming from all around in the car. "Heard you were downtown."

"We're still downtown," Bernie said.

"But you've left HQ."

"Are you watching from a drone?"

"I have other sources," Rick said. "How was your visit?"

"I found out why you're in such a pissy mood."

Rick was in a pissy mood? Wow! How could Bernie know something like that over the phone? Pissy moods give off a very distinctive smell—you don't need me to tell you that—but I've never picked up that smell over the phone. Or any other smell, come to think of it. Was it possible I hadn't been trying hard enough?

"Hang on a minute, Rick," Bernie was saying. "Chet? Big guy?"

"What's he doing?" Rick said.

"Kind of pressing his nose into the speaker for some reason," Bernie said. "Denting it, in fact. Chet! Cool it!"

Wow! Was this interesting or what? Things changed big-time when you got your nose inside this—what was it called? *Speaker,* maybe? It really didn't matter. The point was that on the inside I could actually feel Rick's voice! I could feel his breathing! And buried down a layer or two in that voice and that breathing, I could feel a pissy mood! Could I even . . . ? Yes! I could! I could smell piss! The real thing! I'd been missing so much! From now on, every single time without exception that we were in the car, I was going to plant my—

"CHET!"

Not long after that when I . . . came to, you might say, I found we were in a time-out. We have them on occasion, me and Bernie. They're all about catching our breath, Bernie says, although my breath is always right here with me, so it takes no time at all to catch it. In a time-out, we just sit for a bit like we were doing now, parked near the college. The kids are gone in summer—which is too bad, college kids being so much fun to watch, with their weed and their Frisbees, not to mention their funneling, a game I don't understand at all—so this time-out was on the boring side. I gazed ahead at nothing. Bernie gazed at me.

"You okay, big guy?" he said.

Me? Couldn't be better. Except for the boredom part. Soon—possibly very soon—I'd be needing some action.

"I'd like to finish that call with Rick," he said. "But it won't be easy if someone's tearing the car apart."

Someone tearing the car apart? Outrageous! On no account could that be allowed to happen, not on my watch, amigo, not now, not ever. Who's in charge of security at the Little Detective Agency? You're looking at him. I sat up my very tallest, my eyes, ears, nose, all on highest alert, waiting for trouble to arrive. Good luck, buddy boy.

Meanwhile, Bernie got back on the phone.

"Everything all right?" Rick said.

Bernie shot me a sidelong glance. "I think so."

"Maybe he wants a T-R-E-A-T," Rick said.

While I was on highest alert? Forget about it!

"We're in a brief interlude between them at the moment," Bernie said. "How did you find out about Ellis?"

"It was in the dailies."

"No one talked to you ahead of time?"

"Like who?"

"The chief, for example."

"Hell no. Why would he?"

"Because you were the obvious candidate."

"Not obvious enough," Rick said.

"I disagree," Bernie said. "Heard any scuttlebutt about a quid pro quo?"

"What kind of quid pro quo?"

"Involving Ellis."

"Nope. What are you getting at?"

"I thought Stine was dropping a hint," Bernie said. "Maybe it was about something else."

"How can someone like Stine put up with all this shit?"

"He takes a long view."

"Good for him," Rick said. "But not for me."

"Meaning what?"

"I'm hanging them up, Bernie."

"Don't do that."

"Why not?"

"Just wait it out. I've got a feeling."

There was a silence. Rick said, "Oh, well, then." That made Bernie laugh. Then Rick laughed, too. A bit of a surprise: it hadn't sounded like a funny conversation to me.

"Three people who are proving hard to find," Bernie said as we passed the last condo development, the smell of fresh paint in the air, and came to open country. "First, Mavis. Second, Johnnie Lee Goetz, whose car Mavis was driving, a car she claimed was stolen although she didn't report it. Third, Mickey Rottoni, small-time criminal and former boyfriend of Johnnie Lee."

Wow! Bernie had all that in his head? Just incredible! I took a good close look at his head, beautifully shaped but not the biggest you see out there, in fact just the right size. Did that mean it was crammed full? What if some new idea came to him? Where would it go? I worried a little, but then the answer came to me: Bernie would figure it out like he always did. Did I also wonder how could he figure it out if his head was already full? No, I did not!

We took an exit, hit two-lane blacktop, drove up into the hills, the sun lower in the sky now and behind us, and the Valley shimmering below like it was underwater, impossible of course, with our aquifer problem. Bernie checked Weatherly Wauneka's note. "EZ AZ Desert Tours and Mini Golf, second left after the Zinc Town stoplight." We drove on, Bernie's face darkening a bit, which sometimes happens when he's thinking his deepest thoughts. "Walking tours or ATV tours?" he said at last. Uh-oh. Walking tours, please, the ATV kind being bad for the desert, although that was hard to understand, the desert so much mightier than any ATV. All the same, I sort of had a peek into our next interview, the strangest sensation. I didn't like it one little bit. I prefer the here and now.

We climbed a hill, saguaros just sort of standing there as we passed by. You can't help being reminded of humans when you see them. Not the patient standing part but the shape.

"Damn," said Bernie.

That meant he'd spotted a bullet hole or two in one of the saguaros. I didn't even need to check. I know Bernie.

We entered a little desert town—general store, bar, diner, cowboy art shop, Indian art shop, and no one around. "Zinc Town," Bernie said. "A total swindle way back when. The investors took off half the mountain, never found an ounce of zinc."

I thought about that. We'd dealt with a swindler in the past, an English fellow name of Sir Royce Bentley, who was selling luxury island getaway homes, or possibly the islands themselves. In the end it didn't matter, the homes and the islands not real, and Sir Royce was up at Northern State Correctional, breaking real rocks in the hot sun. He was called something else up there, his name also not turning out to be real. Was Bernie saying Sir Royce was on the loose and back at it? Right away, I was on the lookout for a dude in what I believe is called a *bowler*. A bowler is a kind of hat that turns out to be excellent chewing material. I'd kept possession of Sir Royce's bowler after we closed the case—so we didn't end up with nothing, Bernie said—but it didn't last as long as I'd hoped.

Now in Zinc Town, no one wearing a bowler appeared. We passed a stoplight, turned onto a road that went from pavement to potholes to dirt, and all of a sudden came to a whole lot of fun stuff, normally big but here little, like windmills, lighthouses, tugboats, castles, a Santa Claus, all connected with narrow strips of green carpet. Mini golf! I knew it at once. I loved mini golf, had gone with Bernie and Charlie on several occasions, although my next visit might not be anytime soon.

We pulled up in front of a small sort of ranch house with a sign over the door and . . . and a bunch of dusty ATVs parked out front.

"Damn," said Bernie again.

We got out of the car and headed toward the ranch house. The door opened, and a barefoot kid stepped onto the porch. He wore

jeans and a cowboy hat and looked like a very small cowboy. The
kid eyed me right away, just like every kid I'd ever met.

"Hi, there," Bernie said.

"We're closed," said the kid. "Your dog's big."

"His name's Chet," Bernie said. "He likes kids."

"Chet's big," said the kid.

"I'm sure he'll let you pet him if you want," Bernie said.

"I don't know," said the kid.

"No problem," Bernie said. "Is your mom or dad around?"

The kid shook his head. Then he came down off the porch
and sidled over my way. I lay down. No particular reason. It just
seemed right. The kid put his little hand on my back and went
pat-pat.

"My name's Bernie," Bernie said. "What's yours?"

"Lukie."

"How old are you, Lukie?"

"Almost seven."

"I've got a son who's almost seven."

"What's his name?"

"Charlie," Bernie said. "Will your mom and dad be back soon?"

Lukie shook his head.

Bernie squatted down on my other side, so I was between him
and Lukie. "Does a guy named Mickey Rottoni work here?" he
said.

The pat-patting stopped. "He was mean to me," Lukie said.

"Yeah?" said Bernie. "How come?"

"I played with his putter."

"That doesn't sound too bad."

"It's a special putter," Lukie said.

"What makes it special?" Bernie said.

"It's just special. Mickey said if I ever touch it again—"

A man shouted from inside the ranch house, "What the hell's
goin' on out there?"

Lukie rose and scrambled away from me. I rose, too, and
stepped in between Bernie and the house. The screen door
slapped open, and an old man in a wheelchair rolled out onto the

porch. You saw this type of old man out in the desert from time to time: beaky-faced, wispy-haired, leather-skinned, irritated. His gaze went to Bernie, then to me, and back to Bernie.

"We're closed," he said. "Didn't you tell 'em we're closed?"

"Yes, Poppop," said Lukie.

"When do you open?" Bernie said.

"When there's customers," said Poppop. "And there ain't none, not in this heat."

"We're customers," Bernie said.

"You want a tour? None of the ATVs is gassed up."

"We can take care of that if you've got a pump," Bernie said. Poppop nodded.

"But," Bernie went on, "we want a guided tour."

"I don't do no guided tours no more."

"I understand you have a guide named Mickey Rottoni."

Poppop's eyes narrowed down to just about nothing. "You understand wrong." He did one of those dry spitting things. Human spitting is a huge subject—why men and not women, for instance—but there's no time to go into now, although can I just squeeze in the fact that of all the different spits out there, dry is my favorite? "Never heard of him," Poppop said.

Another big human subject is blurting. Blurting humans get an urgent look in their eyes and an urgent shape to their lips, changes that were now happening to Lukie. "But, Poppop!" Lukie pointed to some hills, not far away. "He took the green ATV, and he didn't—"

Poppop slammed his hand on the wheelchair armrest. "Zip your mouth! Get inside!"

Lukie stepped onto the porch and headed for the door.

"Run, damn you!"

Lukie ran into the house.

Bernie turned to Poppop. "No reason to treat the kid like that."

Poppop had a face made for looking nasty. "You tellin' me how to treat my own flesh and blood?"

"You brought it on," Bernie said. "Where's Mickey Rottoni?"

"Get offa my land," Poppop said. He stuck a hand inside his shirt and drew a gun, not as big as our .38 Special, but guns didn't have to be big, as I'd seen more than once in my career. Poppop's gun hadn't been fired recently. I never miss a smell like that, and would have handled the whole situation differently, possibly getting my teeth involved immediately.

We started backing away. "The boy better not come to any harm," Bernie said.

"You threatening me?" said Poppop.

"Simply stating a fact," Bernie told him.

We parked under the saguaro with the bullet holes and had a picnic supper from the cooler, kibble with some bacon chips—almost more than enough, thanks, Bernie!—for me, and tuna from a can for him. Above us the sky put on a show, running through all kinds of colors, then catching fire, and finally dimming down to black. The moon rose over the hills, and the shadow of the saguaro spread over me and Bernie. That was a little creepy, but I got over it right away. The Little Detective Agency is at its best at night.

We drove back through Zinc Town, headlights off, and parked in front of the EZ AZ Desert Tours and Mini Golf ranch house, not as close as before. I smelled danger. Then I realized the smell was us. Who has it better than me? Bernie opened the glove box and took out the flashlight and the .38 Special. He's a crack shot, in case that hasn't come up yet, can hit spinning dimes in the air, turning them into a kind of music like tiny cymbals. Whoever we were hunting tonight—that part not yet clear to me—was in big trouble.

We walked past the ranch house—no lights showing inside— and were soon on a trail that took us into the hills. What a bright night, everything so clear: the big boulders, the spiky plants, the ATV tracks crisscrossing the trail and heading this way and that through the desert. I couldn't have been in a better mood. Bernie was in the lead, not our usual MO, but I was cool with it. That's how good my mood was! Also I had no idea where we were going or why. Possibly we were just out for a lovely moonlit stroll. But then why the .38? I moved into the lead.

"Smell anything, big guy?"

Uh-oh. Where to begin? With the pack rat that had recently crossed our path? The sidewinder hidden behind a barrel cactus that Bernie's arm almost brushed as he passed by? The gray fox, high on a branch of a mesquite tree at the crest of the hill? How annoying was that, by the way? But did Bernie want to know any of those things? Or would he be more interested in the smell of a human male, a recent scent although not from today, a scent with . . . with a garlic add-on?

I sped up, following the scent of the man with the garlic add-on.

"Good boy," Bernie said.

Eight

I forgot to mention the ATV smell, also recent although not from today. It mixed together with the garlic scent and led us off the trail, up a steep ridge, and across a rocky plateau. And what was this? A member of the nation within had passed this way? A female, to be precise, and with a scent that reminded me of something, something about me, a bit confusing. The next thing I knew, I'd broken into what Bernie calls my go-to trot. The go-to trot is a fine way to travel. You feel so light you can keep it up for a long time, all day and all night if you have to.

Although maybe not you. After a while, even Bernie, probably stronger than you, actually by a lot—no offense—was huffing and puffing behind me. I wanted to slow down for him, but I just couldn't, on account of a sound I was starting to pick up, a soft, low moan that pain sometimes draws out of one of my kind. All that—the scents of ATV and garlic and a member of the nation within, plus the moaning—led me to the other side of the plateau and up a hill. There was a hole in the side of this hill. I was familiar with holes like this. They led to abandoned mines, which Bernie and I liked to explore from time to time. We've found all sorts of treasure on our mine adventures, like an old wagon wheel and a canteen with an arrowhead stuck in it. The fun we had! But I already knew this particular adventure wasn't going to be like that. I've been around.

Bernie switched on the flashlight and shone it into the mine. The first thing we saw was a green ATV, just inside the entrance, the key glinting in the ignition. The moans were clearer now, but no louder, if that makes sense. Pain doesn't make us noisy, me and my kind. We keep it inside. Why? I don't know. We just do.

Bernie came up beside me, shining the light this way and that.

Some mines go deep in the mountain and some do not. This was the second kind. It was also the kind, fairly common, with crushed beer cans and crumpled wrappers on the floor. There was also a rolled-up sleeping bag, a foam mattress, and a backpack—not from the olden days but from nowadays—and beyond them two shadowy forms, both lying still on the hard-packed dirt. Bernie took the .38 from his pocket and aimed the flashlight beam slowly and carefully over every bit of the mine as though he expected to see something. All I saw were the rock-studded earthen walls, a blackened wooden beam or two, and lying not far from the backpack one of those long tubelike things photographers sometimes screw onto their cameras. We moved closer to the two forms, and Bernie shone the light on them.

The nearest form was a man, a man who smelled of garlic and blood—not wet, fresh blood, but the dried, crusty kind. The man lay on his back, one arm out to the side, his hand making the stop sign, his eyes open, dull, still. He had a red hole in his forehead, and blood had leaked onto his face, but I still recognized him: the big, shaved-head dude who'd kidnapped—would that be how to put it?—little Griffie from the Porsche. He gave off one other smell, not particularly strong now although it soon would be, the smell that meant whoever he had once been was now gone for good. Griffie had been here, too, by the way, and recently, although there was no sign of him now.

What came next was the kind of surprise you sometimes get in our line of work. The man's eyes moved the slightest bit in Bernie's direction. Then his lips moved, too, also just the slightest bit. He spoke, his voice low and whispery.

"Golf," he said.

Bernie tilted his head, his ear almost touching the man's lips. "What about golf?" Bernie said.

There was no answer. The man's eyes half closed and stayed that way. Bernie put his finger to the man's neck, held it there, took it away. The no-longer-living smell drifted up from the man's open mouth, stronger now, and very certain.

Bernie rose and shifted the flashlight beam to the second form.

This was not a man, or a human at all, but a member of the nation within, female, lying on her side with blood—fresh blood—dampening the fur on her chest, and her one visible eye closed. Her coat was black all over, except for one ear, which was . . . white. I thought back to Sergeant Wauneka's office and was trying to remember exactly what had gone down on that visit, when the closed eye slowly opened, looking first at nothing and then at us.

Bernie knelt beside her. "Trixie," he said.

Bernie lay the flashlight on the floor of the mine, illuminating Trixie in the cone of yellow light. Then he took off his T-shirt and tore it into strips. Trixie's eye stayed on him. The fresh blood smell got stronger and stronger, made it hard for me to think about anything else. Would licking the wound be the right move? I . . . I wanted to, but Bernie had something in mind, and I'd never want to mess that up, and yet still, what would be the harm of—

"Chet? Just sit tight. We'll be okay."

Sit tight was a tricky one, not a command, really, more like a suggestion. It didn't even mean sit. It meant . . . well, I wasn't sure, but knowing we were going to be okay settled my mind very nicely. Bernie, his hands so gentle, slid the T-shirt strips under Trixie and wrapped them around her. She went on making those soft moans, but so quietly now I hardly knew they were there, like the weakest breeze.

Bernie turned to me. "No way to cover all the bases." He rose, lit the face of the shaved-head man, took out his phone, and went click. Then he came back and bent over Trixie. "She comes first. But maybe we can keep this little scene to ourselves a bit longer."

Ourselves meant me and Bernie, so whatever he was talking about sounded right. He lifted Trixie up in one smooth motion, not slow, not fast, carried her over to the ATV, and laid her on the little platform in back. She watched him the whole time. I watched her watching him, except for when I heard a crunch from high up the hill, beyond the mine, the kind of crunch a boot heel might make. I listened carefully, but it didn't come again.

"Squeeze in next to me, big guy," Bernie said.

In that tiny space? I gave it my best shot, found the only way I could do it was by facing the little platform, meaning that our faces, mine and Trixie's, were almost touching, all the way back to the EZ AZ ranch house. Her eyes were like soft silver in the moonlight, and she only moaned once or twice. A little bit of blood leaked through the T-shirt strips, and I licked it up, the right thing to do, no question. We parked beside the Porsche and got Trixie settled in the shotgun seat. I took the little shelf, no problem. As we drove away, Bernie had a long look at the ranch house, dark and silent. That made sense. Wouldn't Lukie and Poppop be fast asleep? That was as far as I could take it on my own.

I prefer outdoors to indoors, but I'm cool with pretty much any indoor space, except for Amy's waiting room. It's not that I don't like Amy, because I do. She's our vet, a big strong woman with big strong hands that know what's what, but even though I like her, I don't like hanging with her, not in her office, where I always start shaking. Her office includes the waiting room, the parking lot, and a few surrounding blocks. Shameful, I know, but I just can't help myself.

Bernie scratched between my ears, finding the perfect spot, as always. "How about you wait in the car? You'll be more comfortable."

What was this? Bernie waiting inside and me waiting outside? Out of the question. I couldn't have been any more comfortable. Except for the shaking part, which I was going to shut down this very second. There! Or perhaps not. No matter. I made myself immovable. We waited.

The steel door that led to the room I liked even less than the waiting room opened, and Amy entered, taking off her mask and gloves.

"Cautious optimism, Bernie," she said.

"Thank god," said Bernie.

"She's not out of the woods yet."

That was a bit of a puzzler. If we were talking about Trixie, she hadn't actually been in the woods but in a mine in mostly open country. Bernie says that Amy's the best vet in the Valley, so I gave her a pass.

"—a lot of blood," she was saying, "but no organ damage." She handed Bernie a baggie. He opened it and took out a bullet round.

"Thirty-two," he said.

"Promise me you'll catch the bastard who did this," Amy said.

"I can't—"

"Promise."

Bernie nodded.

Amy turned my way, gave me a close look. "Big brother," she said.

"For sure?" Bernie said.

"Can't be sure without a DNA test, but—"

The door to Amy's parking lot flew open, and a woman came running in. I didn't recognize her at first, out of uniform, but it was Weatherly Wauneka, wearing jeans and a T-shirt, her glossy black hair not tied up, instead hanging long and free down her back. The look in her eyes reminded me of the eyes of a mama mountain lion I'd once had a much-too-close encounter with, if we leave out the fact that the eyes of the lion were yellow and Weatherly's were deepest brown, almost black.

Weatherly covered her chest. "How is she? Is it really her?"

"Weatherly," said Bernie. "This is Amy, our vet."

"As I was telling Bernie," Amy said and then went into that whole confusing out-of-the-woods thing again. We'd found Trixie in a mine, not in the woods! Getting the facts straight is a big part of what we do at the Little Detective Agency, almost as important as shooting dimes out of the air or chasing javelinas. Meanwhile, Amy placed a big square hand on Weatherly's back, drew her to the steel door, and led her into that too-bright room on the other side.

We sat in the waiting room. Bernie gazed at the .32 round lying in the palm of his hand. My Bernie! He was thinking hard, poor guy. Whoa! I realized I wasn't thinking at all! I didn't have one single thought in my whole mind, a vast empty space at the moment, and actually quite pleasant, reminding me of the desert. Well, well. My mind was like the desert? How come I was just finding that out now? It explained . . . everything. Amazing! I now knew everything about me. And it was still early morning. Today was going to be a doozie.

The steel door opened. Weatherly came out alone, tears on her face although she made no crying sounds. Suzie cried in that exact same way.

Weatherly saw us watching, gave her head a quick shake, and wiped away the tears on the back of her arm.

"I thought I'd never see her again," she said. "I let myself down, and I let her down."

"Oh?" Bernie said.

"By giving up hope."

"Um," Bernie began, "no need to—"

"Bernie."

"Yes?"

"Thank you."

"You're welcome."

"I can never repay you."

"It's not a thing where, um . . ."

Weatherly stepped forward and gave Bernie a hug. He pat-patted her on the back, at the same time looking at me over her shoulder in a not-totally-comfortable way. Did the hug seem to be taking longer than normal? I thought so. Human hugging is another big subject, maybe even bigger than human spitting, which we didn't go into before, but can I just mention that in a lot of hugs the huggers weren't really feeling each other? They're hugging in a distant sort of way, like Bernie now. Weatherly wasn't hugging in a distant way. She was . . . how to put it? Getting a sense of Bernie? Not that she was moving her hands around or anything like that. In fact, I might have been completely wrong. But then came a change in Bernie, and he was getting a sense of her, too.

I know quite a bit about boxing. After Charlie went away to live full-time with Leda and Malcolm at their place in High Chaparral Estates, we watched a lot of old fights on TV, me and Bernie, both of us on our feet most of the time. Sugar Ray Robinson and Carmen Basilio! Sugar Ray Leonard and Marvin Hagler! The Thrilla in Manila! Don't get me started! The point I was making is that I've observed the behavior of boxing referees and know how to break up clinches, which is what I did now, squeezing in between them.

Weatherly laughed. She turned out to have one of those really big laughs that take you by surprise. "Who have we here?"

Me, Chet. That was who we had here. Surely she knew that already?

"Heh-heh," said Bernie.

"He really is formidable," Weatherly said.

I had no idea what that meant, but I liked the sound. I tried it out in my mind: Chet the Formidable. I'd never remember that. Chet the Jet would have to do.

"What's next?" Weatherly said.

"Head back out there," said Bernie. "Pick up the thread."

"Trixie's staying here, of course, probably for a week, Amy says. And I'm off today."

"Then you can go home and get some rest."

"I'm coming with you."

"Very nice of you," Bernie said. "But I don't really—"

"It has nothing to do with nice," said Weatherly. "I'm already involved in the case."

"True," said Bernie. "But there could be problems, you being a cop and all."

"You don't trust us?" Weatherly said.

"Not all of you, not all of the time."

So that was that, a happy ending. Except Weatherly said, "First sign of a problem, I'm gone without a word."

And Bernie said, "Okay."

Here's an important fact that Weatherly seemed to be missing. The Little Detective Agency is me and Bernie, end of story. My job now was to make sure she learned that fact in no uncertain terms.

Nine

Outside in Amy's parking lot, Bernie reached for his phone. "Before we get started, let's make sure this is our guy."

Weatherly leaned in to see the picture on Bernie's little screen. I leaned in, too, not to see the picture—although I couldn't miss it, the ruined face of the shaved-head dude, lying in the mine—but just to show Weatherly that my leaning-in skills were as good as hers. Or better.

She blinked, possibly because she'd somehow poked her eye on the tip of one of my ears, and said, "Mickey Rottoni, beyond a doubt. Did he steal Trixie to get back at me?"

"No proof of that," Bernie said.

"What's another possibility?"

"Don't have one."

"Then that'll be our working theory," Weatherly said. "Want me to follow in my car?"

Certainly, if you have to come at all. That was the answer I expected from Bernie, although probably without that second part, since he can be a little too nice at times. But what I heard was: "Hell, why not squeeze in with us? We'll drop you back here."

There are things in life you just have to accept gracefully. What's the point of fighting battles you can't win? Actually, there was plenty of point, but no time to figure out the how and why, or even one of them. Instead, as gracefully as possible, I leaped into the Porsche, landing squarely in the shotgun seat, bull's-eye. I sat up tall, facing forward, alert and ready to take on all comers in ways they wouldn't soon forget, a total pro.

"Um," Bernie said.

"Plenty of room for me on that shelf," Weatherly said. "I've got good flexibility."

Bernie shot her a very quick look, the meaning unknown to me. A minute later, we were on the move, a warm breeze in our hair and the seating arrangement as good as it could be under the circumstances.

Out of the Valley, in the desert, two-lane blacktop, open road as far as you could see. I was feeling tip-top, when from behind me Weatherly said, "How fast can this thing go?"

"Thing?" said Bernie, at the same time tromping down on the gas, pedal to the metal. The engine roared like a mighty creature, and the car shot forward like . . . like we were going to take off and fly to the sun!

Weatherly laughed that huge laugh of hers and shouted, "Wow! Wow, wow, wow!"

Bernie ramped us down to where we could hear ourselves think, as humans say. No actual thoughts seemed to be going on in my head, so I soon stopped listening.

We drove up into the hills. Weatherly leaned forward, pretty close to getting in my space. "I'm part Navajo," she said.

"I wondered," said Bernie.

"In what context?"

"No context. Just wondering."

Weatherly sat back. Saguaros appeared, lining the road in a friendly way like they were looking out for us. I spotted the one with the bullet holes, where Bernie and I had had our picnic. Weatherly leaned forward again.

"My grandmother's a tribal member," she said. "It turns out she knows something about you."

"Like what?"

"I call her a few times a week. Yesterday, I mentioned your name. Grammie asked if you were a Little from Mesquite Road. I checked your card and told her you were. Grammie says your family had a whole big spread up there on the west side of the canyon, way back when."

"Long before my time," Bernie said.

"But not before Grammie's mom's time," said Weatherly. "That was my great-grammie. Laura was her Anglo name."

"What was her Navajo name?"

"She had several, over time, but she was mostly known by her nickname, which translated to Laughing Girl in English. She died before I was born, but she was an important figure in the family—actually, still is. Grammie says that she—meaning Laura—knew a young man named Ephraim Little when she was growing up."

"My great-grandfather," Bernie said.

"Do you remember him?"

"No," said Bernie. "But there's a picture of him holding me when I was two or three."

"I'd like to see it."

"Yeah?"

"Grammie says the two of them walked together, your great-grandfather and my great-grandmother."

"Hiking?" said Bernie.

"Possibly that, too," said Weatherly. "But Grammie's an old-fashioned woman, very straitlaced and genteel."

There was a long silence. A roadrunner popped up beside a bush and then popped back down.

"Oh," Bernie said.

Weatherly sat back on the little shelf.

We drove into Zinc Town, cruised along the main street. Bernie slowed down as we passed the Indian art shop and glanced at Weatherly in the rearview mirror. Her gaze was straight ahead. At the stoplight, we took the road that turned to dirt pretty quick and followed it to the EZ AZ ranch house.

Weatherly nodded. "This is where I served Rottoni with the papers."

We parked and got out of the car. "Looks like business has picked up," Bernie said. "All the ATVs are out. I planned on renting one."

We went to the door. Bernie knocked. No answer. Were Poppop and Lukie inside, just lying low? That happens with perps, but although Poppop was perp-like in some ways, there was nothing perpy about Lukie. Sometimes, when perps are lying low, standing absolutely still, I can hear them breathing. I listened my hardest, heard not the slightest sound from inside. Bernie knocked a few more times, peered through a window or two. The house was silent and still.

We walked—me, Bernie, and Weatherly—across the plain and into the hills, not rushing, just at our normal pace. Still, our normal pace, mine and Bernie's, is pretty swift. Some newcomers can't keep up, some can, but just barely, with lots of grunting and groaning, and a few can do it no problem. That was Weatherly's group, the no-problem type. She was also a very quiet walker for a human, maybe the quietest I'd ever seen. She was starting to make me a bit uneasy, not because she wasn't a nice person. Weatherly seemed nice enough. So why—

I shut all that down. Smells were in the air, demanding my attention. *Big guy!* I said to myself. *What do you think's going down right now? A walk in the park? This is a job, buddy boy!* Myself answered back, *Then who's paying?* I ignored myself. Not so easy, but in law enforcement, you do what you have to do.

Smells can tell a story. I assume you already knew that. Sometimes the story can be hard to figure out. You've got the individual smells, say pizza and human puke, and then you've got when they were laid down. If the puke comes after the pizza, then it's a simple little tale: some dude ate pizza that made him sick, and then he puked. But what if the pizza comes after the puke? What have you got then? In my job, I deal with problems like that all the time.

Here's what I had to work with on the trail up to the mine. First, there were the smells of me and Bernie, but they were not the most recent. Later than us—on top of our scents, if you're with me—came the scents of two men, one who had a bit of nervous sweat going on, the sour kind of male human sweat, and the other whose smell reminded me of a strange case we'd worked, something about fake rabbis. Had there been a banquet with some sort of reddish soup? I couldn't remember.

Anything else in the air? Oh yes, we had a very slight snaky aroma, not unusual in these parts. What was unusual was how it reminded me of my collar. I have two collars, a black one for dress-up and another one for everyday. That other one used to be brown leather, but after a somewhat exciting encounter I'd had on a case we'd worked in Cajun country, my everyday collar was now made of gator skin. Do you ever get a feeling in your head, a kind of pressure, when an idea is just about to take shape? I had that feeling now, but it faded away as we approached the cave. Who wants pressure in the head? Not me, amigo. And just like that, poof, it was completely gone.

We reached the entrance to the mine. The sun was high in the sky now, the strongest thing around by far. In the daytime at this time of year, it's like the sun is trying to press you into the ground. At the same time, cool air was flowing out of the mine. There are ways around the sun, if that makes any sense.

Bernie took out his flashlight, stepped inside the mine. I was already there, but Weatherly seemed to be hanging back.

"Weatherly?" said Bernie. "Some problem?"

"No, no," she said. "I . . . I just . . . just don't like mines."

"You don't have to come in."

"I do." Weatherly squared her shoulders—one of the best human moves out there—and followed us into the mine.

We moved out of sunshine and into darkness, the yellow cone of the flashlight so feeble compared to what was going on outside. I felt a truly enormous thought taking shape in my mind, but before it could, I began to see that there'd been big changes in the mine. The backpack was gone. And so was the sleeping bag and the air mattress. As well as the body—the body of Mickey Rottoni, if I'd been following things right. All of them gone. We kept going to the end of the mine, not very far, a wall of rock, hacked at here and there, but still solid. The mine was empty.

"Bernie?" Weatherly said. "I don't understand."

Bernie walked around, stabbing the light beam in one corner and then another, kind of fiercely like it was a weapon.

He turned to Weatherly. Just the lower part of her was lit up, the rest invisible. Her voice came out of the darkness. "I'm angry."

"He was lying right there, just like I told you," Bernie said.

"I know that, Bernie. I just hate when someone does the right thing on a real tough call and then some bastard makes them pay. I'm sorry."

"Nothing to be sorry about. And we don't know that anything tricky happened here. Maybe some hikers came along and took the body down to the sheriff."

"And there's no one securing the crime scene?" Weatherly said. "No one even put up any tape?"

"Maybe they're on their way," Bernie said. "Or—Chet? What's up, buddy?"

Nothing really. I seemed to have gone off to one side a bit. Sometimes a patch of dirt interests me. This particular patch seemed a little less smooth than the rest of the mine floor. Not much of a reason to start digging, you might say, and I'd agree. Not that I was actually digging, more like just pawing around, and with only one of my front paws, not putting any force into it. But once, pawing around just like this, I'd pawed up an old silver spoon that we pawned at Mr. Singh's for fifteen bucks! Not to mention a big helping of Mrs. Singh's curried goat, a favorite of—

"Chet? What you got there?"

Me? Nothing. I knew at once that Bernie was hoping for another old silver spoon, and I hated to disappoint him, so I pawed a little harder and . . . what was this? I did feel a little something.

Bernie hunched down and shone the light into the small hole I'd made. The light glinted on a wire. A disappointment, certainly, but—

"Run!" Bernie shouted.

When Bernie's voice gets like that—not so much the loud part, but the command part—I don't think. I do. "Run!" I ran. We all ran. One problem. I was so much faster than Bernie and Weatherly that there was no way I wouldn't be the first one outside. It was my job to be last. That probably explained the slight confusion at the entrance, the odd bump and even stumble—although there was no stumbling by me. Really, people. Who has more legs, me or you? Facts are facts.

We burst outside and kept running, me hanging back to stay last.

Bernie looked over his shoulder and yelled at me. "No, Chet!"

Bernie yelling at me? Oh no. That had never happened before, not once. I must have done something wrong, but what?

"Go, Chet, go!"

Whew. That was all? Easy-peasy. I bounded ahead, surging forward with enormous leaps, practically flying, my ears flattened back from a wind of my own making. I glanced behind and saw Bernie and Weatherly running hard. Behind them, a little puff of white smoke appeared in the black opening of the mine. Bernie couldn't have seen it, but at that moment, he placed his hand in the small of Weatherly's back to make her go faster, and then: ka-KA-BOOM! BOOM! BOOM!

Ten

Sometime later, we had kind of a crowd around what had been the opening to the mine but was now just more rubble on an already rubbly hillside. There were guys and gals from Valley PD, the sheriff's office, plainclothes, uniformed, Crime Scene, even a few motorcycle guys from Highway Patrol, although not Fritzie Bortz, an old pal with balance issues, now working for the Border Patrol. It reminded me of a cop convention we'd once attended, me and Bernie, with lots of standing around, taking pictures, hey-how-ya-doin', and complaining about this and that. The only missing part was the booze, probably a good thing. There's nothing worse than a roomful of boozy bikers, of course, but a roomful of boozy cops comes close.

No surprise that I knew several of the participants, which resulted in a few nice pats, some first-rate between-the-ears scratching from Nancy Nix of the Vice Squad, and half a roast beef sandwich. Lots of crime scene tape got put up, an earthmover broke down, and folks started drifting away. Then it was just Bernie and me, plus Weatherly, who had no way of getting back except with us. Plus one other dude who'd climbed up to the top of the hill and was now making his way down, a cop with lots of gold on his uniform and receding red hair. The name came to me at once: Captain Ellis. I couldn't have said my mind was on fire—that didn't happen every day—but it was getting the job done, baby. Who could ask for more?

Captain Ellis picked his way through the last of the rubble and came over to us. His pale face was all sweaty. Those redheaded types didn't do well in the heat, although I've only known a few, all of them breaking rocks in the hot sun, come to think of it.

"Haven't seen you in years, Bernie," Ellis said, "and now all of a sudden we're practically living together."

"There's a thought," said Bernie.

But . . . but a bad one, right? Because living with Bernie means living with me. And as I believe I've already mentioned, Captain Ellis's voice had a bit of a grating thing going on, which would make me uneasy after a while. My ears are sensitive, perhaps more so than yours, no offense. Also, he had a sweaty smell that bothered me a bit, kind of strange since hardly any smells actually bother me, certainly not that of human sweat. And why wouldn't he have been sweating, toiling up and down this hill in the heat? But mixed in with the fresh sweat was a hint of the more sour, possibly nervous kind of sweat. Was it the mixture I didn't like? I just couldn't figure it out. And no time now. The problem would have to be set aside for later. I told myself to remember to do so, without fail.

Ellis turned to Weatherly. "I'm puzzled to find you here, Sergeant. I don't recall seeing you at roll call this a.m."

"It's my day off," Weatherly said.

"And an exciting one," said Ellis.

"Excuse me?" said Weatherly.

"Speaking for myself," Ellis said, "I've never had a single day off that involved private eyes and mine cave-ins."

Weatherly said nothing. Ellis gazed at her, smiling slightly. Human smiles—and it took me so long to figure this out!—are not necessarily friendly. So there was a time when I might have missed what was going on right now, which was . . . which was . . . well, a complicated situation, let's leave it at that.

This moment of silence went on a little too long, in my opinion, and then Bernie said, "An explosion, not a cave-in."

Ellis rubbed his hands together. "TBD, Bernie, my friend. TBD."

There's violence in Bernie. It doesn't come out often, just when we need it the most. The rest of the time, it disappears like . . . like it's deep in a mine. Whoa! But not the point, which was about the violence inside Bernie, which we certainly didn't need now. TBD, whatever that was, couldn't have been much of a threat, not like someone was waving guns around—although strangely enough, everyone in this little conversation was packing, except us. Ellis wore something that had recently been fired, out of sight in a shoulder holster under his shirt, to judge from where the smell was coming from, and Weatherly had something smaller, not recently fired, in an ankle holster under the hem of her jeans. Both of them cops, of course, so no biggie, but still, I wished we'd been carrying the .38 Special. If Bernie didn't want to bother, I could . . . carry it myself! What a fantastic idea! And I was only now thinking it for the very first time? Chet! Wake up!

"An explosion," Bernie was saying, "as Crime Scene will be documenting for you by tomorrow. But you've always been the aggressively wrong type, haven't you, Von?"

"What could you possibly be referring to, old buddy?"

Without actually moving, Bernie seemed to close some of the distance between him and Ellis. One of Ellis's hands twitched, made a little motion toward his shoulder, then settled back down.

"I'll try to keep you from embarrassing yourself," Bernie said. "We've got three acts here—the killing of Mickey Rottoni, the removal of the body, the planting of the explosive. Probably the same perpetrator for all three, but not necessarily."

Ellis turned to Weatherly. "Your friend here's always been a real deep thinker, in case you didn't know."

Bernie whipped out his phone and thrust it in Ellis's face, almost hitting him with it. Ellis's face got blotchy, but he held his ground, glanced at the screen, and said, "A picture, photoshopped or not, is not a body."

A muscle in Bernie's face jumped. I'd only seen that once before, and what came next was hard to forget. But this time, Bernie didn't move. Staying still at that moment took a lot of strength. I could feel it under my paws.

Ellis looked at Weatherly again. No muscles jumped in her face, but it seemed to be made from stone. "I am not a deep thinker," Ellis said. "Merely a humble worker who closes cases. All we know for sure about this one is that a gent name of Mickey

Rottoni has gone missing." Ellis smiled his unfriendly smile. "Since I'm in charge of the Department of Missing Persons, I'll be running the case." He touched where the brim of his hat would have been had he been wearing one. "Enjoy the rest of your day off, Sergeant. And, Bernie—always a pleasure." He walked over to an ATV with a blue flasher on the back and drove away, the blue light flashing even after Ellis and the ATV couldn't be seen.

We drove back to Amy's with hardly any talk.

"What was that all about, you and Ellis?" Weatherly said.

"Nothing," said Bernie.

And a little later, she said, "What's next?"

"We'll work the case," Bernie said.

"I'd like to help."

"Is that a good idea?"

"For who?" Weatherly said.

"For you," said Bernie. "You and your career."

"The hell with my career."

One of Bernie's eyebrows rose the tiniest bit. Those eyebrows of his! What communicators! "Lou Stine thinks you'll be chief one day," he said.

I could see Weatherly's eyes in the rearview mirror. She was back on the little shelf, with me in the shotgun seat, as I'm sure you guessed. Her eyes got very bright. She didn't speak until we were in Amy's parking lot, all of us getting out of the Porsche, the normal routine in a back shelf situation. Weatherly turned to Bernie and said, "I owe you."

"For what?" he said.

"Trixie."

Bernie shook his head and was still doing it when she kissed him on the cheek, one of those little kisses you see from time to time. A nice way of saying goodbye, I'd always thought, although not all humans do it, and among the not-doing-it types was Bernie. But now came a bit of a surprise. Bernie kissed her back, maybe partly on the cheek but also partly on the lips. Then it was all on the lips, and not over immediately, plus they had their arms around each other. A good thing or a bad thing? I finally decided bad and was moving in to break things up when they broke it up themselves and Weatherly got in her car and drove away. The whole Valley seemed oddly quiet, even disturbingly so. I barked, just a single bark and far from my loudest, but enough, and . . . what's the expression? Disorder was restored? Something like that.

Our kitchen table stands by a bay window, with a curved bench seat on the window side. When it's just me and Bernie, I sometimes eat not on the floor but right at the table, our little secret. After we got home, we had a nice snack at that table, leftover something for Bernie—I couldn't tell exactly what—and kibble from Rover and Company—where I'd once spent a morning in their test kitchen and am available for retesting at any time—mixed with a bacon bit or two. We both gazed out the window, me because Bernie was doing it and he for reasons of his own. The window looked out on part of old man Heydrich's front yard, where he seemed to have hammered in a new sign, bigger than before.

Bernie sighed. Was the sign bothering him in some way? Did he want one in our yard, too? I sketched out a quick plan that began with uprooting old man Heydrich's sign.

"These forces," Bernie said and then chewed his food for a while. "They go dormant for weeks or months, even years, and then all of a sudden . . ." So this was about the sign? I was leaning yes. He took another bite. "Propagation of the species . . . no denying the power, but still—" He turned to me. "But are we just puppets? And are the strings our emotions?"

I didn't like the sound of this at all. I changed my mind about the sign, and now leaned no.

He went back to gazing out the window. "On the other hand, is that whole approach—call it cerebral or scientific—a dead end? She's flesh and blood, and our time's not infinite."

She? Who would that be? As for the sign—out of the picture for sure.

"So why not pull the trigger, huh, big guy? Or . . . or has it already been pulled?"

This was a bit of a surprise, but maybe gunplay was exactly what we needed right now. I gazed at Bernie: always the smartest human in the room, and he was mine. Were we headed outside to grab the .38 Special out of the glove box? Or was this about the single-shot .410 in the safe behind the waterfall painting in the office? I never found out, because at that moment, someone knocked on the door, a man, to be specific, telling man knocks from women knocks being one of the easiest parts of my job. By this time, I was actually at the door, letting whatever man was on the other side know that I was mad at myself for not hearing his approach and being there before the knock—which was the right way of doing things—and that I was going to take it out on him in no uncertain terms! Or would that be a no-no from Bernie's point of view? I hadn't made up my mind about that before Bernie came up behind me and opened the door. My mind had stopped paying attention in any case. It had become a sort of bright flashing light, sending me a message: CAT! CAT! CAT!

A man stood on our doorstep. He was maybe a bit younger than Bernie, had slicked-back hair, and wore a suit, tie, and a blue shirt with a white collar. Did any of that matter? He smelled of cat. What else did you need to know? A surprising number of people smell of cat, by the way, and there are also those who smell of cat and of my kind at the same time. What sense does that make? But never mind that now. I waited for Bernie to say, "Not today," and close the door in his face.

That didn't happen. Instead, the man smiled a very white-toothed smile and said, "Bernie Little?"

"Correct," said Bernie.

"Nice to meet you. My name's Scott Kyle."

"In that order?" Bernie said.

I didn't get that, and neither did Scott Kyle, unless he was looking confused for some other reason. He blinked and went on,

"And this must be Chet. He's, uh, bigger than I imagined. Aren't you, fella?"

Scott Kyle raised his hand like he was going to pat me and then changed his mind. So far, he was making a poor impression. I'm actually capable of closing the door by myself and have done it on several occasions. Why not now? I couldn't think of one good reason.

"Does he always accompany you on assignments?" Scott Kyle said.

"We're a team," Bernie said.

"I hear you," said Scott Kyle, a good thing because what Bernie had just said was very important. "Is he good on planes?"

"Why?"

"Because the job I have for you involves travel."

"What kind of job?"

Scott Kyle looked past us, into the house. "May I come in?"

That was a tough one. Did a job mean money changed hands? I used to think that, but lately, there'd been a job or two where it didn't. Such as this whole complicated thing that had begun with Mavis! It sure felt like a job, but was anyone paying? When was the last time I'd even laid eyes on any green? I couldn't remember.

Bernie stepped aside to let Scott Kyle in. A tough call but the right one, in my opinion, although I held my ground, forcing Scott Kyle to move around me. Hard to explain why. It just felt correct.

We went down the hall and into the office. We have a very nice office with waterfall paintings on the walls—one of which hides the safe with the single-shot .410 waiting inside—and an elephant-pattern rug on the floor. Once, we'd worked a case involving an elephant name of Peanut. She'd never been in the office, but ever since that case, our elephant-pattern rug smells of her. What's that all about? And here's another puzzle—not a single person who's been in the office, not Charlie or Suzie or any client, has ever mentioned the elephant smell. Don't humans talk about missing the elephant in the room? But they still don't get it!

I like when Bernie sits behind the desk, because that means

business, but he hardly ever does. Instead, he sat on the couch, Scott Kyle taking the visitor chair in front of the desk, and me sitting in the open doorway in case Scott made a break for it. Unlikely with a potential client, but I'd seen it happen, the lady involved hurling a stiletto-heeled shoe at Bernie, probably not a concern today.

"I work for McGregor," Scott said.

"Who's he?" said Bernie.

"McGregor Worldwide Business Consulting?" said Scott. "Surely you've heard of us?"

"It's unavoidable," said Bernie.

Scott laughed one of those nervous little laughs you hear from time to time. I've begun to think they mean the laugher is off-balance. Getting the other guy off-balance is important in boxing. Bernie mentions it whenever he gives Charlie a boxing lesson, those boxing lessons being a little secret by the way, between me, Charlie, and Bernie.

But not on any account including Leda. When was Bernie going to teach Charlie that sweet uppercut? I couldn't wait. In fact, I very badly wanted to see that uppercut this very minute! Do it, Bernie! Do it! Do it on this cat-stinking dude with the two-color shirt!

But Bernie did not.

"I work in the energy department," Scott said. "East European division. Ever been to Ukraine?"

"No."

"Vast potential, and not just in energy. We partner with some very smart and motivated folks over there. They face a big challenge, of course, too obvious to name, but that makes them the little guy, and you have a reputation of looking out for the little guy."

"I wasn't aware of that," Bernie said.

"You're pulling my leg," said Scott.

Whoa. Nothing like that was going on, and besides, it's out of the question in boxing. You get leg-pulling in mixed martial arts, of course, although Bernie's not a fan and therefore neither am I.

But all in all, if the uppercut was off the table, I'd settle for a leg pull or two.

Scott rubbed his hands together. Sometimes that means a human is starting over. "Uh, well, very, um, self-effacing of you. Commendable even, in these self-promoting times. But I should correct myself a bit. When I say little guys, I'm only talking about their relationship to the bear. In terms of financial wherewithal, the top ones can compete on a global basis. And among the top ones, maybe at the pinnacle, is the particular client who's interested in you."

Oh no. I don't mean the money part, which I was pretty sure Scott was talking about. I mean the bear. I'd dealt with bears once in my career—specifically, a mama bear whose cubs I'd been playing with in the nicest way when she happened on the scene. With many things in life—Slim Jims, for example—once is not enough, not even close. But with bears, it was too much. I glanced over at the waterfall painting that hid the safe. We were going to need the .410.

Bernie stayed on the couch, perhaps planning to get the .410 a little later. And why not? We had time, wherever this Ukraine place happened to be. Bernie's very sensible. A lot of people seem to miss that.

"Who's the client?" he said.

"These people have their own ways of doing business," Scott said. "Folkways, if you will."

"You're not telling me the name of the client?" said Bernie.

"Not at this juncture," Scott said. "My brief is to gauge your level of interest."

"Interest in what?"

"Why, the assignment we've been discussing."

"What we've been discussing is too nebulous to be called an assignment."

Nebulous? Whatever that was, I'd never heard it before, not from Bernie or anyone else. A moment comes along in every case when you know you're going to win. This was one of those moments.

"I take your point," Scott said. "You can say, how do we judge another culture, but that won't get us anywhere in practical terms. Would it help if I mentioned the fee?"

"Give it a whirl," Bernie said.

Scott's lips turned up on one side like a smile was on the way, but down on the other like it wasn't. Was he off-balance again? It hit me for the first time that Bernie could box with words! Who's got it better than me?

Scott took out his phone, tapped it once or twice, read from the screen. "One hundred K on signing the employment contract, twenty-five K per week for three months. Should your services no longer be required before that period is up, you will still be paid for three months' work, and in the event of a satisfactory performance, there will be a one hundred K bonus at the end."

Was that a lot? A little? Somewhere in between? I was completely lost. Bernie gazed at Scott. What was he thinking? I had no idea. The silence went on and on, and at last, Scott spoke.

"Naturally, this is an opening position, subject to any negotiation initiated by you."

I understood none of that, and perhaps Bernie didn't either, because he continued gazing—although no longer at Scott Kyle but simply into the distance—and remained silent.

And now Scott did smile. "I hadn't been led to believe you were such a hard bargainer."

Bernie a hard bargainer? So good to hear! In all this time, I hadn't realized that. I felt better about everything.

Meanwhile, Bernie had turned to him. "By who?"

"Various sources," Scott said. "We like to keep the names confidential for the protection of all involved."

"Sure thing," said Bernie. "But we'd need the name of the person we'd be working for."

"I'm not authorized to reveal that information," Scott said. "But in effect, it would be me."

"Do you see the contradiction between those two statements, Scott?"

Scott's eyes shifted. Then he looked at Bernie in a whole new way. It reminded me of the look I've seen in the eyes of a perp or two when we finally slap on the cuffs.

"I think I should speak to Olek." Scott did something on his phone. "He can be here in twenty minutes."

"Who's Olek?" said Bernie.

"He'll explain." Scott rose. "A pleasure meeting you, Bernie. I'll show myself out."

I followed him to the front door, of course, goes without mentioning, followed him nice and close. He glanced back in an uneasy way.

"Maybe I should have brought you a treat."

"It never hurts," Bernie called from the office.

Eleven

From the side window in our front hall, I've got a good view of the side window in the Parsonses' front hall. Iggy was there now, doing nothing much, mostly just letting his amazingly long tongue hang out. After a while he noticed me, went yip-yip-yip, and disappeared.

Bernie came into the front hall. "Anything going on, big guy?"

The obvious answer was no. The unobvious answer was yes, and that happened to be the right one. I knew Iggy.

Bernie turned his gaze toward the sign on the Parsonses' lawn. "The Parsonses are for Erlanger. Heydrich is for Wray. Is there any more we need to know?" He shook his head. "That must sound pretty simpleminded."

Which made no sense at all, unless a simple mind was the best kind, and Bernie had the best kind of mind, no discussion. When it comes to minds, the name Einstein gets thrown around, but you'd be smarter to bet on Bernie. Can this Einstein dude shoot spinning dimes out of the air? How's his uppercut? Do sweet uppercuts happen all by themselves in a—what would you call it? Mindless? Yes, exactly! In a mindless way? No way, amigo. Bernie clobbers Einstein in a first-round knockout. Case closed.

"Instinctively, I've just stayed away from politics, but is that . . ."

He wandered off down the hall and into the kitchen. Meanwhile, Iggy had returned to the side window. He stood there, no longer letting his tongue hang out. Instead, he now had a sandwich, specifically a peanut butter and jam sandwich, very clear from the reddish-brown smears on his face. I'm not at all a fan of peanut butter, which sticks to the roof of my mouth in a very unpleasant way, and I have no interest in peanut butter sandwiches.

But I wanted that particular one, Iggy's peanut butter sandwich. I wanted it very badly.

Iggy seemed in no hurry to actually eat the sandwich. Instead, he was content to simply stand in the window with the sandwich in his mouth and his odd, crooked eyes on me.

"Chet? What's all that barking? Someone at the door?"

Barking? I heard no barking. And if there was barking, it had nothing to do with any—

Knock, knock.

Oh no! Someone at the door and I'd missed it again? What a wretched day I was having! Was it all Iggy's fault? No. I knew better than that. But how come—

Bernie came into the hall. "Good boy, Chet." He gave me a nice pat. "You're the best."

My tail shot straight up in the air, almost taking me with it. Across the way, Mr. Parsons had stumped up behind Iggy, and Iggy, so busy showing me the peanut butter sandwich, hadn't noticed. Mr. Parsons leaned down in his slow, creaky way . . . and grabbed the sandwich! The look on Iggy's face! What a moment! I was on top of the world!

Bernie opened the door. On the other side stood a big guy in a tracksuit and white sneaks. He had short blond hair, broad shoulders, and a crooked nose that reminded me of Bernie's, except it wasn't beautiful, and held a flat cap with short brim at his side.

"Olek?" Bernie said.

"Olek Bondarenko, at your service." They shook hands. Is it worth mentioning that Olek's hand might have been slightly larger than Bernie's? I think not. Much more important was this feeling that I knew Olek from somewhere. If I smelled a human, even just once, or heard one of them speak, then they're in my head forever. Olek's smell was standard human male mixed with a hint of a reddish soup I'd come across on . . . on a case involving fake rabbis! Had I been thinking about that case not so long ago? A case, by the way, that I hadn't understood from beginning to end. Had Olek been involved? His voice was new to me, but the smell? I wasn't sure. The case of the fake rabbis had a way of spreading confusion in my mind.

"Many thanks for seeing me on short of notice," Olek said. "Please to enter?"

"Sure," said Bernie, stepping aside.

But instead of coming in, Olek first turned to a long black car parked in the driveway and snapped his fingers. Finger snapping is an interesting human subject that maybe we can get back to later. Right now, Olek's finger snap brought the driver—a really enormous guy, also in a tracksuit—jogging up our driveway with a bottle gift wrapped in black and gold. He handed it to Olek.

"Anything in addition?" the driver said.

"That's all, Vanko," said Olek.

Vanko jogged back to the car. We went inside, me last, standard MO with a stranger in the house.

"How fine a house," Olek said, looking around. "I am always amazed at the building quality of even the middle-class American home."

"Uh, thanks," Bernie said.

"And perhaps for our little talk, there is outdoor seating area?"

"If you don't mind the heat."

"Mind?" said Olek. "Don't Ukrainians grow up cold to the bones? We are lovers of the heat."

Not long after that, we were out back on the patio. Beyond the patio lies the canyon where we take walks, me and Bernie, and chase after javelinas, Bernie not involved in that part except for that one time with the javelina and the car keys, too complicated to go into now. At the back of the patio stands a very tall gate not leapable by any member of the nation within. What's that expression? In theory? Something like that. Not leapable in theory. And in the middle of the patio sits the swan fountain, now silent and waterless.

Olek walked slowly around the fountain. "Beautiful," he said, reaching out and stroking the swan's neck.

"Uh, thanks," said Bernie.

"It is reminding me of my sister when we were kids. She danced in *Lebedyne Ozero*."

"*Swan Lake*?" Bernie said.

Olek turned to him in surprise. "You speak Ukrainian?"

"I just guessed."

Olek laughed. "Just guessed! That is confirming you are the man for the job."

"What exactly is the job?"

"That we will get to." Olek set the gift-wrapped bottle on the table. "Would glasses be possible?"

"Sure." Bernie went into the house.

Olek sat at the table. He looked at me. I looked at him. "What is the cost of a dog like you?" he said.

I had no idea, didn't even understand the question. But in that moment of not understanding, I remembered the name of the reddish soup that I was smelling off Olek, first encountered by me in the fake rabbis case. Borscht! That was it. Then came the obvious question. Was Olek a rabbi imposter? He didn't look like the other rabbi imposters, not at all, but he smelled like them. I was actually wondering about the wisdom of grabbing him by the pant leg then and there when Bernie returned with a couple of glasses and sat down.

"Here is a gift for you," Olek said and began tearing the wrapping off the bottle. Didn't the gift-getter usually do that? Maybe not, and besides, I had the feeling that Olek wasn't from the Valley, perhaps came from a place where things were different.

"Best Ukrainian vodka," Olek said. "The water is coming from a magical spring in an island in the Dnieper."

"Magical?" said Bernie.

Olek poured vodka—which up until now I'd only seen women drink—into the glasses. "Do you think marketing is only in America?"

Bernie laughed.

Olek raised his glass. "To success!" They clinked and drank. Olek raised his glass again. "To a beautiful future for our two great countries, Ukraine and USA!" They clinked and drank some more.

"What is your opinion of our magical vodka?" Olek said.

"It packs a punch," said Bernie.

Olek smacked his hand on the table. It sounded like a gunshot. "Packs a punch—this is an American expression?"

"Yes."

"I am loving it." Olek drained his glass and refilled it. "I have boxed in my time. How is about you?"

"A little," Bernie said.

A little? Come on, Bernie. Tell him about that sweet, sweet uppercut. Or . . . or even better, how about showing him? I changed my position slightly, moving behind Olek's chair in case he tried to take off. But Bernie stayed seated. Could the uppercut be thrown from a sitting position? I didn't even know how to start imagining that.

"So then we have something in common, you and I," Olek said. "And not only boxing. I, too, am former military man."

"You've done research on me," Bernie said.

"Homework and more homework," said Olek. "'Train hard, fight easy'—General Suvorov. I was army, like you. Saw fighting, like you—but maybe not so organized."

"Oh?"

"We sleep next to a five-hundred-kilo gorilla."

"The Russians?"

Olek nodded and took another drink, wiping his mouth on the back of his hand. "Yes, always the Russians. Sometimes we kill them, sometimes we kill with them."

A dark look passed over Bernie's face. "We did some of that, too," he said.

"But not with the Russians," said Olek. "And you yourselves are also a gorilla, maybe one thousand kilos. A nicer gorilla, sure thing, even friendly." He refilled his glass, topped up Bernie's. "To the friendly gorilla."

They clinked glasses and drank to the friendly gorilla. Then and there, I knew the case had taken a bad turn. I was familiar with gorillas from Animal Planet, had seen one pull a tree right out of the ground, and with only one arm. What else did you need to know?

Olek had begun to sweat a little bit, but not Bernie.

"Now how is the vodka?" Olek said.

"Better and better."

"Always the way—with the right sort of man. And you, Bernie, are the right sort of man. Are you coming to work for me?"

"So we'd be working for you personally?" Bernie said.

"Oh, no, no, no. For the big boss. You have heard of Romanovych Energy?"

"No," Bernie said.

"Is a very big company, Bernie. One hundred billion capitalization."

Bernie said nothing. Was that a negotiating technique? Were we negotiating? Bernie could be a brilliant negotiator when he put his mind to it. Was he putting his mind to it now? I gave him a close look. Now he, too, had started sweating. Maybe it was time to move into the shade.

"Romanovych Energy is controlled by Marko Romanovych, Bernie, number ninety-seven billionaire in the world. That takes a special man, I'm sure you agree."

Bernie nodded. He has a number of nods meaning this and that. I was pretty sure that this particular nod, with an inward look, meant nothing.

"In fact," Olek went on, "a prophet."

Bernie leaned back. "It takes a prophet to be the ninety-seventh richest person in the world?"

Olek set down his glass hard, liquid spilling over the rim. "How can anyone make that kind of fortune without seeing the future? To see the future, you must be a prophet."

"Then he already knows whether I'll say yes or no," Bernie said.

Olek went still for a moment, his face reddening. Then he shook his head and laughed. "Mr. Romanovych likes a joke now and then. You will be a big success for him."

"So we'd be working directly for him?"

Olek put down his glass, rubbed his hands together. "You have been to Kauai, Bernie?"

"No."

"Paradise," Olek said. "Paradise in the middle of the sea. The first time I landed there, I thought, so far from America and yet part of America. What does this tell you, Olek?" Olek wagged his finger. "It tells you all you need to know about America."

"Which is?" Bernie said.

Olek made a big circle with his big hands. "The whole waxen ball, Bernie, the whole waxen ball. Think of that when you soon are flying into Kauai."

"And what would we be doing when we land?"

Olek leaned forward. "Now we come to the nut and bolt of the affair. You will be consultant number one on the infrastructure of security planning."

"What does that mean?" Bernie said. I was with him on that.

"Mr. Romanovych has acquired a three-thousand-hectare property on Kauai," Olek said. "He is important man. Important man needs important protection. Therefore we must have security expert to tell the architects, 'Build higher this wall,' 'Here make a watchtower,' 'So-and-so road must have remote-controlling gates each three hundred meters,' etcetera. This is where you are coming in."

"Why not you?" Bernie said.

Olek poked his own chest, quite hard, a move completely new to me. "I am no security expert."

"Could have fooled me," Bernie said, no doubt one of his jokes. There was no fooling Bernie, as I'm sure you're aware by now.

Olek laughed, meaning he got the joke, which did not always happen with Bernie's jokes, probably because they were too funny for most people. "Yes, Mr. Romanovych will be liking your humor."

"Thanks," Bernie said, "but—"

Olek raised his hand. "No butting. You have been informed the pay schedule?"

"Yes."

"It is not enough for your liking? I am willing to ice up the cake a little more." He turned to me. "And if you are worried about this excellent specimen of dog in a crate on some commercial flight, I am assuring you that all flights will be in aircraft owned by Romanovych Energy and therefore no crates."

No crates? That part of whatever this was sounded perfect. The cake, iced up or not, I could do without.

Bernie rose, walked to the fountain, reached for the tap, and turned it on. Water began flowing from the swan's mouth and splashing into the dry pool below. A little green lizard popped out of the pool and skittered away. Bernie gazed at the flowing water for a moment or two and turned to Olek.

"I'll think about it overnight and call you in the morning."

Olek jumped up. "Who asks for more?" He gave Bernie his card and patted him on the back, the same way he'd poked himself in the chest, meaning hard. "I show myself out, no trouble." Olek opened the side gate and headed toward Mesquite Road.

Bernie locked the gate, then went to the table and screwed the cap on the bottle, although there didn't seem to be much left. Meanwhile, the idea of someone walking on the property, even someone we knew, makes me a little edgy, so I opened the back door of the house—the handle being the easy-peasy kind for human thumbing—and trotted inside. There's a small round window near the front door, kind of high up but not so high I can't see out if I stand on my back legs. Which I did.

What was this? We had a taxi pulling up? That didn't happen every day. The passenger in the back—a woman with a ponytail—leaned forward to pay the driver. She opened the door, and I got a good look at her. Whoa! Not just a ponytail woman but our ponytail woman—namely, Mavis! Had I solved the case? Wow! Chet the Jet.

But then, just as Mavis was about to step out of the taxi, Olek appeared, coming from the side of the house next to the Parsonses' and headed for the long black car parked in our driveway. Mavis saw Olek, but he didn't see her. She sank back into the taxi, closing the door and ducking down out of sight. Olek glanced at the taxi, then got in his ride. It backed out of our driveway and drove off. Mavis sat up and looked my way. She saw me. I started barking in no uncertain terms. She spoke to the driver. The taxi pulled a U-ee and drove away, not in Olek's direction, if you're following all this coming and going, kind of complicated and maybe not important.

Bernie appeared in the front hall. I stayed where I was, looking out.

"What's all the excitement?"

He stood next to me. We looked out together, heads touching, and saw no excitement whatsoever.

"I know what you're thinking," he said, giving me a nice pat. "Practically a paid vacation—and a very well paid one at that."

No! That wasn't it at all! But the patting was nice.

Twelve

"Vodka in the middle of the day," Bernie said when we were back in the kitchen. He stood by the sink and drank right from the tap, no glass. Who wouldn't love Bernie? Nobody, amigo, and the ones who don't—a surprising number—are a complete mystery to me. He looked my way. "The magic wears off pretty fast."

And not long after that, we were out in the canyon back of the house. This was called *walking it off,* a booze-related activity of Bernie's that came after the drinking part was over. We headed up the trail that leads to the hill with the big flat red rock on top. Sometimes Bernie runs the whole way, sort of, but not today. Even so, he was huffing and puffing.

"Not as young as I used to be, big guy," he said.

I didn't believe that for one second, and I was sure Bernie didn't either. To snap him out of it, I ran circles around him, narrowing in closer and closer with every circle, paws really digging in, clods of dry desert dirt flying every which way, plus pebbles and stones and some plants and—

"All right, all right." Bernie laughed and jogged the rest of the way to the top, if jogging was walking-speed movement, only painful looking. He sat on the flat red rock, kind of flopped on it actually, and then just breathed for a while, his chest heaving. After that, we took in the view. On a clear day like this, we could see all the way to the airport, the top of the tower like a small black hat at the bottom of the sky. A plane took off, just a tiny gleam of silver soaring up, and another silver gleam glided down for landing.

"On one side," Bernie said, "we have a client, a clear job description, and a fee that's more than we make in a year." He gazed at me. I gazed at him. "Okay, two years. And that's without the bonus. On the other side, we have no client, no job description, and of course no fee, since there's no client."

No client meant no fee? Had I already known that? I sort of thought so, but now I knew it way better. Bernie's brilliance was like . . . like . . . I couldn't even think of something shiny enough. That's how brilliant, my friends.

"All we have is a jumble—does it even qualify as a case?" Bernie thought about that for a while. I watched him think. Then I scratched behind one ear, which felt pretty good, so I scratched behind the other. A light breeze sprang up, carrying a snaky aroma, but distant. The breeze strengthened, and the air cooled a bit. Do you ever have a feeling where everything comes to a dead stop and life is perfect? I had it now.

"Maybe not a case, but there's a dead and now missing body, a wounded dog, and an attempt to blow us up, and if not us, then someone." Bernie made a fist and pounded it into his other hand. I'd never seen him do that before. It got my attention, big-time. I ramped down on the scratching and sat on his feet, ready to do whatever it took. Bernie was angry. I did my best to be angry, too, but couldn't quite get there. Was that letting Bernie down? I hoped not, but what could I do? How do you make anger happen inside you?

Bernie reached out and stroked the top of my head. His anger leaked out of him, and the breeze carried it away. "How does surfing sound to you?"

Surfing? It sounded wonderful! We'd surfed, me and Bernie, on our trip to San Diego, first on the same board, where we did our very best to share, and then on two boards, one for Bernie and one for Chet. The fun we had! Now Bernie laughed, perhaps at what I seemed to be doing, which had to do with wriggling around on my back for no reason, and said, "Aloha, Kauai."

I'd heard something about Kauai quite recently, and aloha had come up once or twice at the beginning of our Hawaiian pants venture, but I wasn't sure where Bernie was going with this. Then he started singing, "Hanalei Bay, Hanalei Bay, where the big rollers roll in day after day."

Bernie singing! I hadn't heard that in way too long, and I'd never heard this particular number, which sounded amazing. Bernie has the best human voice in the world, so when you combine it with an amazing song, well . . . what else is life all about? I got where Bernie was going with this, where we were both going: San Diego!

Back on the patio, Bernie had his old camo duffel on the table and was hosing off all his flip-flops, of which he had a surprising number. How happy he seemed, still singing about the big rollers. He turned to me with a big smile on his face.

"Should we pack your other collar, Chet?"

What a clever idea! You never knew when a fancy occasion might pop up—such as last year's Valley PD Christmas party with the beer pong tournament, not won by Bernie although he'd gotten to the semis, whatever those were, exactly. I ran into the house, grabbed my leather collar, hanging on a hook in the office, and ran back out. At the same time, someone knocked on the side door of the patio fence, the same door that Olek had left through. That memory led me right to the memory of the taxi and Mavis, and I got a little confused, pausing by the fountain, my black leather collar hanging from my mouth.

Meanwhile, Bernie twisted the nozzle off, went to the door, and opened it. The first thing I saw was the muzzle of a gun, pointed right at his chest. My back legs bunched under me and—

"Chet! Stay!"

But—

"Stay!"

There's a voice Bernie has for really meaning it, and that was the voice I heard now. I stayed.

Bernie backed up a step, but he didn't raise his hands into the hands-up position, the usual human thing when a gun gets pointed at them, and neither did he drop the hose. That hose was going to be important very soon. I know Bernie.

The gunman came inside—a gunwoman, in fact—and closed

the door with her heel, a cool human move you see from time to time, although not from bad guys, in my experience. I knew this woman from the truck company office in South Pedroia. The cat's-eye glasses were unforgettable, and so was her hard face, although I had sort of forgotten that detail. But now I had a grip on it for sure.

"Something on your mind, Sylvia?" Bernie said, his voice nice and calm, like this was just a regular back-and-forth, no guns around.

"Don't want any of your smart mouth," Sylvia said. She made a little motion with the gun. "Here on in, every word that comes out of it is the truth, or else. And make sure that dog behaves. I like dogs. I don't like you."

"Why not?" Bernie said.

Sylvia glared at him. Could someone wear cat's-eye glasses and at the same time be a fan of the nation within? It made no sense, but people who take a shine to me and my kind actually give off a tiny scent when we're around, and I was picking it up now.

"Why not?" Sylvia said. "You've got some nerve." She made another motion with the gun, this one wilder than the first. "What have you done to him?"

I've seen humans at gunpoint more than once, comes with my job. It tends to make them panicky. You can hear it in their voices, high and shaky. All I could hear in Bernie's voice was normal Bernie.

"Who are you talking about?" he said.

Sylvia's eyes narrowed to slits. Since the cat's-eye glasses were slittish to begin with, this was one of the scariest sights of my whole life.

"Don't push me," she said.

Bernie didn't push her. He can be very quick, but pushing was probably on the risky side, what with the way she had the gun—and not a small one, by the way—aimed right at his heart. I could hear his heart beating, nice and calm, and also Sylvia's heart. It was beating nice and calm, too, a bit of a surprise. And then there was my own heart, maybe the nicest and calmest. We had three drumbeats beating out a rhythm that had not much to do with the gun, which maybe would have been the first thing you'd have noticed if you'd paid a visit to our patio, and I hope you do someday. Whoa! What a thought! Among other things, I'd gone past two! I'd been past two before—to four, if I remembered right—but I'd somehow missed three. And now it was mine! This was shaping up as a fine afternoon, if only Sylvia would put her gun away.

Slow and casual, Bernie turned his back to the gun, walked over to the table, and sat down. The vodka bottle and the glasses were still there. For a very strange moment, I felt like I was in his mind, and in his mind was a thought about pouring out two drinks, one for him and one for Sylvia. But I must have been wrong, because instead, he looked at her and said, "Whatever this is, come take a seat. You'll be more comfortable."

"They're right about you," Sylvia said, staying where she was. "You're a ballsy son of a bitch."

Ballsy? Bitch? I got a little confused. Maybe Bernie was, too, because he seemed to redden a bit, although that might have been from the sun, now lower in the sky on the street side of the house and partly blocked by old man Heydrich's enormous palm tree. "Who's 'they'?" he said.

"Never mind that," said Sylvia. "Look at me."

Bernie looked at her.

"Did you kill Mickey?" she said.

"No," said Bernie.

She watched him for what seemed like a long time. "What's the name of the dog?" she said.

"Chet."

"Swear on his head. Swear you didn't kill my nephew."

"I do."

"Say it."

"I swear on Chet's head I didn't kill your nephew, Mickey Rottoni."

Whatever was happening now was pretty puzzling to me.

Puzzles can make my head itchy, way at the back but within scratching distance. I scratched.

"Not even by accident?" Sylvia said.

"I don't know what you're talking about."

"You didn't blow up that mine, maybe not knowing Mickey was there?"

"Hell no. Where are you getting this bullshit?"

"Didn't I already tell you to never mind that?" Sylvia said. "I know the whole story, except for the most important part. Is he alive?"

Bernie shook his head.

"Then where's his body?" Sylvia said.

"I don't know."

"Then how do you know he's dead?"

"I saw the body with my own eyes."

"That's not good enough."

Bernie's phone lay on the table. He tapped at it, then shoved it toward her. Sylvia leaned down and gazed at the screen. For just a moment, I thought I saw how she'd look as a real old lady. Then she drew herself up and said, "Photos can be messed with."

Bernie shrugged.

Sylvia reddened. She glared at Bernie and then turned away. Her voice amped way down. "I want the body. The family wants the body."

"Why?" said Bernie.

"How can you ask that? He needs a proper burial. Mickey was an asshole, but he was our asshole."

Bernie nodded like that made sense. "I think he was living in that mine, at least part-time. Why would he be doing that?"

"No idea," said Sylvia.

"Was he afraid of someone?"

"Wouldn't have been the first time."

"Any idea who?" said Bernie.

Sylvia shook her head.

"What do you know about EZ AZ Desert Tours?"

"A dinky little outfit," said Sylvia. "We shipped them some

ATVs a few years ago. Mickey drove the truck—he was still working part-time for us back then. Turned out, the real business was drugs. The couple that ran it got locked up, and the wife's father took over. Supposed to be legit now. I hear they added mini golf."

"Was Mickey involved in the drug running?"

"I'd be surprised. Lone wolves don't do well in the drug business." Sylvia pointed her finger at Bernie. "So what's it gonna be, yes or no?"

"Not following you," Bernie said.

"No? I thought it was clear. Are you going to find him for us?"

"You want to hire us to find the body?"

"And whoever killed him," Sylvia said, now cracking her gum. I love that sound, but coupled with the fact she still had the gun pointed at Bernie, it made me a little uneasy. "What's your price?"

"Before we go there, who told you about the mine, the explosion, all that?"

"I got my sources."

"We'll need the name."

"I don't blab." Sylvia cracked her gum again.

"How about I give you the name, and then we move on?"

"Try it."

"Von Ellis."

Sylvia nodded a tiny nod.

"How well do you know him?" Bernie said.

"Maybe not well enough." Sylvia lowered the gun, gestured with her chin at the bottle. "What you got there?"

Sometimes my mind gets a bit tired. Not my body—my body is another story, can go on and on forever. But the mind can get overworked, and when that happens, the body lies down. Too bad the mind can't just lie down on its own and let the body keep keepin' on. In short, my mind needed to put its feet up, so my body lay down by the swan fountain on the patio, the soft splashing sounds just perfect for the mood I was in. I had a not-very-nice thought. Please, Bernie, forget about the evaporation effect, whatever it was.

Sylvia, sitting at the table opposite Bernie, tapped the vodka bottle with the tip of her fingernail, a long, gleaming fingernail with a long white part at the end, also gleaming.

"What's this writing?"

"Cyrillic."

"What's it say?"

"Couldn't tell you."

"Where's it from?"

"Ukraine."

"Don't know anything about the place."

"Me, either."

"But it's the best damn vodka I ever tasted," Sylvia said. She picked up her glass and took a sip that turned into a gulp.

"Keep the bottle."

"Gonna bill me for it?"

Bernie laughed.

"What's funny? You think I haven't been billed for shit like that?"

"But you caught it every time," Bernie said. "We charge three fifty a day plus expenses—which actually can include drinks in certain cases, but not this one—with a thousand-dollar retainer."

Sylvia whipped out a credit card and flicked it to Bernie, a move I'd never seen from a client before. I knew right then she was good for the money, not true of all our clients. Bernie caught the card no problem of course, his hand folding softly around it. He went into the house for the little credit card machine.

Sylvia looked my way. "Gonna find him for me, Chet? I'm counting on you."

I'd do my very best to find whoever it was, but meanwhile, didn't we have a problem? How could Sylvia be the client? Wasn't there a client already—namely, Olek? Who was paying us big green to go surfing in San Diego, or possibly somewhere else, the name forgotten? We'd never had two clients at once before. How could that work? Bernie and I would have to split—whoa. I didn't want to go there. So I didn't. Some problems can be solved without moving a muscle.

Bernie came back with the credit card machine. "What can you tell us about Johnnie Lee Goetz?" he said.

Great question. For one thing, I remembered her—nice young lady with her head half-shaved. Hadn't we first met Griffie at her place? Chet the Jet—in the picture. I stretched full out, got more comfortable. My eyelids started in on heavy plans of their own.

"Not a whole lot," Sylvia said. "Apparently, she's good with horses. Works for a trainer up in hill country. Horses was how they met, her and Mickey. He likes—he liked—to bet the ponies, one of his many vices."

Horses? Ponies? Normally an unsettling subject, but now they were shrinking, shrinking . . . and gone.

Thirteen

The Arroyo Seco is always dry, but now it wasn't, and instead had turned into a lovely little stream of bubbling blue water. I drifted down this lovely little stream with my nose just above the surface and my paws not moving at all. Had I ever felt more relaxed? The stream ended in a cloud of white haze. I couldn't see it, although I knew it was there, white haze and nothing but white haze waiting at the end of the stream, a very far way off, so I wouldn't reach it for ages.

After not very long, I began to notice that my stream was speeding up. At first, that was kind of fun—who's not a fan of speed?—but the water kept flowing faster and faster and faster, way beyond the border of pleasantness, so I twisted around and started swimming the other way. Swimming is just running in the water, so if you're a good runner, you're good swimmer—and, of course, they don't call me Chet the Jet for nothing. I swam and swam, my legs really getting into it, churning through the water so fast that—

But no. I was getting nowhere. This stream, lovely at the beginning, turned out to be nasty and also much stronger than me. It had a mind of its own, and the only thought in that mind was, *Sweep Chet away*. In a situation like that, you don't go gently, at least not me. I swam and swam and fought and fought and—

"Chet? Bad dream, big guy?"

I opened my eyes, kept swimming for an instant—and there was Bernie, looking down at me, his eyes worried. I went still. We were out on the patio, the swan fountain quietly splashing nearby. The sun was lower in the sky now, and Bernie had changed from shorts and a T-shirt to into a work outfit, meaning jeans and a T-shirt. I jumped right up. A bad dream? How embarrassing! I'd worried Bernie for no reason. I hurried over to the fountain, slurped up lots of water—even had the crazy thought of drinking the whole fountain dry. But why? No answer came. I stopped what I was doing and glanced around. Where was Sylvia Rottoni? I felt the smallest bit out of the picture, not a good feeling at all. Now would be a good time to sit on Bernie's feet. I turned and saw he was headed into the house. I bounded forward and beat him through the doorway.

"Chet? Whoa!"

One thing about Bernie—he has excellent balance for a human, so no surprise he managed to stay on his feet, or just about.

There was a bowl of kibble with—oh, how nice—some crumbled biscuit treat mixed in, waiting for me in the kitchen. Can you go from feeling no hunger to being out of your mind with it in no time flat? Oh, but yes! Try it sometime!

"Are you even tasting that?"

What a question! I was tasting like you wouldn't believe. Maybe this was one of Bernie's jokes, but glancing over to check the look on his face was not a possibility. Meanwhile, I could hear him tapping at his phone.

"Olek? Bernie Little, here."

Olek's voice came over the speaker. "At your service, Bernie, my friend." He laughed. "On my screen at this very minute is Weather .com. Temperature in Kauai eighty-two Fahrenheit, light breeze, not a cloud in the whole of the sky. And tomorrow is the same!"

"Uh," Bernie said. "A beautiful place, I'm sure, and you can't beat the climate. But it will have to wait, at least for us."

"Explain, please?"

"We're not taking the job," Bernie said. "It's a great offer, and I appreciate it, but no."

"No? No? What are you—" Olek paused, amped down the volume. "Is this about money? Did I not make clear that our offer was not hard line? We are flexible, Bernie. Name me a figure."

"I'm sorry," Bernie said. "The timing's wrong."

There was a long pause. Then Olek again said, "Explain, please?" His voice had grown even softer, but somehow more clear.

"I can't fit it into the schedule right now."

"What is this schedule? Other work?"

"Yes."

"Of the private investigation kind?"

"Correct."

Another pause, this one not as long. "It is a case?"

"Yes."

"I do not ask the details, only does it pay like our offering?"

"Not even close."

I paused over my bowl, not quite done. Was I hearing right? Was it possible that we were walking away from a stack of cold hard cash that Olek was paying us for a job that was all about surfing? For the sake of some other job about which I knew nothing—except that it paid a lot less? I snapped up the last of my dinner, kind of taking it out on the kibble, if that makes any sense, and I believe it does.

"Not even close?" said Olek. "Who would turn down a lot of money for a lot less of money, I ask myself. And the only answer I can think is a man of honor who has already agreed to the small job. Is that our situation, my friend?"

"Roughly," said Bernie. "But it has nothing to do with honor. It's just how we work."

"Very good. I clap my hands. At the same time, why not make happy all the players?"

"I don't understand."

"We, Romanovych Energy, will hire the private investigator of your best recommendation to take over the duties of this other case. Making you free, Bernie, to accept our offer in good . . . what is the word?"

"Conscience."

"Yes. I am liking that American saying. We have something of the same, although different in the end. When all is done and said, isn't that the final truth?"

"We are different in the end?"

"Ha ha. That is such a Ukrainian thought. Do you have Ukrainian blood, Bernie?"

"Not to my knowledge."

"So American to not know. I am Ukrainian through and through."

"Have you taken a DNA test?"

Now came another pause, this the longest. "What is your suggestion?" From the sound of his voice, I could almost think Olek wasn't liking Bernie so much anymore, but that was impossible. Bernie was Bernie, and once you liked him—as I was sure Olek had up to now—you liked him forever.

"Just jerking your chain," Bernie said.

"I wear no chain."

"No, of course not, sorry. And I appreciate your suggestion on hiring another investigator. But it just isn't going to work."

"This other case," Olek said. "For sure it came first? I am meaning first in time."

Bernie glanced my way. My bowl totally cleaned out, I was licking my muzzle and pretty much involved in only that when I saw Bernie was biting his lip. That hardly ever happens, and I've never understood it. Does it mean he has to say something that isn't quite tr—no, I couldn't go there. Bernie is straight up, 24-7, which is an enormous number, way out of my league.

He took a breath. "Yes," he said.

"Then," said Olek, "why no mention of this first case when we are speaking before?"

Bernie's mouth opened, but whatever he was about to say stayed unsaid because the phone went click at the other end. A strange picture popped up in my mind, a picture of a man on a rooftop. His face was about to come into view, but before it could, Bernie said, "Let's roll, big guy."

Poof!

Sometimes when we're on the road and Bernie's thinking his hardest, his hands take care of the driving all by themselves. Like right now, as we headed out of town and up into hill country. Hill country air is softer than Valley air and full of country smells. My nose handled them, while the rest of me concentrated on Bernie's hands. This may sound odd, but they were like two tiny Bernies, each with a tiny mind. Don't get me wrong—Bernie's hands are big as far as men's hands go, big and beautiful if you're an admirer of a bent finger or two, or a swollen knuckle, and I am. And his mind is big and beautiful, too. But back to the minds in his hands, which work as a team, a two-person team just like . . . like me and Bernie! I felt myself at the edge of an enormous thought, but it bumped up against another almost-thought, kind of waiting in line, specifically the thought about the man on the rooftop, and then—oh no!

Poof! Again.

Bernie glanced at me. "You're in a funny mood."

I was? First I'd heard of it. But if Bernie said I was in a funny mood, then that was that. I began to think of funny-mood activities, and was still waiting for the first one to come along, when Bernie said, "Two missing women and one missing body, Chet. Yes, it forms a triangle, and I see that, but what kind of triangle? Isosceles? Equilateral? Oblique? You might think it doesn't matter, except crime is born in relationships, so it helps to picture their geometry."

Me? Think geometry didn't matter? Of course it mattered, if that was Bernie's take. Geometry mattered more than anything, and whenever we ran into it, I'd be ready. I pawed at my leather seat, but in a hidden, quiet way, not to bother anybody.

There are lots of ranches in hill country. They all have long dirt driveways and gates with tall side posts and cool crossbars over the top. The crossbar over the gate we drove through was all about a giant rearing horse with six-guns in its two front hooves and a fat cigar in its mouth. Any chance of pulling a U-ee, Bernie? That was my only thought. But no U-ee got pulled. "Billy Baez's Bucking Bronco Ranch," Bernie said, and drove straight on. "We may be dealing with a horse or two," he added as we passed a small ranch house and followed the driveway to a big barn at the end. "Just so you know. In case of . . . well, just so you know."

Oh, I knew, all right. The air was full of horsey smells, somewhat like cattle, actually, but grassier and way more nervous. Horses are prima donnas, each and every one, always moments away from a panic attack. That makes it so tempting to . . . to . . . I kept that bad thought to myself.

A dusty pickup stood by the barn. We parked beside it and walked around to the other side of the barn, which looked out on a racetrack, a lot like the racetrack in town where we'd once bet—not the house but pretty much everything else—on a sure thing name of Prince Theodore, who'd come in last by so much, arriving all by himself at the finish, that I got the feeling he actually thought he'd won. But he had not, as was very clear the next day when we went to Mr. Singh's place and pawned Bernie's grandfather's watch, our most valuable possession.

On the near side of the track, a cigar-smoking dude leaned against the rail, stopwatch in hand. On the far side a black horse with a brown mane was galloping toward the turn, a bare-chested jockey in the saddle and leaning forward, his face almost touching the horse's neck. Horses, at least some of them, can run. There's good in everyone. That's one of my core beliefs. But can I just squeeze in the fact that I can gallop, too, amigo? We just don't give it that fancy name.

The horse rounded the turn and came pounding down the stretch, the muscles in his chest rippling, his eyes huge and crazy. I had a sudden urge to . . . not compete, exactly, more like simply to get out there and—

I felt Bernie's hand on the back of my neck, very gentle, but there. The horse galloped by us. The cigar-smoking man clicked his stopwatch, peered at it, and said, "Piece of shit."

There was some on the track, no doubt about that, but I had no idea which piece he meant and what he wanted done with it. Rolling in it was always a possibility, of course. I kept that in a corner of my mind.

Bernie and I drew closer. The man heard us and turned, the big-bellied sort of man, so his belly kept turning and then jiggled back into line.

"Billy Baez?" Bernie said.

The man spoke around his cigar. "Who's askin'?" He glanced at us and went back to watching the horse, now trotting down the track, the jockey holding the reins in one hand and checking his phone in the other.

"Bernie Little," Bernie said. "And this is Chet."

Billy Baez, if that was his name, turned his tiny eyes on me, eyes made even tinier from squinting through cigar smoke.

"Sizable animal. Wouldn't be fixin' to put the fear of god into Capitol Hill, now would he?"

"Excuse me?" Bernie said.

Billy Baez twisted his lips to poke the cigar in the direction of the horse, now walking slowly back our way, the jockey still looking down at his phone.

"Capitol Hill is the name of the horse?" Bernie said.

"I don't name 'em," Billy Baez said. "I just train 'em. And between you and me, the goddamn horse could use a bite on the ass, maybe motivate him some."

This interview, if that's what it was, had taken an interesting turn. Although Billy Baez had those tiny eyes, plus a scratchy voice and an overall stink, coming from many places but especially his feet, I was starting to like him.

Bernie gazed at Capitol Hill. "I'm no judge, but he looked pretty fast coming around that turn."

"Oh yeah," said Billy Baez. "And pretty fast is just fine and dandy for a small-stakes career. But the owner didn't pay small-stakes money for him. Small-stakes money won't get you mounts with his bloodlines. Problem is, bloodlines don't always tell you what's here." He tapped his head. "Or here." He tapped his chest.

"So somehow you've got to get him to love speed more than anything?" Bernie said.

Billy Baez gave Bernie a second look. "You an owner? Lookin' for a trainer, by any chance?"

Bernie shook his head. "We're actually looking for Johnnie Lee Goetz."

Billy Baez, who'd been warming up to us—I feel these things, sort of in the air, hard to explain—now went cold real quick. "You some kind of muscle?"

An odd question. No one had ever asked us that before. We had muscles, me and Bernie, nothing weak about either of us, but if Billy Baez thought that was all we were bringing to the table, he had lots to learn.

"I wouldn't put it that way," Bernie said, just showing how alike we were in some ways. He handed Billy Baez our card.

Billy Baez peered at the card, then held it at arm's length and peered again, a puzzling human move you sometimes see. "Who you workin' for?" he said.

"We keep the name of the client confidential," said Bernie.

"Hell with that," said Billy Baez, and he ripped our card in two and threw away the pieces. Not a first in my experience, but I never liked seeing it. "You're workin' for that meathead prick."

"Absolutely no way," said Bernie.

"Huh?"

"Our client's a woman."

Billy Baez, his face already screwed up around the cigar, screwed up some more. "It's not Mickey Rottoni?"

"Nope. What have you got against Mickey Rottoni?"

"You know him?"

"Can't say I do."

Billy Baez nodded. "He hit her. Beat her up but good. That crosses the line, where I come from." He blew out a huge cloud of cigar smoke, hot smoke I felt on my nose.

"You're talking about Johnnie Lee?" Bernie said.

"Hell yeah. A great gal. Not here or there, issue-wise, I guess. But a great gal and the numero uno exercise rider ever worked this ranch."

"I'd like to talk to her."

"Me, too," said Billy.

"What do you mean?"

"She didn't show up for work two days ago—which ain't how she rolls. Johnnie Lee's straight up reliable. She didn't answer my text or calls. I even drove out to her place, two hours each way, for crissake. And guess what?"

"She wasn't there?"

Billy took the cigar from his mouth and stabbed it in Bernie's direction. "Way worse. Johnnie Lee's packed up and gone, no message, no forwarding address, nada."

"Any idea where she went?"

"Nope." He shot Bernie a sideways look. "Tell you what worries me—the idea maybe that bastard did something to her."

"The timeline pretty much rules that out," Bernie said.

"What's that sposta mean?"

"Just that I think she took off before he could get to her," Bernie said.

"How do you know that?"

I was with Billy on this one. The two of us watched Bernie, waiting for the answer.

"From our preliminary investigation," he said.

Billy nodded like that made sense. I didn't get it. Preliminary investigation? What was that? Also where and when?

"But right now," Bernie went on, "I'd like to get a handle on their relationship."

"Like, how do you mean?"

"When did they meet? Did they live together? What was the attraction? How did it go wrong?"

"You talkin' about psychology? Is that a private detective thing?"

"Crime comes out of human relationships," Bernie said. Was I hearing this again, and so soon? It had to be important. I told my mind to hold on to it and not let go, but my mind seemed to be more interested in Capitol Hill, now standing not far away while the jockey hoisted off the saddle. "Maybe not always, but in this case for sure."

"I don't know how they met, exactly. Maybe two years ago. He treated her real nice at first—flowers, jewelry, weekends at Cabo, all that crap. The Rottonis have money, but you wouldn't know it. Mickey's the black sheep and the only one who acts rich, even though he's the one that ain't. They were even talking marriage, but then—this was a couple months back—she showed up here with a black eye and goddamn stitches on her face."

"What happened?"

"He beat the crap out of her is what happened."

"Why?"

"Because he's a no-good son of a bitch, and if there's a god, he'll get what's coming to him."

Sometimes with Bernie you get a pause where maybe he's thinking of saying one thing but changes his mind and goes with another. A pause like that happened now, and then he said, "I meant what provoked him."

"Couldn't tell you," said Billy. "Course I asked, but she wouldn't say. All's I told her was that a man does that once, he'll do it again, only worse. Like a dam's been broke."

"Good advice," Bernie said.

"And she took it," Billy said. "Locked him out, got a restraining order. But he followed her around a time or two, texted her . . . what are those little things?"

"Emojis?"

"Yeah. Threatening emojis. Like an actual threat would violate the restraining order, but an emoji? You see what we're dealin' with?"

Bernie nodded. "Did anything unusual happen in that time period?"

"Like what?"

"Another man showing interest in Johnnie Lee, for example," Bernie said.

"Well, Johnnie Lee's the type to get second looks. Not a show horse, like her friend, but no plow horse neither. More on the exotic side, you might say."

"Her friend?" Bernie said.

"Childhood friend, from where they grew up, which was over in Grantville, New Mexico."

"Tell me about her."

"A real beauty, like I said. Natural-like. No makeup, no fancy hairdo, came up hardscrabble, same as Johnnie Lee."

"What's her name?"

Billy shook his head. "Can't help you there. Only met her the once, not long after she came to the Valley." His eyes got a faraway look. "Although I remember thinking about her name."

"Yeah?" said Bernie.

"Not suiting her. A beautiful girl like that, you'd think her name would be Gisele or Christie or something of that nature. But instead . . ." Billy shrugged.

"Instead, it was Mavis?" Bernie said.

Billy's eyes opened as wide as they could, getting him a little more in line with other humans. "How'dja know that?"

"Just a guess. What about her last name?"

"Not sure I ever heard it," Billy said. "Only meeting her the once and all."

"Where was this?" Bernie said.

A big white convertible drove slowly around the barn, top down and a blond woman wearing big sunglasses at the wheel. Billy glanced over, dropped his cigar on the ground, and mashed it under his foot.

"At Griffin Wray's holiday party, out at his lake house. He always includes the whole crew, so Mavis tagged along with Johnnie Lee."

"You're talking about Senator Wray?"

"Uh-huh. Griffin Wray."

"Griffin," said Bernie, kind of to himself. "I must have known that, but . . ."

Billy gave him an odd look. "The senator owns Capitol Hill.

Well, Caroline's the actual owner." He turned to the white convertible and waved. "That's her now."

The blond woman didn't wave back. She got out of the car and headed toward the rail. The jockey led Capitol Hill toward her.

"She actually knows a thing or two about horses, unlike her husband," Billy said. "I hope he's more clued in on senator type things."

Fourteen

The blond woman ducked under the rail in a smooth, easy movement and walked up to Capitol Hill. The jockey was wiping down Capitol Hill's glossy back with a towel, but he stepped aside as the woman came forward. A small gold purse hung from her shoulder. She unbuckled it and took out a carrot. Capitol Hill snapped it right up and started chomping with his huge yellow teeth. I'm not a fan of carrots, so you might think I wouldn't care at all about this particular carrot. But I did. I wanted Capitol Hill's carrot so badly, and if I couldn't have it, then I wanted the carrot or possibly carrots that remained in the woman's purse. At this distance, my nose couldn't tell if there was more than one. I began shifting my position.

The woman watched Capitol Hill chew on the carrot. Without looking at the jockey, she said, "How's he doing, Cesar?"

"Good, *señora*," said the jockey.

"How was his workout?"

"Real good," Cesar said. He glanced over at Billy. "Real good workout, huh, boss?"

"One of his best," said Billy.

The woman tidied up Capitol Hill's brown mane, twisted it into a curl at the top. Her head turned slightly in our direction. Because of her sunglasses, I couldn't tell who she was looking at, but I got the feeling it was me.

She came over to us, rested one hand on the rail. The late-in-the-day sunshine turned the diamond on her finger—maybe the biggest I'd ever seen—into a fiery little sun of its own. Had I seen another diamond ring recently? Not this size, but . . . but just as the memory was about to arrive, Capitol Hill neighed the most high-pitched neigh I'd ever heard, farting at the same time, also high-pitched, weirdly so. There's only so much you can take, although no one else seemed to notice.

"One of his best, Billy?" the woman said.

"Yes, ma'am."

"That's reassuring," she said. "Sometimes I worry. But why worry for no reason, Billy, if there's no reason?"

"No, ma'am."

She turned to me. "Here's a specimen with championship bloodlines, unless I'm mistaken," she said. She looked up at Bernie, standing behind me. "Is he yours?"

"We're more like partners," Bernie said.

She gazed at Bernie, or seemed to—the sunglasses made it impossible to tell. "Have we met before, Mr. . . . ?"

"I don't think so," Bernie said. "I'm Bernie Little. This is Chet."

"Bernie, Mrs. Wray," Billy said. "Mrs. Wray, Bernie."

"Call me Caroline," she said. "Are you involved in the horse world, Bernie? What my husband calls the equine money pit?"

"The senator's got a great sense of humor," Billy said.

"Most certainly, and in so many ways," Caroline said. "But I was addressing Bernie."

Billy looked down at his feet. He was wearing flip-flops, his toes so thick with dust they looked like they were made of it, through and through.

"I appreciate that world from a distance," Bernie said.

Caroline laughed and pushed her sunglasses up on her head, revealing her eyes. They were big and dark and . . . and other things I didn't understand. I ended up liking her and being a bit afraid of her at the same time. Well, not afraid. I'm afraid of nobody. You'd be the same if you'd gone one-on-one with a gator and come out of it, if not the winner, then at least in one piece.

"Can you ride, Bernie?" she said.

"Not well," said Bernie, which wasn't a lie, since Bernie's not a liar. It just meant he'd forgotten an episode with a horse named Mingo on a case not very long ago where he'd revealed himself to be maybe the greatest rider in the world. But who remembers everything? "I had a horse when I was a kid," he said.

Is there a human expression about being knocked down by a feather? I'd seen a perp knocked over by a whole bird once—the case involving a Thanksgiving turkey and an angry girlfriend—but no cases where it was just the feather part. But not the point, which was about how stunned I was at that moment. Bernie had a horse when he was a kid? I was just finding that out now? One thing for sure: I did not like that horse. I felt a sudden need to be active. Close by stood Capitol Hill, swishing away flies with his tail, a vacant look on his very long face.

"What was its name?" Caroline said.

"Dottie," Bernie said.

"Whose idea was that?"

"The name?" Bernie said. "Mine."

"Any particular reason for it?"

Sometimes—not often—Bernie has this little soft laugh that comes mostly through his nose. I love that one! Why? No idea. But he did it now and said, "I had a pal named Dottie who lived next door. They moved away."

"And then you got the horse?"

He nodded again.

"How old were you?"

Bernie shrugged. "Eight or nine."

Caroline tilted her head as though seeing Bernie from a different angle. Bernie's mom, a real piece of work—she calls him Bernard!—does that same head-tilt thing. I suddenly got the idea she and Caroline might be the same age, although Caroline looked quite a bit younger.

"What is it you do, Bernie?" she said.

"Private investigations."

"How interesting." Caroline lowered her sunglasses back down and turned to Capitol Hill.

Two-lane blacktop, no other cars in sight, pedal to the metal. A sign zipped by. "Entering New Mexico," Bernie said. Something glinted in the distance, and Bernie eased off the gas. Not long after that, a car took shape around that glint, a desert thing I'd seen before, in this case a cruiser parked by the side of the road and partly hidden by some silvery bushes. A kind of bush wasps take a liking to, in my experience. And as we passed by, I caught a glimpse of the cop behind the wheel, batting his hand frantically in the air. A nice sight. We've picked up a number of speeding tickets in New Mexico, me and Bernie.

Meanwhile, Bernie's mind was elsewhere. I can feel when that happens. It makes me a bit lonely, sometimes lonely enough to lean up against him. He glanced at me and smiled.

"Need some help with this one, big guy. New Mexico is to Arizona as . . . ?"

Sometimes Bernie doesn't get enough sleep. When that happens, he tends to worry for no reason, think about things that don't need thinking about. The mind can only do so much even when it's not tired. A tired mind? Look out! I gazed into Bernie's eyes and sent a message. Pull over. Take a nap. I'll watch over you.

"You're having deep thoughts," he said. We sped up, me and Bernie, the only moving things on an endless high plain under an endless blue sky. The nap that got taken was mine.

We came down from green hills on a long curving road and entered the kind of town you often saw in our part of the world, one with better days in the past. They all had a nice little core of solid old brick and stone buildings with a few restaurants, inns, and shops, but the farther you got from the core, the more ramshackle everything became. It was all about mining, Bernie said. We turned a few corners and followed an empty street to a high school at the end. You can tell a high school from the football field on one side and the yellow buses on the other. I love high school when the kids are around. But in summer, like now, when they're not, high schools give me an uneasy feeling.

Bernie parked at the entrance and got out.

"Chet?"

I gazed up at him.

"Tired today? How about waiting in the car? I won't be long."

The next thing I knew, we were walking up to the front doors of the high school side by side, together. Bernie tried the door—locked—but we could see a man in the lobby mopping the floor. He leaned his mop against the wall and stepped outside.

"He'p you?" he said.

He wore a beige uniform and a tag around his neck. Bernie glanced at the tag and said, "Hi, Hector. I'm Bernie, and this is Chet. We're looking for a former student named Johnnie Lee Goetz."

"Why?"

Some humans have quicker minds than others. You can't always tell by how they look, and you can never tell by what jobs they work. This mop-pushing guy was the quick-minded type.

"She has information about a horse we're interested in," Bernie said.

"To bet on or to buy?"

Bernie smiled. I got the feeling he was liking Hector. "That depends on what she tells us."

Hector smiled back. Most of his teeth were gone, but the ones he had were gold. "The other fellow said he had some money for her. I like your story better."

"Other fellow?" Bernie said.

"A few days back. Also looking for Johnnie Lee Goetz, who I never heard of, by the way. Former student, evidently, but I'm new here. Which is what I told him, and that was that."

"Can you describe this other fellow?" Bernie said.

"Why?" This was Hector's second why in a very short time. Normally, Bernie takes care of the whys in interview situations. Was it my job to make sure the mop-pushing guy understood that fact? If so, how?

"Because we're looking out for Johnnie Lee's welfare," Bernie said.

"Are the cops after her?"

"Not to my knowledge. Was the other fellow a cop?"

"Not in uniform, or nothin', but you get a vibe sometimes. I'm getting it from you a little bit. And from this pooch of yours a lot."

"We're not cops."

Hector pointed at me with his chin. "I'd like to hear it from him."

Bernie laughed.

"Not every day you see a dog with a snakeskin collar," Hector said.

"Gator skin, actually," said Bernie.

"There a story to that?"

Bernie nodded. "But the most dramatic parts are known only to Chet."

"I reckon he knows we're talkin' about him—tail's a dead give-away."

Something about my tail? Yes, I could feel it. I myself was perfectly still and calm, correct behavior in an interview. My tail is not always a team player. I got it back in line, and in no uncertain terms.

"Anything else you noticed about the other fellow, beside the cop possibility?" Bernie said.

Hector shook his head. "Fair-skinned, but I didn't get a good look. He wore sunglasses—the mirror kind—and a baseball cap."

"Remember the logo?"

"Diamondbacks."

"How about his car?"

"Black sedan." Hector pointed. "The driver parked it over there and stayed in the car."

"Did you get a look at the driver?"

"Not really. Might have been a big guy—just from his arm resting on the doorframe—but I wouldn't swear." Hector checked his watch. "Anything else?"

"The name of the rodeo team coach."

Hector looked surprised and also pleased. "So it is about a horse after all?"

Bernie was quiet for a moment and then said, "Yeah. Partly."

Oh? That was disturbing. Perhaps it was a new add-on to Bernie's interviewing technique.

"Ms. Wynona Antrim's the rodeo coach," Hector said. "She's a legend around here."

"I'd like to talk to her," Bernie said.

"Hang on."

Hector went inside, locked the door, and disappeared into an office off the main hallway.

Bernie turned to me. "So far, you're solving this case all by yourself."

How nice of Bernie! But way too modest. He's always a big help in our work. For example, I hadn't been sure we'd been making much progress. And now I knew we were. The Little Detective Agency, my friends. Keep that in mind.

Hector came back outside. "She runs a little place outside of town." He handed Bernie a scrap of paper. "One other thing. That possible cop fellow? Might have been a redhead. Hard to tell with the cap and all."

"You're an excellent observer," Bernie said.

Hector shrugged. "Had nothing else to do for a spell. Eighteen years, seven months, eight days, to put it in numbers. Took the time to educate myself a little bit."

Bernie's eyes got bright. "Then maybe you can help me," he said. He cleared his throat. "Arizona is to New Mexico as . . ."

"Donald Duck is to Daffy Duck," Hector said without the slightest pause. He went inside and got back to mopping the floor.

"I'd never have thought of that," Bernie said as we drove out of town. "I was headed in the direction of something stiffer, like Ella Fitzgerald to Billie Holiday. Ducks are way better."

Billie Holiday was in the conversation? I know Billie Holiday. There are times in our life when we listen to her a lot, maybe some of the down times—meaning Bernie's down times, since mine don't seem to come around. Bernie's don't happen often, but when they do, it's my job to boost him back up, and Billie Holiday's a big help. Have you heard "If You Were Mine," for example, and that trumpet at the end? It does things to my ears that you wouldn't believe. And now, out of the blue, ducks were better than Billie Holiday? Ducks quack. This had to be one of Bernie's jokes.

"What we're leaving out," Bernie said, checking Hector's scrap of paper, "are the whys and wherefores of those eighteen years, seven months, eight days. I know the book is closed, and that's the right thing, and yet . . ."

I waited for more, but there was no more. We turned onto a dirt road that dead-ended at a little adobe place with a couple of pickups outside and a few empty tables in the shade. The smell of horse was everywhere, also some mule thrown in, and plenty of chicken. Only the chickens were visible, pecking at the dirt around the tables. They scattered as we passed by. Why did that make me feel pretty good about myself? There are mysteries in everyone's life. I'm cool with that.

We sat down at one of the outdoor tables. A full water bowl lay close by on the stone floor, always a promising touch. Bernie read the sign on the wall. "Lucky Horseshoe Bar." I'd already noticed a big silver horseshoe nailed to the front door. Horses wear shoes. Why is that? Humans wear shoes, too, but that's it, horses and humans. Are horses trying to tell humans, hey, we're a lot alike, you and me, buddy? That had to be it, just another annoying thing about them.

The door opened, and a woman came out. She was short, broad-shouldered, with strong squarish hands and short graying hair. "Menu?"

"Just drinks," Bernie said. "Beer for me—anything local you think is good. And I'm sure Chet appreciates the water bowl."

She looked at me. "Chet's the name of the dog?"

"Yes."

Her eyes shifted to Bernie. She went back inside.

"We don't think about gravity enough," Bernie said.

Uh-oh. I had never once thought about gravity and had no idea what it was. Also, a job like mine already comes with plenty of thinking, too much, if you want the truth. How could there be room in my mind for any new thinking?

"It's like how they found Neptune," Bernie went on.

Gravity and now Neptune? I made no attempt to understand. That didn't mean I wasn't listening. I always listen to Bernie. His voice is like a lovely brook bubbling by.

"They looked at the numbers from Uranus and sensed something unseen pulling at them," he said. "That's how I feel about this case. There's some big body out there distorting the lives of a whole bunch of—"

The woman returned carrying a tray, and Bernie went silent. She set a glass of beer on the table.

"Will that be all?"

"Not quite," Bernie said. "We're looking for Wynona Antrim."

"You're Bernie Little?"

Bernie sat back. "How did you know?"

"We'll get to that. I'm Wynona. What do you want?"

"Well," Bernie said, "I'm guessing you already know what we do for a living."

Wynona nodded.

"Right now, we're looking for someone you coached on the rodeo team a few years back," Bernie went on. "Her name's Johnnie Lee Goetz."

"What do you want with her?"

"Originally, it was help in finding another person. Now the case has gotten more complicated."

"Who's this other person?"

"Mavis," Bernie said. "We didn't get to the last name."

Wynona's face didn't change, and neither did the way she was standing or anything else you could see. But her smell turned just the littlest bit nervous. "Why are you looking for her?"

Was this interview going well? I didn't think so. Normally, Bernie handles the questions and whoever he's talking to comes up with the answers. What we had now was upside down. How was that going to work?

"The question is what Mavis wants—or wanted—from us," Bernie said. "She got in touch and then disappeared."

"So?"

"So we're worried about her."

"Who is 'we'?"

"Me and Chet. The Little Detective Agency."

Wynona looked in my direction. She caught me at a good time, in a moment of discovery, the object of discovery being a Cheeto, somewhat fresh, under the table. I actually prefer Cheez-Its to Cheetos, but why be fussy about things like that? I looked back at Wynona, and made an attempt, perhaps not successful, to take my time with the Cheeto. Something in her eyes—eyes of the no-nonsense kind—changed a little. They didn't go all the way to yes-nonsense, but did seem to warm up a bit.

She turned to Bernie. "Wait here." Wynona went back into the bar.

Bernie took a sip of his beer. "Very nice." He looked around. Green hills rose in the distance, the greenest country I'd seen in some time, not counting golf courses. Wynona returned, carrying a glass of beer, and sat at the table.

"Normally, I never talk about people I know to people I don't know," she said. "I don't even talk about people I know to people I do know, not unless there's a very good reason. Gossip is never a good reason." She raised her glass and downed quite a lot of what was in it, half or more. A bit of froth clung to her upper lip, a look I always like to see. She wiped it off on the back of her hand way too soon. "I certainly don't know you," she went on. "But you come highly recommended from a person I trust."

"Who?" Bernie said.

"We'll get to that," said Wynona. Hadn't she already said that once before? Who the hell was running this interview? One thing was clear: she was not a person to be messed with. And anyone who tried—a horse, for example!—would get nowhere. I remembered then that Wynona coached the rodeo team, and suddenly I understood . . . well, everything, just about.

"Let's start with the kids in this town," Wynona said, "really in this whole corner of the state. It's not like the Valley, so don't make that mistake."

She waited for Bernie to react. I knew he'd have a special

nod for this, but he didn't use it, maybe saving it for another day. Instead, he smiled a quick little smile—looking so young for a second or two!—and said, "I won't."

Wynona gave him a little nod. "Some of our kids leave after high school—either for college or just to taste the outside world—and some stay. Of the ones who leave, maybe half end up coming back. The kids who don't come back are the most self-reliant, in my opinion. They can compete in the outside world, or at least they've convinced themselves they can. People say they're the ones who want to make something of themselves, but I see them more like the old pioneers. Maybe I'm crazy, but I believe there's still a pioneer spirit in America." She drained the rest of her beer. "One day, it's going to burst free and wash away all the crap." She gave Bernie a close look. "You think I'm talking out of my hat?"

Ha! Did she think she could fool Bernie that easily? She wasn't even wearing one!

"I agree with everything, except maybe the bursting-free part," he said. Which had to be brilliant. I got the feeling we were back in charge.

"I can always hope," Wynona said, a bit of a surprise since that was one of my core beliefs and I wouldn't have thought Wynona and I had much in common. "Anyway, that's all preamble to the main point, which is that Johnnie Lee is in that last group, the pioneers. She was hands down the best rodeo rider I ever coached—two-time state cutting-horse champion, three-time state breakaway roping champion, all-around cowgirl in her senior year. Natural talent was only part of it. Johnnie Lee's ambitious. All my rodeo girls are self-reliant and tough, but not all of them have big desires for themselves. More than there used to be, but still not many, not here."

"Have you kept up with her?" Bernie said.

"Only at first. She went to ASU but dropped out after a semester and got a job as a riding teacher somewhere in the Valley. Silence after that until last month, but I never worried. As long as she was working with horses, I knew she'd be all right. I was wrong."

"How do you mean?"

"She was scared," Wynona said. "I heard it in her voice. Johnnie Lee—the Johnnie Lee I knew—was hard to scare. She told me she needed help."

"What kind of help?"

"Protection, she said, but she couldn't trust the police."

"Why not?"

"She didn't elaborate. The conversation was disjointed, to say the least. I suggested she hire someone like . . ." Wynona gave Bernie a direct look. "Like you."

"Like me personally?"

"I hadn't heard of you then. But I called a reporter I knew in the Valley—a reporter who came out here a few years ago and did a story on high school rodeo. This reporter made an impression on me. She recommended you."

"What was the name of the reporter?" Bernie said.

"Suzie Sanchez," said Wynona.

Fifteen

Suzie was in the conversation? What a strange interview! Nothing strange about Suzie Sanchez, of course, one of my favorite humans. Bernie is numero uno, goes without mentioning, and after that is a gap and then comes Charlie, his kid with Leda. Only Charlie in this spot, not Leda, just to be sure you know. After that is a hugeish kind of gap followed by a few people—Suzie, Rick Torres, and Cleon Maxwell of Max's Memphis Ribs, best rib joint in the whole Valley.

Something special happens to Bernie when Suzie's around, not just the change in his scent, which gets a little funkier, but a change inside him, a warming I can feel in a way that's hard to describe. And it still happens when she's around, even though she's now married to Jacques. A fine wedding, by the way. I'd like to think I've been to my share of weddings, but the truth is I don't attend as many as I used to, not after an incident at the wedding of Ziggy Ziggler, an old stock-swindling pal, whatever that is, exactly, who actually ended up marrying one of the guards on his Northern State cell block. But that's just by way of background. The incident I mentioned had to do with an unusual dance, possibly called the *hora*, that I found somewhat exciting. At first. Then it became extremely exciting, followed by out-of-my-mind exciting, and the next thing I knew we were in the car, me and Bernie, with part—certainly not the whole, not even close—of something called the *bridal bouquet* in my mouth.

Bernie and Suzie go way back to when she was a reporter for the *Valley Tribune*. Then she went to *The Washington Post*, possibly a step up, that part of it never clear to me, and they sent her to London. Was there talk of us going there, too? I clearly remember one night after a bourbon or two or several more, Bernie turning to me and saying, "We'd be fish out of water, big guy. How could that work out?" He didn't have to say another word. I'd seen a fish out of water—a brightly colored little fella name of Montego, I believe—whose tank had fallen off a very high shelf, a shelf you'd have thought unreachable by just about anyone. In the end, we didn't go to London. And soon after that, Bernie and Suzie weren't a pair anymore, and when she finally came back to the Valley, she was with Jacques. His hands are a bit like Bernie's, but smaller and showing no signs of throwing many punches. They'd both played college baseball, Bernie at West Point and Jacques at Caltech. That had led to some joking and a visit to the batting cage, and now they were buddies, in a way. But here's an interesting fact. When Bernie's around, Suzie's scent becomes funkier the same way his does around her, and also, the warmness inside gets going, just like his. I mean even now, since the wedding. When she's with Jacques, the warmness is there, no question, maybe even stronger than with Bernie, but not the funky part, which dwindles down. Is there any meaning to all that? I leave it to you.

"Suzie's an extremely impressive person," Wynona said.

Bernie's eyes had an inward look that happens when he's deep in his own head. Right next to me but actually far away, is what I'm trying to get across. It took me a long time to understand that.

"Bernie?" Wynona said.

He blinked and turned to her. "Uh, yes. She . . . she is."

"I looked her up. Bloomberg did a story on her. She's heading up a company that's bringing a whole new approach to news in the Southwest. Citizen journalism on steroids, they called it."

"So I heard."

Wynona gave Bernie a sideways look, then pointed at his glass. "Don't like the beer?"

"I do." Bernie raised the glass and took a big gulp.

At that point, Wynona did one of those amazing things that hardly any humans can manage, sticking two fingers in the mouth and whistling a whistle that's sharp and loud beyond belief. It kind of takes possession of my ears while it lasts, a feeling I love and hate at the same time. I always remember the folks who've got this one in their repertoire and try to be ready when the next time rolls around.

Almost at once, the door to the Lucky Horseshoe Bar opened and a girl popped out, a glass of beer in each hand. She looked older than Charlie but not by much. Charlie is the best kid going, and the fact that there was no way he could have brought the beer over to the table without spilling or maybe even dropping the glasses didn't change that. This girl did it smooth and easy, no problem.

"Thanks, kiddo," said Wynona.

"You're welcome, Auntie Wy," said the kid. "Can I pet the doggie?"

"Have to ask the owner," Wynona told her.

"We're more like partners," Bernie said. "But I know the answer to this one's always yes."

The girl came closer, reached out, and patted my neck. "What's his name?"

"Chet," said Bernie.

"Chet," she said, "your eyes are beautiful."

Kids. How can you not love them? She turned and walked back inside the bar. Wynona watched her the whole way.

"Has something bad happened to Johnnie Lee?" she said.

"I don't know," said Bernie. "Does the name Mickey Rottoni mean anything to you?"

Wynona shook her head. "Who's he?"

"Johnnie Lee's former boyfriend."

"Is he involved in this?"

"Not now," Bernie said. "When was the last time you heard from her?"

"When I gave her your name. Since then, I've called or texted a dozen times. No response."

"We'll need her number."

Wynona wrote on a cocktail napkin, handed it to Bernie.

"Does she have any family here?" he said.

"Her dad was never in the picture. Her mom remarried a few years back and moved away."

"Where?"

"No idea. As for friends, I don't think Johnnie Lee kept up with any, except for Mavis Verlander. I believe they were sharing an apartment or condo in the Valley."

"Was Mavis on the rodeo team?"

"No. She was only here for a couple of years—her parents were at the base. I really didn't know her at all. She was a beautiful girl, could have had her pick of the boys—captain of the football team, all that. Instead, she took up with the class clown."

Clowns were in the picture? An interesting development. I'd seen a number of clowns on TV, the sight always making me do my backing-up-and-barking-my-head-off move, but then I'd actually gotten to know one and he'd turned out to be a nice guy and a very good head scratcher. I felt much better about the case.

Wynona sipped her beer. "Well, that's not fair. Neddy Freleng was the class clown, but he was also head of the drama club—and a very good actor. They did *The Crucible,* and he was amazing as John Proctor. I can still see his face when they march him off to the hanging. Mavis played the servant girl, Abigail something-or-other."

"Williams," Bernie said. "Was she talented, too?"

"Not like him. When you see Mavis in real life, you can't take your eyes off her. But when she was onstage you could. Isn't that weird? And Neddy's the opposite. In the end, they went off to Hollywood with big dreams. I don't think Mavis got anywhere at all, but Neddy did some stand-up. He came back a couple years ago."

"By himself?"

Wynona nodded. "Mavis was already in the Valley by then. Neddy persisted in LA a little longer."

"What does he do now?"

"He's a substitute teacher at De Vaca Elementary, maybe has some tutoring gigs on the side—although there's not much demand for tutoring around here."

"Why not?"

"Good question, although I don't see what it has to do with Johnnie Lee and Mavis." Wynona gave Bernie a sideways look.

"I've never dealt with a private detective before. Are they all like you?"

What a lucky lady! Her very first meetup with a private eye and it's Bernie! I waited for him to say, "None of them are like me, pally, not even close." Instead, he went with, "More or less." Bernie! Come on! You've got to toot your own horn, as his mom was saying on her last visit. Bernie has a ukulele—which he plays beautifully, especially around campfires with a glass of bourbon on a log beside him—but he doesn't have a horn. A ukulele instead of a horn: Was that somehow why the finances part of the Little Detective Agency never seemed to do as well as the rest of the operation? What else could it be? I made what Bernie calls a mental note: be on the lookout for horns, big guy.

"As for tutoring," Wynona said, "parents here are like everywhere—they want their kids to do well. They know how to raise them just fine, but the ins and outs of slotting them for success in the big world is still a mystery. Also that costs extra money. The folks pulling the strings are always the ones with extra money—ever noticed that?"

Bernie smiled. He picked up his glass, clinked it against Wynona's, and drank. "If anyone else comes looking for Mavis or Johnnie Lee, you know nothing."

"Anyone else like who?" said Wynona.

"Like anybody."

Wynona nodded. They clinked again.

"Where do I find Neddy?" Bernie said.

"Poor Ms. Drubbins was the sub teacher in fifth grade," Bernie said. We drove back into town, through a nice neighborhood, into one not so nice, and came to a trailer park. Trailer parks are a great human invention, in my opinion. Lots of outdoor cooking goes on in trailer parks, meaning scraps are there for the taking. This particular trailer park was also quiet and shady, the trailers, of which there weren't many, spread out in a small sort of forest, the trees green and leafy, the air around them moist on my nose. Bernie parked in front of a yellow trailer that was all by itself in the deepest part of the woods. It was up on blocks, a bicycle on a kickstand by the door. "We stuck gum on her chair," he said. "Day after day. It never got old."

I had no idea what he was talking about, but the sound of his voice in this quiet little forest was lovely. We walked up to the door of the trailer, and Bernie knocked. Time passed, and he knocked again.

"Maybe no one's home," he said.

What about that snoring sound? I supposed it could be someone snoring on TV, although actually it couldn't because TVs do all kinds of buzzing and whining when they're on—and also when they're off, by the way—so there was only one possibility: Bernie did not hear the snoring. Was it an especially quiet sort of snoring? I didn't think so. It was human male snoring with a snorting in-breath, followed by a strange pause, just long enough for you to think the snoring was over, and then a high and wheezy out-breath that ended with a hint of lip flapping. In short, unmissable. I barked a bark that was also unmissable. Time, you often hear, is money. A bird in the nearest tree took off and soared away. Whoa! Had I done that? Just with my voice? I barked again, amping it up a little. And caramba! Multiple birds took off from multiple trees! I, Chet, turned out to be . . . what would you call it? A bird whisperer? Well, not really, since I wasn't whispering, more like the furthest thing from it. I was more like a bird herder, herding birds across the sky. What a life! I wondered whether bees or butterflies or other flying things could also be herded in this same way. Their ears had to be smaller than birds' ears, meaning that I'd have to reach back and give it my all.

"Chet! What the hell?"

And inside the trailer, a man was saying the exact same thing. Not the *Chet!* part. Just "What the hell?"

Bernie heard that, no question. His face changed slightly, became the Bernie face for when others are around, not just him and me. Bare feet pat-patted to the door, and then it opened.

You see a lot of big, tough, dangerous dudes in this line of work, but the guy in the doorway wasn't one of them. Big? No. Quite the opposite. Short, but some short types can be very quick and powerful. Take Nguyen "Tank" Tong, for example, who once ran right through the wall of a dive bar down in San Dismas, an amazing feat, and Tank seemed quite pleased with himself until he noticed me waiting on the other side. This little fellow had narrow shoulders—easy to see since he was only wearing boxers—and thin arms with knobby wrists.

Tough? Sometimes hard to tell just by looking. An unshaven face might be a sign, but not this type of unshaven face, which was more hipsterish. Also rumpled, like his hair, and unmarked by any past dustups.

Dangerous? There's a smell that men who are ready for a fight give off, and this guy didn't have it. He smelled like someone who was still partly asleep and also needed to pee. Dangerous dudes tend to be hard around the mouth. This guy's mouth was soft.

He blinked at us, then gave me a second look and backed up a bit. Some humans aren't comfortable around me and my kind. If it's a kid or if we're not on the job, I try to show them I'm just a big softie, maybe by doing one of my tricks, charging around a lawn, for example, with razor-sharp cuts. If we're on the job, I wait for some sign from Bernie.

"Neddy Freleng?" he said.

"Um, yeah?"

"Sorry to wake you."

Neddy rubbed his face. He had one of those rubbery faces that changes shape a lot when it's rubbed. "I wasn't sleeping," he said.

Not the first time I'd heard that one, a very common response from a human awakened by day, although never by night. What's that all about? It can only be that when humans sleep in the day-time, they don't realize it! Humans can amaze you, but not always in a good way, no offense.

"I'm Bernie Little, and this is Chet," Bernie said.

"Uh-huh," said Neddy, covering up a yawn with his hand. Another strange bit of human behavior right there, but no time to go into it, on account of something else was going down. When a dude recognizes our names, there's always some reaction, reaching for a gun, say, or taking off at top speed. "Uh-huh" and a yawn means they haven't heard of us. Then why was Neddy suddenly so nervous? I mean deep inside where you can't see. Human nervousness has a sour smell I never miss.

Bernie handed him our card. He squinted at it. "Cool. I've never met a private eye."

"We're looking for two women you know," Bernie said. "Johnnie Lee Goetz and Mavis Verlander."

Neddy scratched his skinny chest. "I knew them back in high school, and Mavis later than that. But I haven't seen either of them in years."

He stood in the doorway, gazing at us pleasantly, in no hurry to get rid of us or head back inside. I got the feeling we were done with Neddy, so it was a bit of a surprise when Bernie said, "Maybe you'll be able to help us anyway. Can we come in?"

Sixteen

"No problemo, ordinarily," Neddy said. "But it's so messy right now. I've been too busy to clean up."

"Yeah?" said Bernie. "Doing what?"

"Oh, just working on an idea or three."

"What kind of ideas?" Bernie said.

By that time, I was inside the trailer. It just seemed like the right move. Bernie wanted in. That was all I needed to know. Why complicate things?

"Hey," said Neddy. "Your dog's, um—" He turned to me. "What's the matter, buddy? No comprendo plain English?" He laughed a little heh heh out the side of his mouth.

"What's the joke?" Bernie said.

I was with him on that. A disturbing thought popped up in my mind. Could Neddy be the bad guy? We'd dealt with many bad guys, but never one as wimpy as him. Was he even worth cuffing? I'm the type who takes pride in his work and who could be proud of cuffing Neddy and sending him off to break rocks in the hot sun? Was he even capable of breaking one single rock?

"Well," Neddy said, "first rule of stand-up—never explain a joke. If you have to explain, it's not funny."

"You do stand-up?" Bernie said.

"Done stand-up, certainly," said Neddy. "Currently doing? Not so much. I—"

His head swiveled around in my direction. I was now comfortably inside the trailer, in the middle of the living room, which smelled of weed and Chinese food. Chinese food comes in cartons, small ones that you tip over to spill out the contents, and bigger ones you can squeeze your muzzle into. I'm partial to General Tso's chicken, and there was a definite General Tso smell in the air.

"Um, here, boy," Neddy said. "Not a good day for a visit, nice doggie, so how about—"

We have some cool little tricks at the Little Detective Agency. Take, for example, the two-on-one. Pretty simple. We just separate a bit, me and Bernie, making some space between us. Here's how we learned the two-on-one: one of us tossed a treat into the corner of a room and the other one went and got it. That's all there is to it! After a while, you won't even need the treat! That's where we were now, me and Bernie nicely spaced in the trailer and Neddy in between. He had maybe the skinniest calves I'd ever seen. My teeth took no interest in them whatsoever.

"See, uh, Bernie, was it?" Neddy said.

Bernie didn't answer. He was studying a framed photo on the wall.

"Why don't you let me clean up a little and you can come back later, like in a couple hours or so?" Neddy said.

Bernie didn't look at him. He pointed to the photo and said, "You and Mavis?"

Neddy glanced at the photo, rubbed his face, changing its shape a little. In the photo, Neddy was all dressed up in what I believe is called a *tuxedo*. Bernie used to have one, and still does, at least the pants. There'd been a problem with the jacket, as I recalled, not so much owing to the taste of the lapels—made of satin, it turned out, a material unknown to me until one afternoon when I'd ventured into Bernie's closet for reasons unknown—as the texture. Some textures have the irresistible power to flip the switch on what might be called the *clawing urge*. Well, let's not put it that way. How about the *examining urge*?

But forget all that. The point was that Neddy, here before us in his boxers, came close to looking like a different guy in the photo. Tuxedo instead of boxers, and although his hair, so messy now, was also messy in the photo, it was messy in a cool way, all gelled and spiky. As for Mavis's hair, it wasn't in a ponytail, but sort of fluffed out like a tiny golden cloud. She actually reminded me of an actress in a movie Bernie and I once watched, something about two dudes pretending to be women, her name and the movie's name forgotten if I'd ever known them, and the movie itself incomprehensible.

"What's it say on that background screen?" Bernie said.

"Northeastern Utah Film Festival," Neddy said.

"I don't know that one."

"Up-and-coming. On a bit of a hiatus but coming back looooong and strooooong." Neddy smooshed his mouth to one side and whispered in Bernie's direction. "Silicon Valley cash on the way. Very hush-hush."

"Hush-hush cash?" Bernie said.

"Heh." Neddy shot him a sideways look. "Heh heh. That's kind of funny—in an offbeat way, right?"

Bernie shrugged.

Neddy went over to a lumpy chair, shoved away this and that, came up with a yellow writing pad and a pen. "Okay if I steal it?"

This was a first. We'd dealt with way too many thieves to remember, but none of them had ever asked our permission to steal stuff. Not only that but steal stuff from their own home! My ears and tail rose straight up, on high alert, ready for anything. I myself was the same, but just didn't show it. I'm a cool customer, in my way.

"For what?" Bernie said.

"My routine," said Neddy.

"There's stand-up around here?"

"Out at Rumbles on the county line, Thursday nights."

"We'll have to catch your act."

"There's a tip jar—nothing hush-hush about it. Heh heh."

Bernie laughed. Bernie has one of the best laughs out there—not quite as good as Charlie's when he really gets going and falls down, laughing so hard he can't breathe—but this particular laugh didn't even sound like him. As though . . . as though someone else was inside Bernie, doing the laughing.

"You're funny," he said.

"Yust my yob, amigo," said Neddy.

"Ha." That laugh, very brief, sounded more like Bernie. "What about your substitute teacher gig at De Vaca Elementary?"

Neddy went still, the first moment of stillness I'd seen from him. "Who's been talking about me?"

"We never burn our sources," Bernie said. "Especially in a missing persons case."

"Who's missing?"

"I told you—Mavis Verlander and Johnnie Lee Goetz."

"You only said you were looking for them. You didn't say they were missing."

"My mistake," Bernie said. "Didn't realize I was dealing with a lawyer manqué."

Neddy looked very confused, and even though he was almost certainly headed for the slammer, I was with him on that.

"But now that we're on the same page, where are they?" Bernie said.

"Like right now?" Neddy said. "No idea. I haven't seen Mavis in over a year and Johnnie Lee way longer than that. Last I heard, they were roomies out in the west Valley someplace."

"They moved out a few days ago," Bernie said.

"And you don't know where they are?"

"Correct."

Neddy's face got into a thoughtful arrangement. "Did you ask the landlord? Maybe they left a forwarding address."

"Why didn't I think of that?" Bernie said.

"Don't beat yourself up. It's not that obvious, and I'm sure eventually you'd—"

He came to a sudden stop. Was it because of a certain look in Bernie's eyes, a look you don't see in them often but means, *Messing with me, buddy?* Or was it because Neddy had suddenly realized that Bernie was not the type to beat himself up? I'd only seen two dudes beat themselves up, both of them perps hoping that if they took care of their own punishment, we'd cut them loose. One night at the Dry Gulch Steakhouse and Saloon, Bernie had told that story to a judge we knew, a hanging judge—whatever that is, exactly—named Maria Valdez. She'd laughed until tears rolled down her face.

"Let's put it this way," Bernie said. "Where would you start looking if you were me?"

Uh-oh. If Neddy was Bernie? Then . ... then I didn't want to think about it. All I knew for sure was that I was done with New Mexico. It was time to haul ass back to the Valley, just me and Bernie, and never see Neddy again. I moved toward the door, just giving Bernie the hint.

"Hmm," Neddy said. "That's a head-scratcher." Maybe, but no head scratching took place. "Like I said, I haven't laid—"

"How about taking us through your relationship with Mavis?" Bernie said.

"But why?" said Neddy. "I don't get it. Who's looking for her?"

"We are."

"Who's 'we'?"

"Chet and I."

Neddy gave me one of those double takes. I'd never understood them and now found that I still didn't.

"But you're a private eye," Neddy said. "That means you're working for someone who wants to find Mavis. So who is it and why?"

"The identity of the client is something we keep to ourselves," Bernie said. "All I can tell you is that Mavis's safety—and Johnnie Lee's—are the client's only interest in this case."

"Meaning they're in danger? Who from?"

"Any ideas?" Bernie said.

"Why would I have any ideas?"

"Wasn't she your girlfriend?"

"Is that little factoid from your so-called source? Or the so-called client?" Neddy got a clever look on his face. "Any chance they're one and the same?"

Bernie smiled. "You're a smart guy, Neddy. That's going to help us."

"How?"

"Because a smart guy like you is bound to have insights on Mavis."

"Such as?"

"Did she have any enemies, for example?"

"Not that I know of," said Neddy.

"How did the two of you break up?"

Neddy leaned back a little, almost like a boxer avoiding a punch, although he resembled no boxer I'd ever seen, and I knew plenty from down at Stillers Gym. "Whoa," he said. "What are you implying?"

"Not a thing," Bernie said. "Let's hear the story of you and Mavis."

"Huh?"

"It's a narrative, Neddy. Isn't stand-up all about narratives?"

"Are you suggesting our relationship was a joke?" Neddy sat down heavily on the lumpy chair. A tiny poof of dust rose up.

"Was it?" Bernie said.

"Just because it didn't work out?" Neddy said.

"Why didn't it?"

"It wasn't my fault."

"Who said it was?"

Neddy's eyes shifted.

"The name, Neddy," Bernie said.

Neddy sighed. "Johnnie Lee said it was my fault. But she was wrong. Mavis lost hope. How was that on me?"

"What was Mavis hoping for?" Bernie said.

"You know. Success."

"Success in Hollywood?"

"Yeah."

"As an actress?"

"At first. Then it got more like success as a movie star." Neddy shot Bernie a quick up-from-under look. "Now you're going to say what's the difference?"

Bernie laughed. "Maybe Chet and I should just leave and let you interview yourself."

Neddy's face brightened. All Bernie's ideas are brilliant, but some are more brilliant than others. This seemed to be one of the others. If Neddy interviewed himself and we were gone, how would we know what he found out? Maybe I was missing something. But there was another problem with leaving right now—namely, a faint smell coming from farther inside the trailer, a smell that needed looking into.

No worries. I should have known. Bernie hooked a barstool with his foot and drew it closer, just another of his many cool moves. He sat down opposite Neddy.

"We're all ears," Bernie said.

I had a choice. Try to make sense of what Bernie had just said, or not. I went with not.

"Mavis is beautiful," Neddy said. "Her face, her body, everything. And don't say the camera doesn't love her." He pointed to the picture on the wall. "It does. The problem with Mavis is she's such a genuine person."

"Meaning she can't act?" Bernie said.

Neddy frowned. "You're not a very nice man."

Whoa! How off base was that? There was no one nicer than Bernie. Some humans miss the most obvious things. That's not how we roll in the nation within. We're all over the most obvious things like . . . like white on rice! Although I'm not a big fan of rice and actually prefer the brown kind.

"So she can act?" Bernie said.

"I'm not saying that. I'm saying she's so genuine she just can't merge herself into some imaginary life dreamed up by a writer."

"Is that her explanation of what went wrong?"

"I wish," said Neddy. "She thinks she has no talent. We tried everything—classes, yoga, therapy. We made some progress, even had an agent who repped some known B-listers. They still rep me for some reason. Maybe they forgot to fire my ass."

Bernie smiled. "What's the name of the agency?" he said.

"MDC," Neddy said. "Stands for Mad Dog Creative. But the point is, Mavis called it quits." He raised his skinny arms and let them flop back down. "Mavis and Johnnie Lee had kept in touch, so one day—this was two years ago around Thanksgiving— Johnnie Lee told her about a good job opening in the Valley. Mavis interviewed, got it, and that was that."

"What was the job?" Bernie said. Or something like that. I was a bit stuck on Mad Dog Creative.

"PR for a big golf course developer," Neddy said.

"Which one?"

"Don't remember the name, if I ever knew."

"And you stayed behind?"

"At the time, I was involved in a pretty exciting pilot development. It almost got green-lit. Came this close." Neddy held up his thumb and first finger with a tiny space between them. Human hands can talk, by the way, often made more sense than their mouths. "Also I was actually making a dollar here and there on the stand-up circuit. Mavis and I fought about the whole thing from every possible angle. It went on for weeks. Finally—in order to be fair to her—I broke it off." He gazed at Bernie, waiting for some reaction.

"Are there groupies in stand-up?" Bernie said.

Neddy's face, so changeable, made another change, this one the biggest so far. It twisted up in rage—was there really so much rage inside him?—and he sprang up and punched Bernie right on the nose.

Well, not that last part, although the nose was where Neddy was aiming. But Bernie caught Neddy's wrist in midair and held it there, absolutely still. Without getting up, Bernie gave Neddy a gentle push, and he sank back down in his chair. Then Neddy put his head in his hands and began to sob.

"I loved her, you son of a bitch. I still do. I can't stand to see her treated like trash."

"Who's treating her like trash?" Bernie said.

Neddy's sobs amped down, but he kept his head in his hands. "Go away," he said.

Bernie rose. "Thanks for your time."

We were leaving? Without cuffing Neddy and taking him in? I was a little surprised. Then came another surprise. Instead of heading for the door, Bernie went the other way, deeper inside the trailer. Were we doing one of those real fast recons? I love those! I trotted alongside Bernie as we swept through the trailer, finding lots of mess but nothing worth a second look. There was one interesting smell, rather kibbley, although not like my kind of kibble.

We went back into the living room. Neddy was still in his chair. "Snooping through my home?" he said.

"Correct," said Bernie.

Neddy called him something that didn't sound very nice. I took one last look at those skinny calves. My teeth just didn't want to get involved. We went outside and headed for the car.

A trash barrel stood by the roadside. Bernie raised the lid. It was stuffed to the brim. On top lay an unopened bag of kibble, not quite smelling like food for me and my kind, and the happy eater pictured on the front was not one of us. It was a ferret.

Seventeen

"Two ferrets in the same case?" Bernie said as we drove away from Neddy's trailer. "What are the odds on that?"

Odds came up from time to time, a complete mystery to me. The two ferrets part zipped by me, too. There was only one ferret so far, Griffie, first encountered at Johnnie Lee's condo, and now we had ferret kibble in Neddy's trash. So therefore?

"Approaching zero, big guy. Was Griffie here? If so, why didn't he eat his kibble? Or . . . or was he just expected here but never . . ." He tapped his fingers on the steering wheel, a sign he was so-therefore-ing at a very high level. "Griffie belongs to Johnnie Lee, or possibly Mavis. Yet Neddy says he hasn't had contact with Mavis for over a year, and Johnnie Lee for much longer than that." Bernie gave me a quick look. "He's a liar, Chet—but what kind? The big lie kind of liar where you can't trust a word he says? Or the careful little-lie kind who mostly sticks to the truth, although the frame around it is crooked?"

Wow! Bernie at his most brilliant! I wanted him to go on forever.

"And don't forget he's an actor of sorts, maybe not as genuine as Mavis, and therefore better at fooling people. But there was one moment when he was genuine for sure, Chet—when he threw that punch. That was a lucky break for us."

Some dude trying to hurt Bernie was a lucky break? This was a strange case. Also we've never had a case with a ferret before. We had had cases where tough guys like Mickey Rottoni end up with a round red hole in their foreheads. So at least that was a good sign. Not for Mickey, of course. A bad guy, although he'd never done anything bad to me or Bernie. For a moment, I thought, *Poor Mickey*. Then the next moment came, and I was thinking about something else. Slim Jims, if you want the details.

Bernie fished under the seat and came up with a bent cigarette, or at least part of one. He was great at quitting smoking, had done it often. It had been a long time since the last cigarette, but maybe Bernie felt like quitting again. He lit it, inhaled, exhaled, and relaxed, the whole car relaxing around him, and everything in it, including me.

"The main takeaway is that he loves her, Chet. And will protect her if she asked. Suppose he's protecting her from us—that means she asked. So therefore Mavis and Neddy are in contact. My guess is she was here, and not long ago."

Wow! Mavis and Neddy were in contact! All we had to do was . . . was . . .

I could feel the answer coming to me, maybe not full speed or even steady, more like lurching. But before it could arrive, Bernie said, "Why would she want protection from us?"

A tough one. We were the ones who did the protecting. I waited for Bernie to figure it out and was still waiting when the phone buzzed.

"Hi, Bernie. It's Weatherly."

"Well, hi," said Bernie, a very warm hi for him, especially on the phone. He cleared his throat and tried again in what sounded more like a business-type voice. The Little Detective Agency is a business, don't forget, a highly successful business except for one tiny part, which I won't go into now. "Um, hi. Hello. Bernie speaking."

"Right," said Weatherly after a slight pause. "I recognize your voice. I just wanted to thank you again. Trixie's back home."

"Good to hear."

"She has to take it easy for a few weeks, but she's doing fine."

"I'm glad."

"One other thing," Weatherly said. "I've been suspended."

We slowed down a little, like . . . like the car was dealing with this news. I'd learned all about suspensions from the career of Fritzie Bortz, former motorcycle cop and now Border Patroller riding shotgun in a white SUV, and even sometimes in the back seat. But how did the car know? Whoa! I'd strayed into odd territory. Lucky for me, I'm pretty good at straying right back out.

"Go on," Bernie said.

"They took my gun and my badge."

"What for?"

"Insubordination."

"Was it Ellis?"

"Not openly."

"Of course not," Bernie said.

Then came a silence. I could sort of feel the presence of Weatherly during that silence. She was steaming.

Bernie glanced at me, or rather at my neck. Hey! My neck fur was standing on end, and I hadn't even realized it! What was that all about? Bernie checked the rearview mirror. We were alone on the highway, which I already knew just from the sound, empty of all machines except us.

"I was wondering," Bernie said, "if you'd like to . . . that is, um . . . how about a bite to eat?"

Wow! Great idea, and so sudden, right off the top of his head. My neck fur settled right back down. The Little Detective Agency, ladies and gentlemen. What can I tell you?

"When?" said Weatherly.

"Tonight at eight?"

"Okay."

"Dry Gulch all right with you?"

"The place with that cowboy sign?"

"Uh, yeah. Or if that's not—"

"See you there."

Click.

Bernie sped up a little. "Is there something wrong with the cowboy sign?"

The huge wooden cowboy out front of the Dry Gulch Steakhouse and Saloon? I loved the wooden cowboy, had lifted my leg against him too many times to count, even for someone good at counting, like Charlie, say, who could now go all the way to 106, which took pretty much our whole walk around the block, just him and me. I wore a leash! He held one end! He really is the cutest kid.

But back to the huge wooden cowboy. He had a big square jaw and eyes that sparkled—although only at night—and he was hunched over a bit, reaching for his gun. What could be wrong with any of that?

We drove into the Valley, took one of the first exits, and were soon in South Pedroia. The heat was rising up from the ground more than it was coming down from the sky, a late-in-the-day summertime thing in our part of the world. We headed into the oldest part, those narrow streets lined with brick warehouses, the heat now coming in from the sides as well. Lots of interesting smells in the air—which gets pissier as the day goes along, which you may not know—and among them a strong smoked-oil sort of smell you find wherever big trucks get together. So before we even pulled up in front of Rottoni Transport—the security rollers over the doors all down for the night—I knew where we were. There was no one around but our little bare-chested buddy, leaning against a wall and talking on his phone, a cigarette bobbing up and down in his mouth and a bottle sticking out of his shorts pocket. His name almost came to me. Wow! Was it possible I was getting better at the job? I knew one thing for sure: we'd be rolling in money one day. I—but not Bernie—have rolled in poop from time to time. Would rolling in money be much different? I couldn't wait to find out.

Bernie parked not far from our pal. As we got out of the car, he said, "Griffie is the key to this case, big guy."

Uh-oh. How was that possible? Griffie was a ferret. His smell was unbearable, even to me, who likes just about every smell I've come across. Was Bernie joking? No time to figure that out, because we were now pretty close to the bare-chested dude. He saw us, said something quick and quiet into the phone, tucked it in his shorts, and glanced down the alley. Not a very long alley, and it seemed to end in a brick wall. As for what he'd said into his phone so quick and quiet, I'm the type who hears the quick and quiet things, in this case, "Yikes, gotta go."

He looked at us, his face running through several expressions, none happy to see us.

"Hey, there, Rico," Bernie said.

Rico! I'd almost had it.

"If that's your name," Bernie went on, confusing me a bit. "You owe us twenty bucks."

"Uh, I don't remember nothin' about no, uh . . ."

He backed away. I seemed to be quite close to him, one of our best techniques in a situation like this. As for the twenty bucks, there were a number of people around town we'd lent money to, although we never asked for it back. Was Bernie tweaking our business plan at last, as Ms. Pernick, our accountant, had suggested? Rico seemed the unpromising type in so many ways, but you had to start somewhere, as humans like to say.

"Can you get your dog to back off, mister?" Rico said.

"First," said Bernie, "we're partners. Second, he's more likely to back off when he sees the twenty bucks."

Rico blinked. "But it's a dog."

"He."

Rico shrugged. "Okay, he's a dog. What's a dog know about money?"

"You'd be surprised," Bernie said. "But one thing's for sure. He knows about being owed." Bernie held out his hand.

Rico licked his lips. "You keep sayin' I owe you, but what for, man? Is this a shakedown? I got friends, if you didn't know."

"Like who?" Bernie said.

"Guys you don't want to mess with, believe me."

"Name one."

"Not gonna open that can of worms."

That was what humans call a no-brainer. There's not a chance worms are in my vicinity without me knowing it, and no worms were anywhere near. Was Rico just trying to be difficult? I moved in a little closer. He was nicely placed, tight to the wall now, possibly on his tiptoes. This is a fun job, my friends.

"You remember us, don't you, Rico?"

"Sure, sure, kinda."

"We met right here."

I placed a paw on one of his feet, quite gently.

"It's comin' back to me a little," he said.

"What did we talk about?" Bernie said.

"You . . . you don't remember?"

Bernie laughed. I love when he enjoys himself. Was there any-thing I could do to Rico that would make Bernie laugh harder? I began to give that some serious thought.

"What's funny?" Rico said.

"You," said Bernie. "What's your last name, Rico?"

"None of your goddamn business."

"Wrong on that one. Let's see your ID."

"Don't have it on me."

"What would fall out of your pockets if we held you upside down and gave you a shake?"

Oh boy! We hadn't done the upside-down-shake in so long I'd almost forgotten it! But why not? It had to be one of our very top techniques. What was that other guy's name? Swiftie something-or-other? A speedy little human who might have really thought he could run away from me. The fun I'd had, closing in, dropping back, closing in. And we get paid to do this? Well, not always. But forget that part. The point was that when we turned Swiftie upside down and shook him, all sorts of things fell out of his pock-ets, including a chunk of stolen moon rock, a complete mystery to me, and a Slim Jim, no mystery at all, and soon taken care of. Rico had no Slim Jim, but I still wanted to get started on the upside-down shake. I'm a team player, in case that wasn't clear already.

Rico glanced this way and that, looking for help, or an escape route, or something. But he was on his own.

"Okay, you win," he said. "My last name's Carter."

"Like the president?"

"What president?"

Bernie smiled. How nice to have a job you enjoy! "Doesn't

matter," he said. "What's important it that the other day your last name was Miller."

"That must have been some kind of . . . um . . . ," said Rico.

"No arguing with that," Bernie said. "And we're fine with you calling yourself whatever you want—as long as you're straight with us. Otherwise, we're taking you for a long ride." Bernie nodded toward the Porsche. He didn't mention that Rico would be on the shelf in back, meaning it was . . . how to put it? Understood. Something like that.

Rico licked his lips and licked them again, like his mouth was drying up. "You got no right."

"Ever heard that might makes right?" Bernie said.

Rico shook his head. "Nope, but it makes sense," he said. He took a deep breath. "Is this about that ferret shit?"

That was a puzzler. If anything of that nature was around, who would be the first to know?

"Ferret?" said Bernie. "Last time, it was a giant squirrel."

Uh-oh. Two puzzlers in a row. I handled that by stepping on Rico's foot a little harder.

"Ow," he said.

"Chet?" Bernie said. "Let's give Rico a bit more space. Maybe he'll concentrate better."

Really? In these situations, I'd always thought the opposite. This had to be a special case. Who else could have figured that out so soon? Nobody, people. And I get to work with him every day!

"So," Bernie said. "Ferret or squirrel?"

"Ferret," said Rico.

"Does the ferret have a name?"

"Yeah, but—no." Rico looked down. "No name that I know of."

Bernie nodded, a pleasant nod that showed he and Rico were getting along just fine. That's what it showed Rico, is what I mean. I know Bernie better.

"You described the man who took the ferret as a, quote, 'little black guy. Jeans and a T-shirt. Wore one of them do-rags. Red. Not the real bright kind, more like Alabama.' End quote. Sticking to that description? Making sure you got the red exactly right was a very nice touch."

"Uh, thanks," said Rico.

"You should have been a novelist," said Bernie.

"Yeah? What's that?"

"A writer who makes up stories."

"Any money in it?"

"Once in a blue moon," Bernie said. "But let's focus on the whole made-up part."

"Like, uh, what, exactly?" said Rico.

"The little black guy in the do-rag," Bernie said. "Too generic for a first-rate novelist? Maybe, but I'm no expert."

Ha! Of course Bernie was an expert on novelists, whatever they were. In fact, I got the feeling they were like us, at least on the finances end.

"So, um, you're, like, suggestin' that . . . ?"

"The little do-rag black guy was a figment of your imagination."

Rico's eyes brightened. "My mom always said I had a great imagination."

"Yeah? Where does she live?"

"Over in Rio Vista."

"What part?"

"You know Rio Vista?"

"Pretty well."

"Know Carson Park?"

"Sure."

"She's right across the street from the statue of the guy on a horse."

"Kit Carson," Bernie said.

"I wouldn't know about that," said Rico.

We seemed to have a nice and relaxed back-and-forth going on, which happens in some of our interviews, often the best ones. I could sort of feel their two minds. Bernie's was huge, and Rico's was tiny.

"I'd like to meet her," Bernie said.

"Who?" said Rico.

"Your mom."

Rico shook his head. "You don't know her. She's got a mean temper. This vein in her neck?" He pointed to his neck. "It's always throbbing—baboom, baboom, baboom. Ready to explode, is what I'm saying."

"Interesting," said Bernie. "Let's go check it out."

"Huh?"

"Now's a good time. We'll grab some flowers on the way."

"Whoa!" said Rico. "No way. Wouldn't be smart."

"How come?"

"We're not gettin' along too good these days."

"What's the problem?"

"Not sure how to say it. Like when two people disagree about something?"

"A misunderstanding?"

"That's it! Yeah. My mom and me are having a misunderstanding."

"About what?"

"Five hundred bucks. Now she's sayin' it was a loan—plus fuckin' interest!—but at the time, it was a gift, no question about it."

"No problem," Bernie said. "Let's get right over there and straighten out the whole thing."

"Wait just a sec."

"We settle disputes like this all the time, me and Chet."

"Well, you're not settling this one, bud."

Bernie reached out and took Rico by the arm. Not hard or anything like that. He just wrapped his hand around the skinny arm, up at the biceps part. "You'll thank us in the end," he said.

Rico glanced down at Bernie's hand. Then he looked up at Bernie. I felt the tiniest breeze. "There wasn't no black dude. It was a big, shaved-head white guy, like you said."

"Name of?" said Bernie.

Rico gave Bernie a squinty look. "Maybe you already know?"

"We'd like to hear it, just the same," Bernie said.

"Mickey Rottoni," said Rico.

Bernie let go of Rico's arm. "Friend of yours?"

Rico rubbed his arm. "We get along, sure."

"When was the last time you saw him?"

"That time, right here."

"Take us through it."

"How?"

"Like a story. An afternoon in the life of a ferret."

"Hey! That's pretty good."

Not to my way of thinking, but I could feel we were on a roll, so I let it go on by.

"Well, to start with, you guys rode in and went up to the office. I was out here, just doin' my job."

"Which is?"

"Takin' care of things, sweeping up, makin' sure what's sposed to be locked is and what ain't sposed to be ain't."

"So you work for Sylvia."

"Sorta. She's way up on the . . . what do you call it?"

"Corporate ladder?"

"Yeah. And I'm way down. But I get along with all the Rottonis—Mickey, too. He's not a bad guy, just ambitious. The American dream, all that. Anyways, he comes up, sees your car, and does this double take. Then he says to me, 'Hey, what's goin' on?' And I tell him about you and the dog, goin' inside. Then he spots the ferret, cuts him loose, and says to me, 'You don't know nothin'. Hundred bucks, next time I see you.' And I go, 'What's with the ferret?' And he winks at me and goes, 'His name's Icing on the Cake. You didn't see him neither.' Kind of a strange name for a ferret, but the whole thing's kind of strange." Rico's forehead wrinkled up. "'Specially now that I'm tellin' it like a story."

"Did you get the hundred bucks?"

"Haven't seen Mickey since. But he's good for the money. I'm expectin' fifty at the very least. He's got one of those long memories. Good and bad."

"What's the bad part?" said Bernie.

"He don't forget when somebody goes sideways on him," Rico said. "Wanna hear an example?"

"You're way ahead of me."

"Huh?"

"An example would be nice."

"Okeydoke. Take that restraining order his girlfriend got on him. Guess what Mickey did to get back at the cop who served the papers?"

"Kidnapped her dog."

Rico blinked. Then he blinked again. "If you know, why ask?"

"Straight out of the textbook," Bernie said.

Rico nodded. "Shoulda known. Textbooks was never my thing."

"There's still time," Bernie said. "And that fifty you've got coming? Think of it as seventy. You don't owe us anymore."

Rico looked surprised, and then very pleased. "My real name's Donny," he said.

"You're Rico to us," said Bernie.

Eighteen

"Let's remind ourselves," Bernie said. "Only one ferret per case. Call it the ferret rule. Our ferret is Griffie. Therefore Icing on the Cake isn't a name. It's a descriptor."

The ferret rule? I didn't like the sound of that. How could ferrets rule? It made no sense. And what about Icing on the Cake? Not a name, according to Bernie, but instead some other thing that had zipped right on by? All that was way beyond me, although I'd had some experience with cake icing—for example, at a New Year's Eve party we dropped in on, not for long, where they'd had a giant cake. The problem was—and I knew this the moment I walked into the room—that a woman was hiding in it! I did what I had to do, as you can imagine. But the point is, I know icing. If icing was going to turn up in this case, who'd be the first to know? Me, Chet the Jet! We had a big payoff waiting for us, I just knew it. What was I supposed to do? Remind myself? That was it. I reminded myself how good we were, me and Bernie.

We took a ramp up onto the freeway, headed toward the orange tip of the sun, just visible over the edge of . . . of whatever that edge is, where you can't see any farther. The edge itself was very hard to get to—in all our time on the road, we'd never quite reached it. There's lots to look forward to in this life.

"The point being," Bernie said after a while, "if Griffie's the icing, what's the cake?"

A terrible thing to admit, but Bernie would get no help on this from me.

He sighed. "How about we go over the timeline, big guy?"

Uh-oh. The timeline only got brought up when we were having trouble with a case. And here I'd thought we were sailing!

"We—well, actually you, big guy—found Griffie at Johnnie Lee's place on Aztec Creek Road. We also know, pretty much for certain, that Griffie was expected at Neddy's trailer in New Mexico but never showed. After Aztec Creek Road, we had Griffie, and then Mickey had him. Stay with me here. Did Mickey bring him to the mine near AZ EZ, where he seemed to be—I want to say hiding out, but let's just call it living? In which case, someone else grabbed Griffie and . . ." His voice trailed off, just in time, as far as I was concerned.

Meanwhile, Bernie seemed to be in a good mood. He took his hands off the wheel and rubbed them together like we were getting down to business. For a while, his knee did the steering. Bernie's the best wheelman in the Valley, which I should have mentioned already. Once Rumblin' Ronny Leibnitz, a smuggler of this and that, offered Bernie big bucks to drive for him and got pretty upset when Bernie turned him down. "No one says no to me," he told Bernie.

"No?" said Bernie.

At that moment, I remembered something about the timeline. "Stay with me." Wow. And of course I would, for as long as Bernie needed me and then long after that.

Bernie put his hands—actually just one hand—back on the wheel. "How can we test timelines?" He leaned forward and fished around under the seat, eventually discovered what I already knew, that even the last bent little cigarette stub was gone. "How about we impose timelines on the known physical space and see what pops up?" My eyelids suddenly got very heavy. Bernie may have stepped on the gas.

I had a fun dream about Rumblin' Ronny Liebnitz and huge cakes and woke to find we were on a dirt road that seemed familiar, the last light of the day in one low corner of the sky. Ahead stood a small ranch house with a flatbed truck out front, loaded up with ATVs. Aha! EZ AZ Tours! Chet the Jet, in the picture. We parked by the flatbed truck and got out of the car.

Lukie was sitting by himself in the cab. He looked out the open window.

"Hey, Chet," he said. "Is that you?"

What a smart kid! My tail started up right away. Was he planning on hopping out of the cab and playing some game, chase, maybe, or fetch? I was ready for anything.

"Yes, Lukie, it's us," Bernie said. "How are you doing?"

"Okay," said Lukie, his skinny little arm resting on the door-frame.

"Headed someplace?"

"Uh-huh."

"Anywhere special?"

"Colorado," he said. "Where Uncle Bill lives. But don't tell anybody."

"I won't," Bernie said.

"My cousin's there."

"That's good."

"Debbie."

"Nice name."

"She thinks I'm cool."

"So do I," Bernie said.

The door to the ranch house opened, and Poppop rolled out in his wheelchair, a suitcase in his hand and a bolo tie around his neck. He closed the door, made sure it was locked, then started toward the flatbed truck. That was when he noticed me and Bernie.

"What the hell?" Poppop let go of the suitcase and wheeled toward us, surprisingly fast. "Who the—" And then he recognized us. "Didn't I tell you to stay away from here?" He got between the cab and Bernie, leaned forward, and gave Bernie a push. From time to time, some bad guy or other had tried the same thing, although never from a wheelchair. All of them much younger and stronger than Poppop and all of them regretting it very soon. Now Bernie just let himself be pushed, taking a step or two away. Meanwhile, Lukie shrank back in the cab.

"We can't do that," Bernie said. "Why would you want us to?

We're trying to find out what happened to your employee, Mickey Rottoni."

"He run off somewheres," said Poppop. "And he was only part-time."

"Who told you he ran off?" Bernie said.

"Everybody's sayin' it. And a Valley cop came out here personal to explain it to me. Mickey disappeared himself on account of owing a ton of money to loan sharks, and you're in on the scam."

"What Valley cop was this?" Bernie said, his voice quiet.

"A high-up—captain, maybe. Red-haired guy."

Bernie glanced in the cab. Lukie was still in the shadows away from the window, but I could see he was sitting up very straight.

"How about we move away a bit, keep this private?" Bernie said.

"Forget it," said Poppop. "You go on back under the rock you come from. We're done talking."

Where was Poppop getting his information? We came from a nice house on Mesquite Road. And now, after saying that not very nice thing, was Poppop planning to just get in the cab and drive off? I changed my position slightly.

"The cop was lying to you," Bernie said, his voice nice and even like this was a friendly back-and-forth, which I knew from Poppop's smell that it was not.

"Could care less," Poppop said. "I'm outta here."

"Where are you going?"

"None of your concern."

"What about the business?"

"Sold out," said Poppop. "I retired. You sayin' I got no right to retire?"

Poppop rolled toward the driver's side of the cab and found me right there waiting. Not that I was going to do anything. I was just in the proper place if Bernie needed me. The last little bit of daylight made it look like Poppop's eyes were on fire.

"Chet," Bernie said in that same nice and easy tone. I went over and stood beside him. Poppop opened the door, swung up inside, hauled the wheelchair up, and folded it, without seeming to strain hardly at all. But as Poppop began driving away, Bernie noticed the suitcase still on the ground. He picked it up and heaved it onto the moving flatbed, easy-peasy. Lukie watched us through the back window of the cab, his pale little face fading, fading, and gone.

We stood together outside the ranch house as the night went fully dark and the stars came out.

"Any point in following them to Colorado?" Bernie said.

A tough question. I'd actually been to Colorado, on the same case where I'd tasted a gold nugget, a successful trip—we'd even gotten paid—except for the part with the bears.

Finally, Bernie shook his head and said, "We've got other fish to fry."

That was a stunner. When fish are anywhere in the vicinity—and that includes in a stream or in the freezer—I know about it. We had no fish with us of any kind. And also no frying pan. I waited for some sort of explanation, but before it could come, I heard the soft purr of a car, still pretty far away but coming in our direction. I barked my low, rumbly bark. I'd . . . how to put this? Trained him? Something like that, even if it sounded a little odd. I'd trained Bernie on that bark, and he responded right away.

"Chet?"

He glanced around, turned his head to one side—a cute human thing for when they're trying to hear better—and said, "Someone coming?"

So quick on the uptake! But that was Bernie. We jumped in the car and drove slowly, headlights off, to a shed not far from the ranch house. Bernie parked behind it. We got out and moved to a corner of the shed, where we could peek out at whatever was going down—just another one of our techniques at the Little Detective Agency.

At first, nothing at all was going down, except for an owl hooting in the distance. Owls take over the sky at night, and once, I'd seen a white one flying off with a snake, the snake putting up a fight, although not for long. The night can be very special.

Meanwhile, the car noise grew louder, and then headlights appeared on the Zinc Town road. Not long after that, their beams swept across the face of the ranch house and a big black SUV rolled up, parking exactly where we'd just been.

Two big men got out, both of them wearing white sneaks, but otherwise all shadowy. The engine kept running, the headlights still on the ranch house. The men walked toward the house, stepping into the light. The smaller of the two—but still big— was Olek, his short blond hair more moon-colored by night. The really enormous one was his driver, Vanko, if I was remembering right, the dude who'd brought the special vodka that Sylvia Rottoni had enjoyed so much and that Bernie had maybe enjoyed too much. Vanko carried a small box, the size of our tool kit back home. Was it full of cash? Had they come to offer us more money? That was my first thought, but from the way Bernie had gone so still, I got the feeling it was wrong.

Olek and Vanko walked up to the front door. Vanko opened the small box and took out what looked like a drill. So it was a tool kit? How disappointing!

Vanko got to work with the drill. Olek lit up a cigarette and glanced around, first down the road, but then he started to turn toward us. Bernie made a quick and tiny click-click sound. It meant, *Back and down.* We got back and down.

We lay by the shed wall, listening for footsteps. Or at least that was what I was doing. As for Bernie, I wasn't sure. Wasn't Olek a sort of buddy? And if not that, he was certainly not an enemy. So there I was, stuck again at the beginning of a so-therefore. Vanko's drill whined in the night. Then it stopped, and quieter metallic sounds started up. Bernie crept forward on his stomach. I did the same. We peered out, our heads side by side.

Olek and Vanko were still at the front door, Vanko nailing up a small sign and Olek watching him. They stepped away. A big padlock now hung on the door. Olek tested it, said, "Okay," and the two of them started back to the SUV. They got in and drove down the Zinc Town road.

We rose and went to the ranch house door. Bernie read the sign. "'Under new management. Closed for repairs.'" He tested the padlock with the exact same motion as Olek, like most of his mind was somewhere else. Then he stood there for a moment or two, his gaze on the Zinc Town road. Bernie nodded to me. We ran to the car.

Nineteen

"This case began with us getting followed," Bernie said. "Now we're doing the following. Feels right, huh, big guy?"

That was how the case began? How interesting! Once, we had a case that began with lingerie falling from the sky. But no time to go into that now. The point was that Bernie felt right. When Bernie feels right, I feel right. Whoa! Don't two rights make something or other, something important? I felt a real big thought on the way.

While I waited for it to arrive, I helped Bernie with the driving, which I do by sitting straight up, eyes on the road. We were on two-lane blacktop in hilly country with lots of curves and no traffic, just the occasional red glimpse of taillights far ahead. Our headlights were off—maybe something I should have mentioned off the top. In short, we were doing some distant following on a moonless night with no headlights, and going pretty fast, maybe something else I should have mentioned. You might say, "Hey, Chet, that sounds pretty dangerous. Aren't you scared?"

You don't know us.

"They're not in any particular hurry, Chet," Bernie said after a while, sitting back, one hand on the wheel. "It's just that they like to drive fast. Is it a Ukrainian thing?"

For a moment, I was puzzled. Then it hit me. Wasn't that vodka Ukrainian? Speed and vodka: I saw at once how they fit together. Bernie was right, as usual. Speed had to be a Ukrainian thing. Were Olek and Vanko passing a bottle back and forth in that big SUV, now angling up a steep rise with a tall shadowy cliff on one side, a cliff that finally merged with the night? There wasn't a doubt in my mind.

Not long after that, we were on the same steep rise ourselves.

A breeze came curling down from the top, carrying the sweet and heavy smell of a big white flower you only see at night. When we got to the top, Bernie stopped the car. Were we going to hunt around for the special night flower? We'd done that once, Bernie carrying a real big one with inky tips on the petals in a red plastic beer cup back to Suzie. She'd laughed with delight, and at the same time, her eyes filled with tears. I missed her.

I know what you're thinking. With Suzie now married to Jacques, who would this new flower be for? I was thinking the same thing, and also—what about Olek? Bernie didn't get out of the car—meaning the whole flower thing was off the table— but he did do something I'd hardly ever seen from him—namely, stand up on his seat. I stood up on mine. Chet doesn't need to be told twice, or even once when he's really cooking. We peered out at one of those huge desert views that come along from time to time in these parts.

Wow. Our world, mine and Bernie's, went on forever, maybe longer at night than in the day. Over on one side we had the Valley, all shining and gold, going on and on to the edge I mentioned before. Straight ahead was rough and hilly country with clusters of light here and there, some of them pretty big, but nothing like the Valley. On the far side stood mountains, the tallest one with two peaks and a level dip in between. Our road twisted down and down, dark and empty, finally meeting one of the Valley freeways on one side and some smaller roads on the other.

"Where are they?" Bernie said, his voice low.

Meaning the red taillights? Ah! What an excellent question! That was Bernie, of course.

"No way they made it all the way down."

Bernie switched off the engine. Now we had silence to go with the darkness, usually a very good combo for us. We got out of the car and stood side by side. Darkness, yes, but not quite silence. From down below—but actually not that far, only a switchback or two away—rose a very faint little snick, and then again. Snick snick. I have quite a lot of sounds in my head, in case that wasn't clear already. This particular snick was the sound of a match getting struck. It came from behind a rocky outcrop between the switchbacks. I sat right down.

"Chet?" Bernie's voice got even quieter. He followed my gaze, then kept his own on that outcrop. After a while, cigarette smell came drifting up to us. Bernie sniffed the air. "Smell anything, big guy?" he said in that same low voice.

Poor Bernie. But no worries. I had him covered.

We waited, I wasn't sure for what. Waiting is part of the job. It might look like we're doing nothing, but we're not. Once Bernie said, "They also serve who only stand and wait." I've thought about that from time to time, getting nowhere, but I knew it was important.

Down below, a lit cigarette butt came spinning out from behind the outcrop and landed in the road, glowing faintly. An engine started up. Headlights flashed on. The black SUV drove out from behind the outcrop and headed down the road.

"We're dealing with pros." Bernie patted the top of my head. "Good to know."

Was it? Well, that was nice. I felt very happy. On the way down we ran slowly over the still-glowing cigarette butt, squishing it under one of the tires. From the look on Bernie's face, I got the idea that maybe Olek was in fact some sort of bad guy. Was Olek mad at us because we didn't take the job? How many times has Bernie said that it helps to have a theory of the case? And how many times have I failed to get what he was talking about? The same number! Wow! What an amazing thought! But it wasn't even the amazing thought that was amazing me at that moment—namely, that I finally understood what theory of the case was all about! Plus I had my very own theory of this case! Which was . . . was . . . was that Olek was mad at us for turning him down. Whew. Almost lost it there for a second.

Headlights off, we followed those two red taillights down through the switchbacks, keeping some distance but closer than before.

"Only obsessives would try that trick again, and we're not

dealing with obsessives," Bernie said. I love when he talks like that, so in command, and could listen to it forever. Whatever obsessives were, it sounded scary, but they weren't in the picture. We were good to go.

Down we went, then up, then down some more, closing in on the freeway. Soon, I could hear the freeway traffic, but the red taillights didn't take the freeway exit, instead turned onto another two-laner. This one took us out of the hills and across a flat plain, the tall two-crested mountain in the distance. The black SUV sped up, and so did we. I see pretty well at night, but was Bernie having problems? I glanced over. He was deep in thought, one hand on the wheel.

The black SUV started up the two-crested mountain, the red taillights disappearing and reappearing. Bernie made no attempt to get any closer. "Ponderosa Mountain," Bernie said. "Only one way up on this side. Skied up here as a kid, big guy." He smiled at me. "Once, the chairlift got stuck, and I was alone with Lizzie Wheeler for an hour. Couldn't think of one single thing to say. Ten degrees and blowing like crazy. Lizzie was shivering, so I wrapped my jacket around her. 'Thanks, um, what's your name again?' Lizzie was a year ahead of me, the most beautiful girl in the school. 'You're welcome,' I said. Forgetting to mention my name!" Bernie laughed and laughed. What was funny?

We began climbing Ponderosa Mountain. It got steeper and twistier. Now Bernie had both hands on the wheel. You didn't see that every day. Up ahead, the beams of the SUV shone on a line of metal chairs hanging in the night sky. I'd seen some skiing on TV but hadn't realized how dangerous it was. Those chairs so high and flimsy looking! Did Bernie ever get his jacket back?

Not long after that, I began smelling water. The road straightened out, and a lake appeared in the headlights of the SUV, the two peaks of the mountain rising on either side and the road turning to gravel. The SUV came to a stop and bright lights flashed on from the nearby trees, gleaming on a metal gate that blocked the road, tall fencing on either side. Bernie stopped the car and switched off the engine.

Olek got out and unlocked the gate, his sneakers crunching on the gravel. The SUV drove on through. Olek locked the gate. The bright lights went out. Then Olek suddenly looked in our direction. We weren't far away, could easily have been seen in the daytime, but it was night and he was human. Olek got back in the SUV. It moved toward the lake. Farther along the shore, lights went on in a big house.

We sat where we were. Bernie thought. I felt him think. The SUV's headlights blinked through the trees, closing in on the big house. We were actually closer to the other side of the lake, although there didn't seem to be a road going that way. After a while, Bernie backed the car behind some bushes. He opened the glove box and took out the binoculars, then paused for a moment. Was he thinking of the .38 Special, locked in the office safe back home? I was.

We got out, crossed the road, and headed into the woods on the near side of the lake, the trees of the piney kind you find up high in our part of the world. The night was even darker in these woods. I led. Bernie followed. I trotted along a route that seemed quite clear, at least to me. I smelled the way, heard the way, saw the way, in that order. It's hard for me to get lost.

The lake began to appear in glimpses through the trees. Lakes and streams, even on the darkest nights, somehow make a little light of their own. The water smelled lovely. Were we going to be able to squeeze in some swimming? You can always hope, and I always do.

Meanwhile, we were getting closer and closer to the lake. We came even with the big house on the other side, stepped through an opening in the trees, and onto a small sandy beach. An owl hooted, far away. And then again, much closer.

We gazed across the water at the big house. The wind was rising, ruffling up the surface of the lake, each tiny wave topped with reflected gold from the lights of the big house. We got our first good look it at, tall and wide, with lots of windows and balconies, plus a rooftop deck, a ground-level deck, and a pier jutting into the water, with a large powerboat tied to the end. Two people seemed to be standing on the ground-level deck, possibly a silver-haired man and a blond woman, but they were far away and I couldn't be sure.

Bernie raised the binoculars, fiddled with the little things to fiddle with, trained the binoculars on the big house. He went still, not even breathing.

Bernie has a voice for when he's talking to himself. You can't actually tell it apart from the voice he uses to talk to me, when it's just the two of us.

"The Wrays," he said.

Twenty

The Wrays. That had to be important. Out of the blue, I thought of two things, bumper stickers and horses. Was that a good start? I didn't see why not.

Caroline Wray, if I was properly in the picture, was standing at the railing, maybe looking out over the lake, her arms crossed. Senator Wray was off to one side, glancing at her once or twice like he was thinking of saying something, which he ended up not doing as far as I could tell.

A new figure appeared on the deck, big, broad-shouldered, blond. This had to be Olek, not just from the way he looked but also from the way he moved, real easy and sure-footed. Actually, a lot like how Bernie moved, especially when his wounded leg wasn't acting up.

The senator and Caroline both turned to him, Caroline letting her arms fall to the side. Olek spoke. I could tell that from the way his mouth moved, a tiny black hole that opened and closed, opened and closed. Senator Wray raised a hand like he was going to say something, but Olek made a sort of chopping gesture with his own hand, and the senator just stood there, his hand slowly dropping down. Caroline didn't look at either man again. She walked across the deck, head up, and disappeared into the house.

Olek moved to the railing. His gaze swept the lake from one end to the other, slowly passing right over us. We didn't move a muscle. Olek turned and went into the house. The senator watched him the whole way, then moved to a side table and poured himself a drink. Have I mentioned that the breeze was blowing across the lake, from the house toward us? This might amaze you, but I could smell what the senator was drinking—namely, bourbon. I was even pretty sure that it was the kind Bernie liked, the bourbon with red flowers on the label. Not that I could see the flowers from where I was. Please don't expect too much from me.

The senator came forward, set his glass on the rail, and stared out over the water. They'd all done that, taken a nice long look into the night. I felt good about that. We were the night, me and Bernie. Then quite suddenly, the senator picked up his glass, drained it in one swallow, and hurled it into the lake. The splash was golden in the reflected light. The senator turned and headed into the house, slamming the door behind him, the sound of the slam coming to us twice, the second time as an echo. After that, Bernie lowered the binoculars and started turning away, so he didn't see a fish jump out of the water, surprisingly high and quite near where the glass had splashed down. A big black fish, flexing its whole body, like it had plans. We headed back to the car.

"In silent movies, note cards explain the tricky bits," Bernie said as we drove back into the Valley. "Where do we get our note cards?"

What's worse than Bernie having a problem and me not being able to help? I couldn't think of anything. As for movies, you can try sitting on the remote, which boosts the sound amazingly, but other than that, I had nothing to offer.

Bernie glanced over at me and smiled. "A lot to chew on, huh, big guy? Why don't we—oh my god!" He checked his watch. "What time did we tell Weatherly?"

Something to chew on? That sounded perfect. I was certainly hungry—famished, in fact—if that was what Bernie was getting at. I started panting and kept on panting until the huge wooden cowboy came into view, a lovely sight, no matter what someone had been saying about it quite recently. Did I care about exactly who? I did not. Maybe it helps to know yourself in this life. I, Chet, cared about steak tips.

Some restaurants don't welcome me and my kind. That's a bit of a puzzler. Restaurants serve food. Me and my kind love food. Lots of humans are food lovers, too, but they can be fussy. Take Leda, for example, who sends something back at every meal. You don't see that with my guys.

The Dry Gulch Steakhouse and Saloon is the welcoming sort of restaurant. Bernie and I were barely inside before I heard, "Hey, Chet's in the house," and "Alone, or did he bring what's-his-face?" and lots of other funny stuff that Bernie enjoys, but he was only partly enjoying it now. Mostly, he was scanning all the tables. Looking for Weatherly? That was my guess. But she wasn't inside, or out on the back patio, where the smells coming from the barbecue pit were making me a bit dizzy. Bernie got busy with his phone. "Pick up, pick up." But no one did.

We stood out on the patio, the wooden cowboy towering over us, the air so barbecuey, happiness all around. Who invented all this? No time to figure that out now, because I could tell Bernie wasn't enjoying himself. His eyes had an inward look, and not just inward, but worried. I made a move to slide over and sit on his feet, but at that moment, a man in the far corner of the patio called, "Hey, Bernie!"

I'm pretty good with voices—perfect, in fact. Once I hear one, I've got it forever. The man calling to Bernie was Jacques Smallian. Have I mentioned Jacques already? He's half-American and half-French, an investor of some sort, also a onetime baseball player, just like Bernie. He's smaller than Bernie, although not much, but the same body type. Their faces are a little alike—especially the noses, although Jacques's, not quite as big, didn't appear to have been involved in any dustups, rather different from Bernie's in that way. Jacques was Suzie's partner in their new start-up. Also he was her husband, possibly the most important fact about him. Is it a surprise that Bernie likes him? Maybe that's the most important fact.

We went over to Jacques's table, and there, sitting in the shadows at the very edge of the patio, was Suzie. Those black eyes shining like the countertops in our kitchen—especially after a nice polishing, which hadn't happened in some time—and the way her face always seemed about to smile: I hadn't seen her in way too long. Who wouldn't have hustled right over to greet her? The waiter had everything all mopped up in no time.

What a nice table we had, a corner table with a low brick wall on two sides! I lounged on the wall, gnawing on a nice, fresh barbecue bone, and then another after that, and possibly one more. Suzie and Jacques had been drinking wine, but when Bernie ordered a beer, Jacques said, "Let's make it a pitcher," and they all switched over to that. I had water in a big bowl with ice cubes floating in it, just another wonderful Dry Gulch touch.

"So, Bernie," said Jacques after a while, "how are things on the exciting side of life?"

"I wouldn't call it that," Bernie said.

"I know you wouldn't," said Jacques. "Somehow that makes it all the more appealing."

"We could trade pla—" Bernie began, suddenly cutting himself off. "Um," he said, "meaning someone else's, uh, occupation can look greener on the other, ah, side." He reached for his beer and took a big gulp.

Then came a few moments of quiet eating. A sort of uncomfortable cloud that had appeared faded away.

Suzie filled everyone's glasses. "But when you get to the other side," she said, "it's not the other side anymore. That's why some people can't settle down."

"Meaning anyone in particular?" Bernie said.

"Absolutely not," said Suzie. "Well, not true. I met a man last week from up in Quintana who's been married eight times, twice to the same woman."

"One of your nonvoters?" said Jacques.

"Yes," Suzie said.

"Nonvoters?" said Bernie.

"It's one of the ways we're covering the election," Suzie said. "We're getting a panel of nonvoters and canvassing them on a weekly basis."

"Suzie's idea—and I think it's brilliant," said Jacques. "Any idea what percentage of citizens in this state voted in the last presidential year?"

"Um," said Bernie.

"You'll be shocked," Jacques said. "Active voters always are, Bernie. The percentage was forty-nine point nine."

Bernie cleared his throat.

Jacques gave him a long look. "Don't tell me you qualify for Suzie's panel?"

Suzie laughed. "Not Bernie," she said. "I'd bet anything he voted at least once when he was in the service—to set an example for the troops." She turned to Bernie. "Am I right?"

He nodded. "But they saw right through me."

"How do you mean?" said Jacques.

"Politicians aren't in high repute in the military," Bernie said, "especially in war zones." He picked up his beer glass, then paused with it in midair. "What kind of a guy is Wray?"

"Griffin Wray, the senator?" said Suzie.

"Yeah," Bernie said. "And his wife, Caroline."

"You know her?" Suzie said.

"Met her once, briefly," Bernie said. "Him, too, on a separate occasion."

"In what context, if you don't mind saying?" said Jacques.

"By accident," Bernie said.

"Any special reason you're asking about them?" Jacques said.

"If there is, you're not going to find out," Suzie said. "But I'm happy to give you a quick thumbnail, Bernie. Wray is much smarter than people—especially his enemies—think. He came from not much. Dad deserted the family, Mom waitressed, sold real estate, worked retail. They never had a lot, but Wray was a good student and very popular in high school—student body president—and that continued. He was student body president at U of A and landed a good job with McGregor right out of college."

"McGregor?" Bernie said.

McGregor rang a very faint bell, but I was much more interested in Suzie's thumbnail. Not interested, really, more anxious, even scared. I love Suzie and have known her a long time, but not once had she offered to give her thumbnail to Bernie or anyone else. Who could blame her? I'd seen thumbnails torn off thumbs on two occasions, both times quite similar, now that I think of it, where a huge perp, in one case No-Neck Fleck and in the other Muscles Mulvaney, a.k.a. the Mullet, had swung from the heels at Bernie and somehow caught a thumb on boat hook—both times a boat hook! Think of that!—ripping the thumbnail right off. They'd both started bawling their heads off and surrendered at once.

Suzie sipped her drink, then folded her hands on the table. I kept my eyes glued on those hands. Was she reconsidering the thumbnail offer? Suzie was a very sensible person, far more so that either No-Neck or the Mullet.

"McGregor Worldwide Business Consulting," she told Bernie.

"Maybe a bit distant from your world, Bernie?" said Jacques.

"My world keeps expanding." Bernie smiled. "Whether I'm ready or not." Suzie shot him a quick glance, kind of surprised. "I didn't realize McGregor had any connection to the senator."

"A deep one," Suzie said. "Caroline's maiden name is McGregor. Her grandfather started the company—just a one-person PR firm in Chicago at first. It was her father who really got it going. Caroline came out here for college, which was where they met. They got married, moved to Chicago, and lived there until he—"

"—or they," said Jacques.

"TBD," Suzie said. "Until the decision was made—let's put it that way—to come back here and get into politics. It's possible that was on his mind from the start, but Caroline's money made it realistic."

"It sounds like you've been doing some thinking about them," Bernie said.

"An election puts us on the clock," Suzie said. "One crazy thing is that Wray and Erlanger both switched parties when they were in their twenties. The polls show them neck and neck. It's a bit surprising—Wray's brought piles of investment money into the state, and he's a far better debater. Erlanger comes off as a bit of a dweeb, even an elitist. Then there's the divorce. The whole state was glued to it."

"Yeah?" Bernie said.

"But not you?" Jacques said.

"I must have missed it," said Bernie. "But divorce is pretty common."

"Not Erlanger's," Suzie said. "It started as a ménage à trois gone wrong and ballooned from there. Wray will have a field day with it."

"What's Erlanger's background?" Bernie said.

"Before Congress, he was a law professor at Northern State, and before that a real estate lawyer," said Jacques.

"Does he have any Ukrainian connections?" Bernie said.

Jacques turned to Suzie.

"Not that I know of," she said. "Why?"

"We had a job offer from a Ukrainian," Bernie said.

"Go on," said Suzie.

Bernie shrugged. "We didn't take it."

"Are you suggesting it involved Erlanger?" said Jacques.

"Oh, I don't—" Bernie cut himself off, thought for a few moments. "I don't know."

"Wray?" said Jacques. "Does it involve him?"

"I don't see how."

"But maybe?" Jacques said.

"Jacques?" Suzie said. "The third degree won't work on Bernie."

Jacques's eyebrows rose in a way that reminded me of what Bernie's eyebrows could do. Did his eyebrows also have a language of their own? Not as—how to put it?—loud as Bernie's eyebrow language? The answer was yes.

"You call that the third degree?" Jacques said.

Bernie laughed. Then they were all laughing. They drank more beer.

"How about this?" Suzie said. "Since you didn't end up taking the job, can you say what it was?"

Bernie laughed again, shook his head, and gave Suzie a quick look that reminded me of looks he used to give her way back when. Did Jacques catch that look of Bernie's? I thought so. His face went blank.

"You win," Bernie said. "Security work."

"For some Ukrainian magnate?" said Suzie.

"That kind of thing," Bernie said.

"Let me guess," Suzie said. "The money was good, but you couldn't see going to Ukraine."

"We wouldn't have had to," Bernie said.

"No?" said Suzie.

"It was Hawaii."

"Oh?" said Suzie.

"Kauai."

"Ah," said Jacques.

"Oh and ah?" Bernie said. "What's going on?"

"The globalization of corruption," Jacques said.

"Meaning what?" said Bernie.

"Influence now gets peddled in all directions," Jacques said. "It's like a very complicated web, almost with a mind of its own."

"Tell him the rest," Suzie said.

"Well," said Jacques, "that part's a bit melodramatic, late-night musings more than anything else."

"I can take it," Bernie said.

"Okay, then," Jacques said. "This complicated web of influence wants to get us all inside and keep us there forever."

"Maybe I can't take it after all," Bernie said.

Everybody laughed, meaning the whole web thing was just a joke of Jacques's, maybe a bit like a Bernie joke. Good to hear, because although Bernie's the toughest guy you'll meet, he hates walking through spiderwebs. He says yuck and echh and other un-Bernie-type things. But no actual web seemed to be in the picture. We were good. Another barbecue bone soon arrived. This was turning into a nice evening.

Twenty-one

The next morning, we were up early, both of us bright-eyed and bushy-tailed, as humans say, although in fact, just like every morning, Bernie awoke without a tail. If that happened to me, well, I don't want to even think of it, but Bernie wasn't bothered at all. He sang in the shower, running through some of his favorites—"Death Don't Have No Mercy," "Devil in Her Heart," "A Fool Such As I." What a great mood he was in! And he hadn't closed the bathroom door, not that that would have made any difference now that I could open every door in the house. Soon I was in the shower, too! Had I forgotten once again about the problem of the shower curtain and how the whole thing with all the poles and screws and rings can come crashing down? Show me the dude who can remember everything.

Bernie made coffee and filled two mugs, which was a bit odd, since there were just the two of us and water's my drink. Humans have so many different drinks! Would they be better off cutting back a bit, maybe all the way to water only? You tell me.

"Let's be unpredictable today," Bernie said.

Whatever that meant, I knew it was fabulous! We went outside, Bernie carrying the two mugs of coffee, and headed over to old man Heydrich's place. *Unpredictable* meant paying a call on old man Heydrich? His sprinklers were on, his grass so soaked there were puddles here and there. Was the plan to dump the second mug of coffee on old man Heydrich's head? No wonder Bernie was in such a good mood!

He knocked on old man Heydrich's door. It opened right away, something we see from time to time. Does it mean we're on the right track? That's always been my take. Was it possible we'd come to cuff old man Heydrich and drag him off to the big house? After maybe leading off with the coffee-dumping thing? That would be a first.

"Good morning, Mr. Heydrich," Bernie said. "Coffee?"

Old man Heydrich's eyes—small and shining, and also his eyelids were lashless, the whole effect on the disturbing side—went from Bernie to the coffee mug and back.

"What's in it?" he said.

Bernie smiled. "Fresh black coffee. Add whatever you like." Bernie looked past Heydrich to quite an interesting sight, a setup with a big desk, a padded chair on rollers, and a whole bunch of screens. Hey! Was that the front of our place on one of the screens? And our driveway, with the Porsche sitting there? And a view of Mesquite Road? And the houses across the street? What was going on? It couldn't be good. The coffee, Bernie—now!

Heydrich noticed where Bernie was looking and moved slightly to one side, maybe to block his view. I was already in the house, the first house I'd ever been in where there wasn't the slightest smell of food.

"That's all right, Mr. Heydrich," Bernie said. "I was aware of your little surveillance system. In fact, that's why we're here. Just waiting for the right moment, if you want the truth."

Heydrich's mouth opened, closed, opened again. Had I ever seen thinner lips? Yes, and quite often, but only on snakes. "How—how did you know? Did you break in when I was out?"

Bernie laughed. "Why would we bother when you've got your cameras sticking out all over the place?"

Old man Heydrich's face went bright red. He began to . . . splutter? Is that when the words get tangled up and some spit's part of the bargain? If so, then what came next was spluttering.

"Cameras? Sticking? How dare you even suggest—?"

"For example," Bernie said, "there's that new one in your weathervane, hiding behind the W. A very nice touch. The one in the sprinkler is pretty good, too, and the one that sometimes pops up from the sewer grate is a tiny technical marvel. On public property, unfortunately. The city'll have to send out a team.

Would anyone be shocked if they wanted to inspect the whole array? You know how they are."

Heydrich's mouth did some more opening and closing. Gurgling sounds came out. He shot a quick glance at a little cupboard in the corner. Bernie strolled over to it. I'd already sniffed out what was in the cupboard, of course, but had Bernie somehow sniffed it out, too? He really can be impressive, my Bernie. He opened the cupboard and took out a handgun, bright blue with a wooden grip, and strange sort of clip sticking out the top.

"My, my," Bernie said. "A Red 9—a real collector's item. Favored by the Luftwaffe, if I recall?"

"I have all the proper permitting."

"I don't doubt that." Bernie snapped out the clip, stuck it in his pocket, and put the gun back in the cupboard. "Mind closing the door, Chet?"

Sure thing! We'd been working on this for some time. The way it went was first Bernie says, "Close the door." Then I give it a push with my head. After that comes the Slim Jim. Our only problem was that Bernie had no Slim Jim at the moment. I closed Heydrich's front door anyway, a fun thing to do all on its own, Slim Jim or no Slim Jim. But of course I knew a Slim Jim would be coming my way later on. I'd remind Bernie, if necessary.

"This is outrageous!" Heydrich said. "Breaking and entering like a common criminal."

"Call the cops," Bernie said.

What a great idea! We had so many pals at Valley PD. Many, many treats were suddenly a real possibility. Heydrich just stood there, the redness slowly draining from his face. The phone, old man Heydrich, pick up the phone! But he let me down.

"First," Bernie said, "let's discuss the bumper sticker you say you dropped in our car."

"What the hell?" said Heydrich. "This is all about politics?"

"Not in the—" Bernie began and then cut himself off. I thought I felt something shift inside him—in his mind, if I had to guess. He has a very big mind like . . . like a huge house! What a thought! With many, many rooms! And I'm always in the kitchen, the kitchen of Bernie's mind! Wow! I'd shocked myself. I sat down, a funny little freep sound coming out of my mouth. That was a bit embarrassing. I went very still, making myself pretty much unnoticeable.

"Maybe we should discuss politics," Bernie said.

"My politics are my business," said Heydrich.

"Agreed—although you're not shy about publicizing them."

"You have a problem with that?"

"None," Bernie said. "How well do you know Senator Wray?"

"Personally?" said Heydrich. "I don't know him personally at all."

"What about Caroline Wray?"

"No."

"Or any members of her family, the McGregors?"

"No. Why are you asking me all these questions?"

"Because of the bumper sticker," Bernie said. Heydrich looked about to do some more spluttering, but Bernie raised his hand. "Ever been to Ukraine?"

"No."

"Got any Ukrainian buddies?"

"Certainly not."

"Why so emphatic?"

"Emphatic?" said Heydrich. "*Emphatic* is not a word I expect from someone like—from someone in your profession."

Bernie smiled, not his usual warm and happy smile but a cold one you hardly ever see. "Dig deep—I know you can handle it," Bernie said.

Heydrich didn't like that, not one little bit. He actually glanced over at his little gun cupboard. Had he forgotten that the gun was now unloaded? Did he really think he could get there, load up, and bring that funny-looking gun into play before I could stop him? I realized he was a perp, but not the kind I liked. He was wearing baggy cargo shorts and had those chicken-type legs you often see on older guys. I would take no pleasure in doing the necessary when the time came.

"Ukrainians are what they are," Heydrich said. "I prefer not to discuss it."

"Did a Ukrainian get you to put that bumper sticker in our car?" Bernie said.

"Are you crazy? Why would I do anything for Ukrainians? They're the enemy of my people."

"I thought you were American."

"Of course I am. Does that make Americans my people?"

Bernie gave Heydrich a long, long look. "That's the whole point," he said.

Heydrich frowned. His face was sort of always frowning, so maybe better to think of it as frowning a little more. Bernie stepped past him and went to the screens. I stayed where I was, on Heydrich's other side, just basic procedure. We're pros, me and Bernie, as old man Heydrich was finding out.

Bernie sat at the desk, drew the keyboard closer. "Not familiar with this software," he said, "but I'm guessing . . ." And he went tap, tap, tap, tap.

"Wait one damn minute!" Heydrich moved toward Bernie, coming up behind him if you can picture what I mean. This was not an acceptable situation. "Aieeee!"

Bernie turned slowly.

"Aieeee! Aieeee!" Heydrich cried. "Your goddamn dog bit me!"

"Language," said Bernie.

"Huh? Your dog bit me! Is that better?"

"A little," Bernie said. He rose and inspected the back of Heydrich's leg. "But not entirely accurate. I'd say Chet mouthed you more than bit you."

Mouthed? I'd only mouthed? Oh no! How bad of me! What could I do to make up for this . . . this failure? That was the only way to put it.

"Mouthed?" Heydrich screamed, his eyes sort of bugging out in a way that reminded me of a guy Bernie and I sometimes saw on the History Channel. "Then where did all this blood come from?"

Bernie crouched down, peered more closely at Heydrich's leg. "This?" he said, pointing. "I'm not sure we can call that blood."

"What is wrong with you? Wet! Red! Blood!"

I was actually on Heydrich's side in this argument, a strange development. And it did look and smell like blood to me, although maybe not a lot. Bernie reached over to the desk, picked up one of those little cloths for wiping computer screens, and dabbed at Heydrich's leg.

"All better," he said. "No harm no foul. Tender is the bite, ha ha. Take a seat, Mr. Heydrich, and walk us through this."

"No harm no foul?" Heydrich repeated that a few times, but each quieter than the one before, and soon they were sitting side by side, working together like a team. The little cloth lay on the floor. I gathered it up and busied myself with it, for no particular reason.

"Whoa!" said Bernie. "Stop right there."

I looked up. The front of our house was on one of the screens. What a lovely house! Not the fanciest house on Mesquite Road— not the fanciest street in the Valley, far from it—and then there's that roof-leaking problem, but guess what? It hardly ever rains in these parts, which is how Bernie took care of it. Bernie! Always the smartest human in the room, and our house the best house. I could have looked at that picture all day, but now on the screen things started moving.

First, we had a taxi pulling up outside. A passenger sat in the back. Somehow, the screen closed in on her: a very nice-looking woman with a ponytail. Hey! It was Mavis! And weren't we searching for Mavis? And here was Bernie kicking back and watching TV! You, too, would have barked your head off.

"Chet, easy there," Bernie said. And old man Heydrich actually had his hands over his ears, one of the most pleasant sights of my whole life, but work comes before play. That's one of our rules at the Little Detective Agency, or should be, as perhaps Leda had suggested on more than one occasion. I ran to the nearest window, got rid of a plant or two that was in the way, and peered out. What was this? No taxi?

I took a few steps toward Bernie. He was still gazing at the screen. And Heydrich seemed to be upset about something. Did he actually shake his finger at me? So much to deal with. Even more than I'd thought, because there on the screen was the taxi! Still parked in front of our house! The taxi was and was not there? If that was how things were going to be in this world of ours, then . . . then . . . I couldn't even begin.

Bernie glanced back at me. "Schrödinger's cat, huh, big guy?"

He turned to the screen, missing an odd look from Heydrich. But I didn't really care about that—or anything else. Because . . . because cats were suddenly in the picture? Wasn't a ferret, or possibly two ferrets—I wasn't quite clear on that—enough? Cats had cropped up in a few cases before, never with a good result. Once, I'd had to come to some sort of accommodation with a supposedly beautiful cat from Hollywood, name of Brando. The most difficult challenge of my whole career? I couldn't think of a harder one.

Meanwhile, Bernie's attention was on the screen, as though this new development wasn't bothering him in the least. Bernie can be a real cool cat at times. Uh-oh. What was going on? My own mind tormenting me? How do you put a stop to that?

I ran back to the window. Still no taxi on the street, no action whatsoever. I took another look at Bernie's screen. Plenty of action there. First, Mavis leaned forward to pay the driver. Then she opened the door and started to get out. But what was this? Just as her foot touched the ground, a man stepped into view on the far side of our house, like he was coming from the patio, and not just a man but a man I knew. Olek! I whipped around to the window. No Olek, no Mavis, no taxi. But there they all were, on the screen. Mavis caught sight of Olek and shrank back into the taxi, ducking down out of sight. Olek didn't see her. His eyes were on a long black car parked in our driveway, a car I'd completely missed until that moment. Olek glanced at the taxi, then got in the long black car, which drove off down Mesquite Road, away from the taxi. Mavis popped up into view and gazed at our house. The taxi pulled a U-ee and drove off down Mesquite Road in the other direction. I came close to remembering something or other.

"What do you make of that, Mr. Heydrich?" Bernie said.

"Why should I even care?" said Heydrich.

Then came a huge surprise—even a shock—and quite scary. Bernie . . . how to put this? Got angry? Got very angry? Got furious? Blew his top? Yes, that was it. Bernie suddenly blew his top at old man Heydrich. He sprang to his feet, his chest heaving, his face flushed, his strength so huge and obvious that if he'd pulled down the whole house, I wouldn't have been surprised.

But Bernie didn't pull down old man Heydrich's house, probably a good thing what with all of us inside it. Instead, he raised his voice—it rang like a giant bell—and said, "Then why are you doing all this?"

Heydrich, still in his chair, raised his hands to protect himself, but Bernie didn't go near him.

"Answer me!"

Heydrich made himself very small and in a very small voice replied, "To protect against bad elements."

"Bad elements? Are we bad elements, me and Chet?"

Despite how afraid he was, some sort of clever idea must have occurred to Heydrich, because his lips curled up in a little smile, and in a slightly louder voice, he said, "Your words, not mine. Perhaps you don't realize I'm protecting the whole neighborhood, including you."

Without warning and with one sweep of his mighty hand, Bernie sent the nearest screen flying. It happened to hit all the other screens, sending all of them flying, and the crashing wasn't nearly done before Bernie said, "Send me the bill." And we were out of there. My very first time inside old man Heydrich's house. All in all, I wasn't against a follow-up visit, just not anytime soon. One good thing: the cat, possibly named Schrödinger, had not appeared.

Back home, I was just the slightest bit nervous around Bernie. Imagine that! But why was he so quiet, just pacing around and glancing out a window from time to time? I paced, too, a little behind him. Suddenly, he laughed and turned to me. "I forgot the mugs."

The mugs? Oh, right, the coffee mugs. And there I was, in the picture.

"I liked those mugs, especially the one with the surfing parrot."

Did Bernie want me to make a quick visit back to Heydrich's and retrieve the mugs? Retrieving is right up my alley, as you might have guessed. I often have to stop myself from retrieving—for example, that time when a perp name of Gene "the Genius" Gendrich pulled the pin on a toy grenade that turned out not to be a toy—and then put it in his mouth!— before Bernie snatched it away and hurled it as far as he could. I'd managed to stop myself from retrieving it, thanks to Bernie, his very strong hands, and my collar. The mug, of course, was not going to blow up. But then there was the issue of the parrot. I'd had an encounter earlier in my career with a parrot named Cap'n Crunch. Parrots are birds, so they have those tiny angry eyes, but also they can say things like "Get lost," and "Big fat ugly." It's a bad combo.

Bernie opened the fridge and gazed inside. I gazed with him. There wasn't much to look at. All we had was a beer or two, some lemons, and a wrinkled-up onion, but gazing into a fridge is a nice way to spend some time, the air so cool.

"Do you feel things shifting under us, Chet?"

We'd been through an earthquake or two, me and Bernie, and I can always feel them coming and he never can, so it I suppose it made sense for him to ask. But why now? There was no indication of any shifting whatsoever, the earth in one of its rock-solid moods. I pressed against Bernie's leg.

"Thanks for reminding me." He reached into his pocket, fished out a cocktail napkin I sort of remembered from somewhere or other. Bernie peered at the smeared inky writing on the napkin and took out his phone. "Johnnie Lee? Bernie Little here. Pick up, please. Your friend has misinterpreted a couple of things. We can help. Pick up."

He waited. No one picked up. Bernie pocketed the phone. "Did I sound believable?"

What a question! Who was more believable than Bernie?

"But can you blame them?" He thought for a moment. "How about we try pulling at a very tentative thread?"

I had no objection, although I didn't see the point. Of course I've had threads caught in my mouth before—who hasn't?—and they can be very bothersome, but the inside of my mouth was threadless.

"I know what you're thinking," Bernie said. "All our threads are pretty damn tentative."

No, no. That wasn't it at all! How frustrating! All I could think to do was grab that wrinkled-up onion, but Bernie closed the fridge door before I could.

"But doesn't a dying man's last word have to mean something?" he said.

"So many last words," said Bernie as we drove out of the Valley, "happening every day, every hour, every minute. But how often is it 'golf'?"

Golf? Aha. Far from unknown territory. I'd been around golf courses in my time, knew, from having heard it so often, that golf was all about putting. That made sense to anyone who'd ever been on a putting green. The feeling of a putting green under your paws is like no other. You want it to go on forever. At the same time, a strange urge starts to overcome you—specifically, a desire to dig the whole thing up. Then there's the golf ball itself, not the best ball out there, but at least a ball. Balls in general are kind of a hobby of mine. Lacrosse balls have the best mouthfeel, basketballs are simply too big unless you deflate them a bit at first—turning your head slightly sideways to get the right teeth involved being the best method—baseballs are the most interesting once you get inside, and the insides of golf balls are somewhat of a disappointment, bad tasting and bad smelling. There. A quick . . . how to put it? Overview? A quick overview of the subject, the point being that when it comes to golf, I'm up to speed. Also, when it comes to speed, I'm up to speed! Was that a sort of joke? Sorry, not my department, Bernie handling the jokes at the Little Detective Agency. I take it back, the same way, for example, when once I snatched a chew toy I didn't even want away from Iggy, and Bernie noticed and said, "Chet?" and I immediately laid that chew toy, or its remains, on the Parsonses' door step just like nothing had happened.

Bernie glanced at me. "Something on your mind, big guy?"

Not a thing. A complete and comfortable blank. We were good to go. Any reason not to grab some shut-eye? Not that I could think of.

When I opened my eyes, we were on the potholey part of the road to EZ AZ Desert Tours and Mini Golf. Soon I'd be seeing those little windmills, lighthouses, tugboats, castles, a Santa Claus, lots of fun stuff. Suddenly, everything became clear. Bernie and I were going to treat ourselves to a round of mini golf. The best treats are the ones you share. Well, no, but it felt good to think the thought.

"Uh-oh," Bernie said. I gazed ahead and immediately thought the same thing: *Uh-oh.* Why? Because there were no tiny windmills and all of that. There was no mini golf. There were no ATVs. There was no ranch house. All that remained was the desert floor, scraped flat, with a few scraps of tar paper shifting around in the wind, plywood shards, bent pipes, a smashed-up toilet. A big dumpster truck sat in the middle of the emptiness, raising a dumpster with its metal arms and thunking it down on the flatbed at the back. Bernie stopped beside the cab and looked up at the driver.

"What's going on?" he said.

"Haulin'," said the driver, his meaty arm hanging out the door.

"Right," said Bernie. "But why?"

"Can't just leave a mess like that out here. Wouldn't be environmental."

"True. But what happened?"

The driver shrugged. "New ownership. Tore it all down. Planning a solar farm—least that's the word." He pointed into the distance. "If you're looking for tours, the closest place is ten miles other side of Zinc Town, on old number seventeen. If it's mini golf, I can't help you." He stepped on the gas and rumbled away.

We got out of the car and walked around. Bernie kicked at this and that. He picked up a blackened brick and tossed it away. He didn't look happy, but then I got lucky and noticed a golf ball with a red stripe on it, just lying there. I grabbed it and held it out for Bernie.

"You're the best," he said. But he still didn't look happy. Then he peered a little closer at the ball, dirty and scuffed up like so many. The next thing I knew, Bernie was flipping open the toolbox, not the big toolbox we had at home but the small one he kept under the front seat in the Porsche.

"Pipe cutter would be perfect," he said, rummaging around in the toolbox, "but of course we . . ." He pulled out what appeared to be the broken blade from a small saw. "Don't recall seeing this before. How in hell . . . ?"

And soon, he was holding the ball steady on a somewhat flat rock with one hand and trying to saw through it with the other. There was a bit of blood—not even as much as had seeped out of Heydrich's leg—a bad word or two, and some forehead sweat beads falling on the rock, but then—

"Ta-da!"

We were looking at two halves of the golf ball. Inside was the blue rubbery interior, no surprise. Bernie poked at the blue rubbery interior and tossed them away. "Worth a try." He looked a little happier. And happier still when I retrieved both halves of the golf ball and dropped them at his feet.

Twenty-two

"What should we call them, Chet? The macro people and the micro people?" He picked up the halves of the golf ball and stuffed them in his pocket. "How about we work the macro side for a while?"

Macro and micro people? Bernie was on his own. He reached inside the car for the phone, tapped at it. From the other end came a voice.

"McGregor Worldwide."

"Energy Department," Bernie said. "East European Division."

"One moment, please."

Another voice spoke. "EED."

"Scott Kyle, please," said Bernie.

"May I ask who's calling?"

"Bernie Little."

"One moment, please."

Then came some music, not "If You Were Mine" or anything like that. We stood in the emptiness where EZ AZ Tours and Mini Golf had been. In the distance rose some green-gray mountains, and off to one side, the desert floor shimmered almost like a lake. Some folks, especially newcomers from back east, wherever that is, exactly, often get excited and say things like, "Hey! Is that water?" Well, I used to think, *Does it smell like water?* Now I don't think anything, just wait peaceably for whatever's coming next. Folks from back east can be lots of fun.

The voice came back on. "Mr. Little? I'm sorry. Mr. Kyle is not available."

"Can you have him get back to me as soon as possible?" Bernie said. "It's urgent."

"I'm afraid not. Mr. Kyle is away on assignment."

"Somewhere with no phones? The moon?"

Silence on the other end.

"Or is he hiding out in Ukraine?"

More silence. Then: "Have a nice day, sir."

"Sure," said Bernie. "Maybe we'll run into each other some-time. Be sure to introduce yourself."

Again, silence, but it didn't sound so empty this time.

Bernie clicked off. He looked at me. "I know. That was un-necessary. I'm getting frustrated." He reached out, scratched between my ears. "And isn't that when we have to be our most composed?"

I missed most of that, perhaps all too wrapped up in the de-lightfulness of getting scratched behind the ears, especially by someone who knew what he was doing, like Bernie. But it would be dishonest to not mention that I'd run into two between-the-ears scratchers even better than Bernie in my career, Tulip and Autumn, two friendly young women who work at Livia's Friendly Coffee and More in Pottsdale, specifically in the More part, which turns out to be a house of ill repute, the meaning of that still unclear to me, perhaps because all Bernie and I did there was buy fresh beans.

"On the other hand," Bernie said, "sometimes it's a good idea to stir up the hornet's nest, see where they go."

I gazed at Bernie. He looked good—well rested, not hung over, certainly not sick or feverish. A joke, perhaps? Could there be anything good about hornets? Wasn't stirring up the nest the last thing you wanted to do? As for seeing where the hornets go, they always go to the same place, right at you. Take it from me.

Bernie walked around the car. I walked with him. He rubbed out a smudge or two on the fenders with the hem of his T-shirt. "Forget the hornet's nest part," he said. "What I meant was we have to find a way to bring the case to us." He gazed around. "Will we ever be able to find out the actual person who owns this place now? Good luck with that. But let's just think of it as Olek for the time being. What was the point of destroying it? I'm actually tempted to ask him. What if we said we'd changed our mind, were ready to hop on the next plane to Kauai?"

He took out his phone. Wow! So surfing was back in the picture? And Olek was a pal? I'd been getting the feeling that Olek was not a pal, but humans can be complicated.

I heard a tiny click, and then I felt someone on the other end of the line, but whoever it was didn't speak.

"Hi," Bernie said. "It's me. Bernie."

"I see that on the screen."

Hey! It was Weatherly. Nice to hear her voice, and I'm sure she was thinking how nice it was to hear Bernie's. Would she also like to hear mine? I was just about to give her a sample when someone barked on her end. A rather impatient-sounding bark and quite a surprise. I barked, not the mild-mannered bark I'd been intending but a bark that sent a message to that other barker—a she-barker, by the way—in no uncertain terms. And would you believe it? She barked a no-uncertain-terms bark right back at me! What else could I do but amp things up? I'm sure you'd have done the same. I amped up my usual no-uncertain-terms bark into something altogether more . . . just plain more! And . . . and she did the same! Did she really imagine she could outbark me, Chet, the best barker in the Valley when I really get going? That was outrageous! I barked a bark she didn't need the phone to hear. She barked back the same kind! Stealing my idea! It . . . it was like . . . like a female version of me! Oh, what a thought! I barked a bark to clear the air of thoughts like that, now and forever. She barked back the same kind of bark. I barked. She barked. I barked. She barked. I—

"Oh, for god's sake!" said Bernie and Weatherly at the same time. "Put a lid on it!"

Here's an interesting fact: Weatherly lived in Upper Canyon, not too far from us. I'd even been quite near her place once, although not with Bernie. It's possible Bernie's not even aware of the little—what would you call it? Day trip, perhaps? Good enough. The little day trip I took with Iggy. This was back when the Parsonses' electric fence was new and before they realized it wasn't working. What a glorious—if all too brief—period in our friendship, mine and Iggy's! On the particular morning in question—as some of my pals at Valley PD might put it—Bernie was sleeping in very late, a bourbonish scent flowing on his breath to every corner of the house, Iggy was yip-yip-yipping in his front yard, and I was on the patio out back, not far from the gate, in those days still considered unleapable by any member of the nation within.

Sometime later, Iggy and I had followed the canyon all the way to where Rio Calor crosses it, and what did we find but actual water! And not only that but some Girl Scouts having a picnic! Hungry Girl Scouts with a fondness for burgers and sausages! Iggy went a little too far—his main problem, really—and the two of us ended up in a green van belonging to Freedy Ramirez, early in our relationship with Freedy, who then was only an assistant dogcatcher but has now risen to director in chief of the entire dog-catching department here in the Valley. The only reason I bring all this up is that Freedy had parked the van at a lookout over the canyon, and on the other side of the road from the lookout stood a car wash with a big sign featuring lots of foam and a happy lady in a bathing suit, and now we were passing right by it. Bernie turned onto the next cross street and stopped in front of a small lemon-colored house with a lemon tree in the yard and a nice shady porch. Weatherly was sitting on the porch, but she rose as we got out of the car.

You can feel some people from a distance—usually a very small distance, and lots of people can't really be felt unless you're actually touching them. Does that make sense? Never mind if it doesn't. The point is that few can be felt from quite far away—Bernie's the champ at that—and Weatherly was in that group. The Weatherly feeling grew stronger and stronger as we walked up to the porch.

"Hi," Bernie said.

"Hi," said Weatherly, looking down at us.

"Sorry about last night," Bernie said. "Things got a little hectic."

Weatherly nodded. Whoa! Her nod reminded me of one of Bernie's, specifically the nod that can mean anything.

"But," Bernie added, "I plumb forgot."

One of Weatherly's eyes narrowed very slightly. Was she having a bit of fun?

"Plumb, Bernie?" she said.

"Uh, well . . ."

"It's okay," Weatherly said. "You don't owe me anything. You're the reason I've got Trixie back."

"How's she doing?" Bernie said.

"Better every day. She just fell asleep." Weatherly tilted her chin toward one corner of the porch. I saw a bushy black tail sticking out from behind a big potted plant.

"I've got news about what happened to her," Bernie said.

Weatherly gave Bernie a long look. "Come aboard," she said.

We climbed the steps. I went right over and checked things out behind the potted plant. Oh, poor Trixie! Not the cone! But it was the cone, all right. There are many great human inventions—the Porsche, for example—and also some bad ones, of which the cone is one of the very worst. Trixie lay on her side on the porch floor, her head in the cone—a clear plastic cone so I could see her eyes, open and staring at nothing. I squeezed in behind the potted plant and lay down beside her. A nice, shady spot as it turned out. My breathing fell right into rhythm with Trixie's.

"What's your news?" Weatherly said.

"Mickey Rottoni kidnapped Trixie to get back at you," said Bernie.

"For serving the restraining order?"

"Yes. According to my informant, he was one of those types."

"Who can't rest if they think they've been insulted?"

"Exactly."

There was a silence. Then Weatherly said, "I thank you, Bernie."

"You're welcome."

"Something to drink?" she said. "Iced tea?"

"Sounds great."

Weatherly went into the house. Bernie came over and gazed down at me and Trixie. A lovely look appeared on his face, impossible to describe. He went back and sat on a wicker chair. Weatherly came out with iced tea and sat on the chair beside him.

"I hope you didn't wait too, uh, very long," he said. "Um, at Dry Gulch."

"Not long," Weatherly said. "Forget about it." She raised her glass and clinked his. "I did see that Suzie Sanchez was there."

A tiny wave of iced tea slopped over the edge of Bernie's glass. "You know her?"

"Not at all," Weatherly said. "I've seen her on TV a few times."

"She's married."

"I know," Weatherly said. "I've done some research."

"On Suzie?"

"On you."

"Oh?"

"Not out of nosiness," Weatherly said. "I wanted to check out the case of that little girl, Gail Blandina."

Gail? They were talking about Gail? I'd been close to falling asleep, but now I wasn't. That was the broom closet case, our very worst, the only missing kid case where we'd failed. Not that we didn't find Gail. We found her, but not soon enough. Later that night, we'd taken care of justice ourselves, me and Bernie, also a onetime thing in our career. After it was over, Bernie had said we had to forget what we'd done and never think of it again. But that had never been easy, and it wasn't going to be any easier if Weatherly planned on talking about it. I rose and moved closer to Bernie.

His voice got very quiet. "Why would you be doing that?"

Weatherly sat back. I'd seen that same sort of sitting back before, when somebody was sensing something in Bernie for the first time. "It's a long story," Weatherly said, "maybe not that interesting."

"Anything about Gail Blandina is interesting to me."

Weatherly put down her glass. "This was just before my suspension."

"For insubordination?"

"Correct. Ellis just couldn't let it go."

"I'm not following you."

"Forget it," Weatherly said. "It doesn't matter. Nothing someone like him could say about someone like you would"—she smiled a sudden smile, surprisingly big, sort of triumphant—"would ever convince someone like me." The smile faded and she looked directly into Bernie's eyes. "Not after what you did for Trixie. And how you did it."

"I did the normal thing," Bernie said. "And I still want to hear the story."

Weatherly took a deep breath, let it out slowly. "Ellis wanted to convince me that you were lying about Rottoni. He said either you never found him and faked the whole thing or you killed him and hid the body where it will never be found. His money was on that, the second possibility."

"And why would I do either one?" Bernie said.

"Quote—you're a tricky operator."

"And why the second one particularly?"

Weatherly nodded. "I asked him that. He told me to check out the Gail Blandina case. Which I did. The poor kid was held for ransom, the department was getting nowhere, the family hired you, and you found her in less than a day. But too late. The kidnapper never turned up, and the case is still open. 'Why isn't anyone working on it?' Ellis said."

Bernie sat very still, not a single movement visible, except for a vein in his neck, throbbing like I'd never seen. Then very slowly he rose. "Can I leave Chet here with you for a little while?" His voice sounded hoarse, like he'd been shouting or didn't feel well.

I rose, too.

And so did Weatherly. "Bernie? What is it?"

Bernie didn't seem to hear her. He moved slowly toward the steps.

"Bernie?" She gripped his arm. "What are you going to do?"

"I'll be back in a bit," Bernie said, his voice kind of strange, like it was no longer connected to him.

Weatherly stepped around, faced him, now gripped both his arms. "You're scaring me. Why aren't you taking Chet? What's going on?"

Weatherly stood right at the edge of the porch, her heels actually over the edge. She was maybe not as tall as Suzie but looked quite a bit stronger. Nothing like Bernie, of course, especially right now. He was huge and wild and dangerous. And what was this about not taking me? He'd never needed me more in his whole life. I just knew it.

"Bernie? Where do you think you're going? Not downtown? I hope it's not downtown. How will that end? It won't be good."

Bernie was looking past her, or maybe nowhere at all. Was he even hearing her? She squeezed his arms, digging in with her fingernails. Now, at last, he gazed down at her. He said something that came out as a hoarse little whisper, impossible to understand.

"Come on, Bernie," Weatherly said. "Come inside and tell me the whole thing."

He shook his head harder, suddenly reminding me of Charlie.

"You don't have to tell me," Weatherly said. "Just come inside." She put her hands on his chest and gave him a little push. He didn't let himself be pushed. "You're a smart man, Bernie. Play the long game." She gave him another push. This time, he let her. The next thing I knew, they were in the house.

And I was not! Normally, that would be an intolerable situation. But somehow, this once, I was okay with it. How odd life can be! I went and lay down by Trixie. She thumped her tail. I thumped mine.

Twenty-three

I was familiar with many games, but the long game was new to me. Had Bernie and Weatherly been playing the long game? If so, had he enjoyed it? It was hard to tell. As we drove home, or at least in the direction of home—I knew the direction home from pretty much anywhere in the Valley—I gave him several looks, just checking his mood. He had a dark look on his face and was deep in his thoughts, those beautiful hands taking charge of the driving all by themselves, but what kind of thoughts he was having, I couldn't tell. One thing for sure: his body was very relaxed. That was nice to see.

Up ahead, I spotted Bandstand Park, where they sometimes had concerts for kids. Once, there'd been a concert where the whole band had been dressed up as ducks! It had taken me a while to put that together, and not long after, we'd had to leave quite suddenly, but Charlie had certainly enjoyed my . . . what would you call it? Performance, perhaps? Close enough. "Did you see what he did to that drummer duck, Dad? Did you see? Did you see?" And every time he thought about it for days and days, he'd laughed so hard, he fell down and rolled around. Even in school, apparently. There might have been a call from his teacher, Ms. Minoso. "Maybe Chet and I could visit the classroom," Bernie had suggested. A great idea, but there'd been only silence from Ms. Minoso.

Bernie slowed down. There were no ducks on the bandstand, no musicians of any kind, just a silver-haired man with a mic, lots of red, white, and blue balloons, and a big crowd, many of them wearing buttons on their chests.

"Well, well," Bernie said. We pulled over and parked. "In the mood for a speech?"

A speech? It hadn't been on my mind at all. I had only slight experience with speeches—in fact had attended just one, Bernie's keynote speech at the Great Western Private Eye Convention not too long ago. Some convention folks must have been called away during the speech because the crowd thinned out a bit, but there was definitely lots of applause. I was sure I heard at least some. Pretty sure.

We crossed the park, came to the crowd, much larger than I'd thought at first. Most folks were standing, but some sat on folding chairs up front. A short, round woman wearing a straw hat with a balloon attached by a long string made room for us.

"What a creature!" she said, taking me in for the first time. "Too bad dogs can't vote."

"They're waiting for the right candidate," Bernie said.

Was that one of Bernie's jokes? If so, I got the feeling it was pretty good. But the woman didn't laugh. She frowned instead, a tiny sweat bead trickling down her nose, pointed to the stage, and said, "There he is, standing in front of your face."

I followed her gaze. Hey! The silver-haired man was Senator Wray! Hadn't he called me a handsome pooch on our visit to the new PD HQ? I took a good look at his face and realized he was a bit of a handsome pooch himself. Was he somehow involved in the case? All at once, I thought I understood it completely. A voice in my head cried out, "Next case!" Whoa! What was that? A voice I'd never heard before and never wanted to hear again.

Meanwhile, Bernie was still talking to the woman. "I didn't realize he was a dog person," he said.

The woman blinked. "He's an every-living-thing person," she said.

"Ah," said Bernie. "And does he have a dog at home?"

"The senator's not a dog person in that sense. In that sense, he's a ferret person."

"Oh?"

"You don't know about Griffie?" the woman said.

"Griffie?" said Bernie.

"He's the cutest little guy." The woman raised herself on her tiptoes. "Sometimes he pops up out of the senator's pocket during one of these appearances, but I don't see any pocket bulge, do you?"

"Afraid not," said Bernie. Then, quietly, maybe just to himself—and to me, of course—he said, "So where's Griffie?"

The woman heard. "Tell you what—if he takes questions at the end, I'll ask him."

"Good idea," Bernie said.

We moved off to one side, got closer to the stage. Senator Wray had the sleeves of his blue shirt rolled up and wore a bolo tie. "—can't do it without you," he was saying in his . . . how to put it? Handsome pooch voice? Yes, that was it exactly. He began pointing at folks in the crowd. "Not without you! And you! And you! And you! You, too, gentleman with the fat cee-gar! You, too, lady spittin' image of Bette Davis! Gonna need all of you, each and every one, if we're gonna get done what needs to be done here in our beautiful Valley and way back there in the corridors of D.C."

"Boo!" went some people in the crowd. "Boo!" Booing is a human sound for when they don't like something. Bernie says humans are related to monkeys! Has to be one of his jokes, but when you see a whole bunch of humans booing, you could almost believe him.

The senator held up his hand. "Yes, sir! What needs to be done. Wanna talk education? Ed-ja-cay-shun? Let's talk ed-ja-cay-shun, my friends. Who's brought over fifty mil of federal money back here to the state, earmarked for the ed-ja-cay-shun of our young-sters? Remember this—the youngsters of today are the oldsters of tomorrow! What's more important than that, folks?"

Bernie glanced down at me. "We're doomed," he said, which I didn't get at all. Meanwhile, the crowd began to chant, "Wray's okay! Wray's okay! Wray's okay!"

We kept moving, still among the standers but closer to the stage—along one side, if you see what I mean. And the standers, kind of a thin line by now, curved around the sitters on our side and ended up quite near the stage. One of the very closest standers, leaning against a trash barrel, seemed a bit familiar. A little narrow-shouldered rubber-face dude who needed a shave and a haircut, or maybe just a comb. Instead of trying to remember the dude's name, my mind wanted to think about a broken comb I'd seen in a gutter a few days ago. But then, beside me, Bernie went still, and in that moment, it came to me: Neddy Freleng! The comedian guy, possibly a onetime boyfriend of Mavis, who lived in a trailer over in New Mexico. Was he waiting to go onstage and do his routine? That was as far as I could take it on my own.

But maybe Bernie had a different idea. I could tell he was on high alert. How, you might ask, when his ears don't suddenly point up and he has no tail to signal with at all? I go partly from a slight change in his smell—it gets more peppery—but mostly just from a feeling of what's going on inside him. We headed away from the crowd, moving slow and silent, practically invisible, and made a sort of circle ending up almost right behind Neddy.

Neddy didn't notice a thing. His gaze—his whole body, really— was focused on Senator Wray. The senator wasn't looking our way. He was talking about his dreams, or possibly the American dream. I didn't quite get it. Whatever it was, it seemed to be making Neddy very nervous. Human nervousness gives off a sweaty scent, not the fresh scent that comes after, say, a long hike but a sour, sweaty scent that gives me a funny feeling way up my nose. And Neddy's sour scent was the sourest I'd ever smelled. He wore a white T-shirt, damp with yellowish sweat under the armpits, and it was also damp, although not yellow, between the shoulder blades. Neddy wore cargo shorts, and his bare legs were trembling. I decided that whatever dreams the senator was discussing had to be scary ones, and was about to tune back in to his speech when something about those cargo shorts caught my attention.

Not the cargo shorts themselves, which seemed like ordinary cargo shorts, baggy with lots of pockets. Leda hadn't let Bernie wear cargo shorts while they were together, but after the divorce, he bought a pair or two. Then along came Suzie, and cargo shorts were gone again. But not important. The important thing was the smell coming from one of Neddy's front pockets, not the smell of a gun recently fired but a gun recently cleaned. I sat right down, eyes glued to that front pocket.

Bernie shot me one quick glance, all he needed. We're a team, me and Bernie. Don't forget that. Those that do tend to end up wearing orange jumpsuits. Bernie moved to Neddy's other side, standing about a step behind him, making Bernie even with me, on the gun side. Many humans would feel a bit uneasy in the middle of that kind of setup—although by no means all, a surprising number of them often strangely unaware of what's going on around them—but not Neddy. Was it because we were already in a crowded situation? Once, I heard Bernie say the best place to hide a tree is in the forest. No getting past Bernie's brilliance, of course, but did that have anything to do with what was going on with Neddy? Or was the little guy just too amped up to notice anything? He had something on his mind, no doubt about that. I could feel it, like a small black cloud hanging over us.

"—so just think about it, folks," the senator was saying. "Anybody here really believe Les Erlanger's gonna bring home the bacon for you?"

"No, no, no!" cried people in the crowd.

"Who's gonna bring home the bacon?"

"Wray! Wray! Wray's okay! Wray's okay!"

An interesting moment. What was Wray all about? Did we like him? Yes? No? Suddenly, the answer was clear. We liked him. He was going to bring home the bacon. And Erlanger, whoever he happened to be, was not going to bring home the bacon. What else was there to know? But whoa! Why was I even thinking about this? We had a real nervous guy trembling in front of us, with a gun in his pocket. Meanwhile, the crowd was chanting, "Wray's okay! Wray's okay! Wray's okay!" It got louder and louder, folks jumping up and down and pumping their fists in the air. A few were even peeing in their pants, which was crazy. And just when it couldn't get any louder or crazier or pissier or plain wilder, Neddy stuck his hand in his pocket, pulled out his gun, and raised it up, pointing straight at Senator Wray.

Or almost. That last part—the raising up and pointing—may not have happened at all, or if it did, you had to be real quick to see, meaning quicker than the dude who grabbed that gun right out of Neddy's hand, possibly taking a bit of skin, or perhaps a tiny chunk of flesh, along the way. That dude was me. Bottom line: nobody saw it.

Well, except Bernie. And in our little corner of the screaming, fist-pumping crowd, now that things were happening, they happened fast. First, Neddy cried out in pain. Second, he shot a terrified glance at me and then at Bernie. Then he bolted, springing into the crowd like he'd been flung from a slingshot—slingshots a big subject I hope we can get to later—and vanishing among the bodies. Not really vanishing. There's no vanishing from me, Neddy smelling the way he did at present. I could have tracked him to the ends of the earth, which I'd heard of but not yet visited. The point being that Bernie didn't even seem to be in a particular hurry when he took the gun from me and slipped it into his own pocket. Only then did we turn to follow Neddy.

That was when Senator Wray, raising his voice above the crowd, said, "Well, well, well, I believe we have a couple of local celebrities in the house."

And what was this? He was pointing our way? And not just our way, but right at us? With his other hand, he shushed the crowd.

"Ladies and gentlemen, one of the Valley's greatest champions of law and order, Mr. Bernie Little! And his four-footed sidekick, Mr. Chet! Well, who's sidekickin' who, right, Bernie? Ha ha ha."

All eyes were suddenly on us? Oh yes. I could feel them.

The crowd got pretty quiet, except for a sort of buzz, that human buzzing for when they think some fun is on the way.

Senator Wray raised his hand toward us and made the come-here motion. "Come on up, Bernie. And Mr. Chet! Let the folks see you."

Twenty-four

So much confusion! I won't go into the details because there's a chance I'd never get out again. But one thing stuck in my mind: *Mr. Chet!* The senator meant me, of course, but no one had ever called me that before. Part of me liked it—*and now here's the star of our show, Mr. Chet!*—and part of me did not. It turned out that the not-liking it part of me was the bigger part. Just call me Chet, pure and simple.

Meanwhile, folks up ahead were making way, and folks behind were encouraging us to "get on up there," one or two even giving Bernie a gentle push.

"Can you believe that dog?"

"What's his name?"

"Mr. Chet."

"Nope, that's the big shambling fella. The dog's Mr. Bernie."

And more like that, only adding to the confusion. Plus Bernie was muttering stuff like "No, thanks, thanks very . . ." and "Very nice, but we really . . ." and the next thing, I knew we were up on the stage. The senator came bounding over, a huge smile on his face, grabbed Bernie's hand, and shook it and shook it. The look in his eyes was probably the coldest I've ever seen.

Senator Wray turned toward the crowd. Hey! I'd had no idea it was so big! What a very nice sight! I came close to a bit of prancing around. Then I noticed Bernie noticing the crowd. The sight didn't seem to make him want to do any prancing at all. In fact, he appeared to get a little smaller. I must have been mistaken. How could there ever be anything small about Bernie? I put that thought away forever and followed Bernie's gaze to the park boundary where Neddy, a tiny figure at this distance, was opening the door of a small yellow car. He drove away.

"My lucky day!" the senator said. "Folks, this is why I love campaigning. My opponent—as you know if you've ever had the pleasure—not!—of seeing him on the stump, does not enjoy campaigning!"

Whatever that was, it brought laughter and more "Wray! Wray! Wray's okay!" The senator raised his voice. "But I love people! I love the stump! Thanks for taking the time in your busy lives! And once in a while, you find you've got an unexpected friend or two among the crowd. Folks, remember that Hollywood star—who'll remain nameless—that got himself into a pickle here in the Valley some time back? Or those bad guys from back east who were messing with our aquifer—our precious water, my friends? This here's the team that cracked those cases. How about a big hand for the private eye you never want on your tail, the Valley's own Bernie Little! And his buddy with the teeth you won't forget, Mr. Chet!"

"Bernie! Bernie! Mr. Chet! Mr. Chet! Wray! Wray!"

"So glad to see you two here, Bernie," the senator said. "Very grateful for your support. Course, everyone knows I've always been a strong supporter of law enforcement—how about the new Valley PD headquarters downtown, my friends—"

"Wray's okay!"

"But it's real good to see law enforcement sayin' to me—right back attcha, Senator! So a great big Western thank-you, Bernie! And a great big bowwow to you, Mr. Chet! Any message for all these fine folks, Bernie?" The senator stuck the mic in Bernie's face.

The most beautiful face in the world, in case I haven't made that clear by now. And it had never been more beautiful! It was the most beautiful sight in this whole . . . what would you call what had going here at Bandstand Park? Thing? Close enough. Bernie's face was the most beautiful sight in this whole thing, and without it we'd have only . . . well, I didn't know what we'd have. That was as far as I could take it on my own.

Beautiful Bernie, but maybe not totally on top of the situation. That could happen to Bernie, but only in the presence of a certain kind of woman, in my experience. This was new. I made what Bernie calls a *mental note* to keep an eye on Senator Wray every chance I got.

Bernie just stood there, the mic in his face. He opened his mouth. Would it have surprised me if he'd then closed it, opened it again, and said, "Ah" and "Uh" and "Um"? No, not at all. But it didn't happen that way. Instead, Bernie looked directly at the senator—like he was on top of the situation after all!—and said, "I can't speak for law enforcement."

Senator Wray's eyes were still icy cold, but I caught a slight flicker in them, the meaning unknown to me. He pulled the mic back and said, "Well, course not, Bernie, my friend, and no one would ever ask you to. I'm sure we're all grateful for your service. How about you tell all these fine folks about this magnificent specimen we got up here with us?" He shifted the mic back toward Bernie.

Bernie looked over at me. I was standing fairly close beside him, but not touching, and actually considering shifting over to the other side of the senator, so we'd have him between us. But why? Did the senator have anything to do with anything? I remembered him on the deck of the lake house, draining his glass and throwing it into the water. Soon after that, the big black fish leaped right clear of the surface, body flexed in a powerful way that had caught my attention. And now I understood. The fish was angry at Senator Wray for treating the lake that way. I began to get the picture. And moved closer to Bernie, so now we were touching.

Bernie stopped looking at Senator Wray and faced the people. He smiled. "There are many things I could tell you about Chet," he said, "but I'll just mention one." Hey! His voice was so clear, positively ringing out across Bandstand Park. "He knows us much better than we know him." Now Bernie turned to the senator and looked him in the eye. He also took the mic away from Senator Wray, not all of a sudden or with much force, just more like they were sharing. The senator's mouth fell open, and he let go of the mic, easy-peasy.

Still looking at Senator Wray, Bernie spoke into the mic. "Chet can see into the human heart. He can tell the good from the bad."

One of the senator's eyes almost shut completely, the eyelid quivering. It made him look very fierce, like one of those big birds that snatches up small animals. We're not small animals, me and Bernie, which the senator now knew, if he hadn't known already. He smiled a big white smile—and snatched the mic back.

"Well, folks, what an amazing dog!" he said. "But he's got nothing on you. You're the people! Of the people, by the people, for the people. What's good and what's bad is up to you! And who's been on the side of good—on your side!—his whole career?"

"Wray! Wray! Wray's okay!"

The senator raised his voice over the cheering. "Let's have a big hand now for our wonderful guests! Thank you for all you do, Bernie and Mr. Chet!"

We headed off the stage to lots of applause. I considered prancing around but oddly enough wasn't in the mood. We just took the short set of stairs and moved off to the side, Bernie getting clapped on the back and me getting petted a bit, and very soon, we were in the car.

I looked at Bernie. He looked at me. "Consider the hornet's nest stirred up," he said.

I didn't know what to think. This whole visit to Bandstand Park had been confusing, but one thing I knew for sure: the place was hornet-free.

Bernie took Neddy's gun from his pocket and stuck it in the glove box. He started the car, then paused. "Mr. Chet," he said. "I kind of like it."

I did not. I turned and looked out my window.

We hit the road, perfect timing on our part. There's nothing like a long car ride after a puzzling meetup. I curled up, got comfy, felt the power of the Porsche and the power of the earth itself, coming up through the wheels. A mighty invisible hand placed itself gently on my eyelids and closed them. Rumble, rumble, rumble. Ah, heaven, wherever that happened to be. A voice in my head—Charlie's actually, which was a first—said, "Of the dogs, by the dogs, for the dogs." Heaven? Was I there?

When I awoke, we were in a little forest, and the sinking sun, blobby and red, was behind the trees somewhere like it was floating just above the ground. It couldn't be floating, of course, since air isn't water. And yet, balloons did float in the air. Hadn't I seen some very recently? Oh yes, at Bandstand Park. I sat right up.

And there was Bernie, behind the wheel, steering us safely from wherever we'd been to wherever we were headed. He glanced over at me. "Grab some nice, refreshing shut-eye, Chet?"

Yes, I had. I felt refreshed, no doubt about it. Basically, I have two . . . what would you call them? While I waited for the answer, Bernie reached for the stick and changed gears. That was it! Gears. I have two gears, fresh and refreshed. Oh, and then there's sleep. Can't leave that out. So my life is all about fresh, refreshed, and sleep. Works for me.

Bernie slowed down and parked in front of a yellow trailer up on blocks. Hey! I knew this trailer. It was Neddy's. So it made perfect sense that Bernie flipped open the glove box and took out Neddy's gun and put it in his pocket. Neddy's place, Neddy's gun—were we cooking or what? We hopped out of the car, me actually hopping. Everything here at Neddy's looked the same as before, except for his bicycle, previously up on its kickstand, now lying flat on the ground, handlebars twisted in a funny position.

We went to the front door and listened for a moment, which we did by me listening and Bernie watching me listen. I heard nothing. Actually, that wasn't quite true. What I heard was the sound of an empty home, not quite the same thing, although I couldn't possibly explain. Uh-oh. That wasn't quite true either. Was I making out a very faint sound of running water? What a complicated case this was! And who was paying? It came to me right away: Sylvia Rottoni. I felt better. We were good to go.

Bernie knocked. "Neddy?" No response. "Open up, Neddy.

We've got something of yours." Still nothing. Bernie knocked harder. More nothing. Bernie tried the door. It opened.

Had things been messy at Neddy's place on our first visit? That was how I remembered it. You couldn't call it messy now. It was wrecked. There's a big difference. Bernie drew the gun and held it at his side. After a bit of confusion, we entered the trailer, me first.

It still smelled of weed and General Tso's chicken, both smells fainter now. Everything that before had been right side up—chairs, table, desk—was now upside down and smashed, mostly to bits. Same in the bedroom and in the bathroom, where the toilet was in smithereens. A small puddle was spreading on the floor. Bernie reached behind what was left of the toilet and shut off the tap. The sound of running water stopped. We went into the bedroom.

Neddy's bedroom was wrecked the most. Someone had broken all the breakables, torn the drywall off the walls, sliced up Neddy's mattress, scattered books and papers all over the floor. Bernie wandered around, toeing at this and that.

"Don't see what else we can—" he began, then paused and picked up some sort of magazine with a purple cover. "High school yearbook," he said in a voice he uses for talking to himself, meaning to me, too, goes without mentioning. He leafed through the high school yearbook, stopped, took a close look at something, went back, took another close look, leafed through some more, and stuck the yearbook under his arm.

"No blood anywhere, Chet?"

I just stood there, mouth open a bit. If there'd been even one drop, I'd have let him know.

"Sorry, big guy, just making sure." Bernie looked around. "So what is this? Sending a message? Simple frustration?" He turned and started back through Neddy's trailer to the front door. I followed. It was never my intention to follow him all the way, of course, since one of my core beliefs is all about being first through any door. But as we passed through the kitchen, I sniffed a Slim Jim. So unexpected, and yet there was no doubt about it. Slim Jims have been a part of my world forever, more than enough time to learn one thing very well: resistance is useless.

I rooted around on the floor and, in a corner by an overturned hot plate, came upon a Slim Jim with only a single bite taken out of it. Was there someone out there capable of saving a partial Slim Jim for later? Neddy, perhaps? The more I learned about him, the trickier he got. I came to a sudden realization. Neddy was a perp. We'd be closing this case pretty soon. I snapped up the Slim Jim and trotted after Bernie.

By that time, he was already at the front door. We'd left it open, so he walked right on through. Here I should probably mention that the door was the kind that opened outward, a kind Bernie didn't like for front doors. "Not secure," I'd heard him say to at least one client. But the important fact was that Neddy's door opened outward. Bernie stepped through and—boom!— the door slammed shut! At the same time, there was a horrible thump that shook the whole trailer, followed by a loud grunt. Not just a grunt, but Bernie's grunt, a grunt of pain.

I sprang to the door.

Twenty-five

And crashed right into it! The door didn't give at all. It was shut tight. Meanwhile, some sort of fight was going on outside. I heard grunts and groans and the crack of punches landing and growls, too, one of which was Bernie's, and another from someone else, a growl deeper than Bernie's and every bit as fierce. Bernie! He needed me! I threw myself against the door with all my strength, hard enough to shake the whole trailer.

But the door didn't give.

At the same time, something crashed into the trailer and shook it again. Then came a grunt that scared me, a grunt of real pain from deep inside Bernie. Not his head? Not his poor head! Eliza—the doctor who'd fixed Bernie up after the horrible saguaro case, and then been his girlfriend for a while and now wasn't, a complicated story I hadn't really understood at the time and now understood even less—had warned us about Bernie getting hit in the head ever again. Was someone out there hitting him in the head? I raced to the nearest window, the only one on the front side of Neddy's trailer.

And what was this? The window was covered by one of those slatted blinds, so I couldn't see out? I swatted it away, ripping the whole thing off the wall, and leaped out—

But no. The window wasn't closed. That wasn't the problem. It was wide open. But outside hung one of those metal security grates. I heard Bernie's voice in my head: *Why bother with window security when your front door's an outie?*

Oh no. There was Bernie, lying on the ground, his nose bloody. Standing over him, both fists balled, was a huge blond guy in a tracksuit—namely, Vanko. His nose looked just fine, and his eyes—reddish, like everything out there, from the last light of the sun—were the eyes of someone enjoying himself.

I pawed at the security grate, got nowhere. Vanko gazed down at Bernie and said, "Where is our little friend Neddy?"

Bernie got his hands on the ground, pushed himself up to a sitting position. "You tell me," he said.

"Ha ha," said Vanko. "You're a funny fellow. Here is what we do with funny fellows." He shifted on one foot—real quick, like an MMA dude, but I'd never seen an MMA dude the size of Vanko—and with the other foot kicked Bernie in the face. Maybe not square in the face. Bernie's real quick, too, don't forget, and maybe he managed to twist away just a bit, his face getting kicked in a more grazing way, or at least not full-on. But it was enough, more than enough, to knock him flat again.

This was unbearable! I pawed at the grate, pawed my hardest, still got nowhere. I raced around in a tight circle and hurled myself at it. Bang! The trailer trembled, but the grate didn't budge. A howling sound rose up in the trailer. Vanko heard it, turned toward me, and laughed. That was when Bernie reached out and grabbed one of Vanko's legs, giving it a hard twist. Vanko lost his balance and fell, but when he fell, he fell right on Bernie! Ooof, went Bernie, the ooof you hear when the wind gets knocked out of a human. They're not much good for fighting right after that.

I hurled myself at the grate again, ran in a tight circle again, hurled myself at it once more. And again. And again. And again. And again. And each time I did, I saw a new sort of still photo of what was going on out there in the deep red light. Like Vanko elbowing Bernie in the neck. Like Bernie somehow throwing one of those kidney punches and rolling out from underneath Vanko. Like the two of them on their feet, circling each other. Like Bernie on the ground again, Vanko sitting on him and reaching for something he had under his shirt, behind his back. Like: a knife, a knife with a thick, heavy blade, maybe the ugliest I'd ever seen.

Splinter! Crash! Suddenly, the grate fell away. I hadn't even been aware of any weakening, was aware of nothing but what was going down outside. Now I leaped through the opening and bounded, once, twice, and straight at Vanko. Somehow, despite the evening being so full of wild barking and howling, he heard me coming, twisted around, and jabbed at me with his ugly knife. I bent my body up and over the point of the blade like a horse taking a jump and . . . forget the part about the horse. Just leave it at me dodging the knife, or just about. I did feel the point graze my chest, but very lightly, not worth a thought.

What I needed to think about was Vanko, who was on the move. First, he cracked Bernie in the jaw with the butt of the knife handle. Then he jumped up and came right at me. In my whole career, no one—not the meanest, baddest perp— had ever charged me like that, even ones that had a knife. The gun-toters didn't have to charge, of course, able to pick you off from a safe distance.

But never mind that. Vanko ran toward me, the knife blade the only bright thing in the gathering dimness. Bernie says there's a right way and a wrong way for holding the knife in a fight. The wrong way is with the stabbing grip, blade pointed down. We don't worry about those guys. The right way is with the sticking grip, blade pointed straight out. Those are the guys we worry about. Vanko turned out to be one of them.

Not only that, but Vanko was enjoying himself a little too much. We like a good dustup ourselves from time to time, me and Bernie, but do our tongues sort of stick out a bit in the midst of it, and do our eyes go suddenly soft and damp in a creepy way? I don't think so.

Bottom line. I did not like Vanko. And he did not like me. Human hatred has a smell you want to stay away from, and right now, it was everywhere. He charged, point of the blade out front. And I charged him. Oh yes. I'm not the type who scares easily, if at all. I sprang. He stuck at me with the knife, aiming right for my heart. I tried to twist away in midair but—uh-oh, how quick he was! I realized something pretty bad: there was a chance I wasn't going to be able to—

But here was Bernie, from out of nowhere and at the very last instant, or even later, in midair, diving at Vanko like some sort of man-shaped rocket. His shoulder hit Vanko in the lower part of the back, making a boom that I associated with car wrecks, and Vanko got knocked up high, right over me, knife and all. Yes, somehow he managed to keep hold of the knife, maybe not quite in proper sticking position, but close, as he bent backward from the force of Bernie's blow and did a sort of complete backflip, although not quite, since he landed facedown. The part about how he kept his grip on the knife is important, because when he hit the ground, Vanko screamed a terrible, deep bellowing scream that went on and on. I remembered the worst TV show Bernie and I had ever watched, a show about bullfighting. I'd never heard of bullfighting, and Bernie changed the channel right away, but not before I saw too much. Now, outside Neddy's trailer, I leaned forward and puked out everything that was in me.

Bernie, on his knees, moved over to me, put his hand on my back. "You okay?"

Perfectly fine. That was the cool thing about puking. You feel bad just before and when you're doing it, but the moment it's over, you bounce back to feeling your tip-top self. At least that's how it works for me.

But what about Bernie? His face didn't look so good. His nose was bleeding, and while it had always been a little crooked—beautifully crooked, by the way—it seemed crookeder now, perhaps not beautifully. I was considering making it all better with a quick lick when Bernie struggled to his feet and went over to Vanko. I followed.

Vanko lay on his front, twisted sideways in a way that looked uncomfortable. His head was turned toward us, and the one eye we could see was open. Now he wasn't screaming or making any sound at all, but that bullfight scream of his seemed to hang in the air, refusing to go away. A dark pool was spreading on the ground from under him, a pool that somehow caught the very last of the red sunset, although the sun was completely gone. I didn't see the knife anywhere.

Vanko's eye shifted, first to Bernie, then to me, and back to Bernie. His lips moved. Bernie leaned in closer to hear. I could hear just fine from where I was. And it really didn't matter, because when Vanko spoke, his voice wasn't particularly soft.

"I will see you very soon," he said.

The light went out of his eye at once. What used to be him just lay there as he'd been lying, but everything had changed. Vanko was gone, and this . . . this was what got left behind.

Bernie sat down beside me, kind of heavily, with a thump. He rubbed his forehead. Uh-oh. That was very worrisome. Then he smiled a quick little smile and put his arm around me.

"What would I do without you?" he said.

The question made no sense. The whole situation was unimaginable. I gave his poor nose a quick lick. Did he wince the slightest bit? I did it again, even more gently if that was possible. What was this? He winced again? But no problem, because this time, he laughed—a brief sort of bark, quite pleasant on the ears—and said, "First, let's get this fixed."

I wasn't sure what Bernie meant. When it came to fixing things—under the hood of the Porsche, for example—we'd had more bad luck than good. But he made no move toward the car. Instead, he took hold of his nose, said, "On three. One, two, YIKES." That *yikes* came when he gave his nose a quick, violent twist, making a loud crack that reminded me of wishbones on Thanksgiving. Thanksgiving was my favorite holiday, and I hoped it still would be after this.

Bernie patted his nose. "Ah, that feels better. How does it look?"

Beautiful. The most beautiful nose in the world. We were doing pretty good, me and Bernie.

He rose to his feet, nice and easy, no struggle this time, went over to the body, and turned it over. The knife was stuck deep in Vanko's chest, and at an angle that was unpleasant to see.

"Everyone's being so clever," he said. "How about we get clever, too?"

A genius idea, even if I didn't quite get it. But that was Bernie every time.

Getting clever turned out to be complicated. First, we listened for anything we should be hearing, me listening and Bernie watching me. Then we went through Vanko's pockets, Bernie going through the pockets and me watching him. All we found were a set of car keys. Bernie pressed a button on the fob, and headlights flashed on through the trees.

We walked over to the car, a black SUV. I sniffed around it. Bernie opened up and searched inside. "Nothing," he said. "No papers, no registration, not even a gum wrapper." He tossed the keys onto the driver's seat and closed the door. We returned to the body. Bernie took a deep breath and said, "This won't be easy."

He was so right. Lifting up the body and carrying it to the Porsche? That didn't look easy. Somehow arranging the body so the three of us would fit? That looked even harder. Getting me to agree to riding on the tiny shelf in back, supposedly the only way this was going to work? Hardest of all. And just when we were set to go, something lying on the ground in front of the trailer caught my eye. I hopped out and—

"Chet!"

—raced over, grabbed the thing, and brought it to Bernie: the purple-covered magazine, possibly called the *high school yearbook*.

"Chet."

It felt like way past dinnertime. Were we headed for home? If so, we didn't go there immediately. First, we came close to getting a speeding ticket, one of those things we do in New Mexico. We were zooming on a long, straight desert road with big rocky outcrops here and there, not much traffic, and the moon rising in a starry sky. A perfect night, except for this passenger of ours making things a bit uncomfortable. But not the point, which was all about suddenly hearing these strange little squeaks going back and forth, the kind of squeaks you hear sometimes when bats are around— although not you, in fact—but not exactly that. More machinelike, if that makes any sense, and if it doesn't, that's the best I can do.

I'm not fond of bats. I'm not a fan of any birds at all, but here's something that will shock you: bats aren't birds! I know because once I heard Bernie tell Charlie, "No feathers. They're mammals just like us."

How disturbing was that? Bats were like Charlie, Bernie, and me? The thought made me uncomfortable in my own skin, and I told myself to forget it, now and forever. Which I clearly hadn't done. So maybe you'll understand why, on that long stretch of desert road, I started barking.

Bernie lightened up on the gas. "Something bothering you, big guy?" He gave me a close look, slowing down more. We passed one of those rocky outcrops at what Bernie calls *grandma speed*—although once an actual grandma and part-time drug runner name of Grannie Helmholtz got clean away from us on the Old Sonoita Road driving a sedan with a flat tire, maybe two—and what was lurking on the other side of that outcrop? Yes, a cruiser, lights off but the cop's face green in the dashboard glow. The cruiser stayed where it was.

"Chet? Did you somehow . . ."

I waited to hear what I'd somehow done, but Bernie never said.

Second, we stopped off at the empty space where EZ AZ Desert Tours and Mini Golf had been, not actually stopping but slowing down.

"Why do I keep thinking about golf?" Bernie said.

Because we were joining a golf club? You had to be rich for that. So we were going to be rich? Maybe soon? What good news!

But first, didn't we have to do something about this passenger, whose heavy leg was pressing into my side, making me uncomfortable in many ways?

No explanation came from Bernie. We sped up a little and followed the bumpy trail into the hills, just like we had on a night that felt long ago but probably wasn't. It was a bright night just like this, but it seemed different. Was that because the mine at the end of the trail—where Mickey Rottoni had parked his green ATV, if I was remembering right—was now just a rubbly mess on the side of a hill?

We parked below the rubble. The remains of yellow crime scene tape blew here and there in the breeze. The moonlight made things a lot like daytime, except in black and white. Once, Bernie tried to explain to Charlie how black-and-white movies were better than color.

"Dad. Please."

I missed Charlie, although this was probably not the kind of outing for him. We got out of the car and made our way into the rubble, me because Bernie was doing it and Bernie for reasons of his own. He picked up a big rock—in fact, huge—and stood still for a moment like . . . like a mighty statue! And also a thinking statue—I can feel his thoughts so easily on nights like this.

"How smart do we have to be, Chet?" he said. "Is there really such a thing as being too smart for your own good?"

Uh-oh. I hoped not. Did it mean being the smartest human in the room wasn't good? If so, we were in trouble. I forgot this little bit at once.

Bernie dropped the huge rock to the side, picked up another. What luck! We were digging a hole. Bernie handled the big rocks, and I got busy with the dirt underneath. Soon, we had a nice-looking hole, not the deepest we'd ever dug, but we were just getting started.

Or maybe not. Bernie dropped one more rock, then straightened up. "That's enough," he said. "Doesn't have to be perfect."

No? I like perfection in the holes I dig, but if Bernie says no perfection, then that's that. We went back to the car. Bernie hefted Vanko on his shoulders and carried him up the slope, possibly staggering just the slightest, although I might have been mistaken. Please change that to me being mistaken for sure.

Bernie did his best to lay Vanko gently in the hole. The moonlight glinted on the knife, still in his chest. We covered him up under dirt and rocks. Then we just stood there side by side. We were both not quite at our best. Bernie was dealing with big questions in his mind. I could feel them. I had a question of my own, a question that wouldn't seem to go away: Why couldn't we have dug the hole deeper? Even just a little bit, nothing like perfection? I pawed at the ground, specifically at a small bump that needed smoothing out. Could Bernie possibly be bothered by that? I glanced at him. He wasn't even watching. I pawed some more, first with just one front paw but then gradually letting the other front paw pitch in when it got the notion. Anything worth doing is—

Hmm. What was this? The end of a sort of sticklike thing, a stick with a leather—what would you call it? Grip, maybe? That seemed right. A stick with a leather grip? Who wouldn't want to chew on something like that? I got a nice firm hold of the stick and with a few quick head shakes twisted it out of the ground.

Bernie looked down. "Chet? What you—?"

He reached out. I let him take the thing.

"A putter?" he said.

A putter for sure. I knew putters from mini golf. Bernie turned it in his hands, hefted it, felt it, studied it from this angle and that. There was some writing on it. Bernie read it out loud.

"Tiger Woods."

Tiger Woods? Come again? I tried to make sense of that and got nowhere. But one thing for sure. This case had taken a dangerous turn. I knew tigers from Animal Planet and had seen what they could do.

Bernie! Get rid of that putter! Throw it away!

But he did not. Instead, he carried it to the car and took the Swiss Army knife from the tool kit. He made a slice in the leather grip and unwound it. Was he looking for something? Underneath the leather grip was only the metal shaft of the putter, glinting in the moonlight. The part you hit the ball with, maybe called the *blade,* was dull gold in color and didn't glint as bright.

Bernie turned to me. "What did Lukie say? It was a special putter? Something like that." He laid the putter and the unwound leather grip on the little shelf in back.

Twenty-six

Back home, we went straight to the kitchen and ate standing up, my usual stance for eating, although not Bernie's. I had kibble. Bernie had slices of tomato and Slim Jims between crackers.

"Dessert?" said Bernie. He tossed me a Slim Jim slice or two. I had the crazy idea of pawing a bit of kibble his way. We're a lot alike in some ways, don't forget.

After that, we went right to bed, Bernie in his bedroom and me next to the front door, where the night air squeezes in through the crack and breaks over my nose in tiny waves. A busy day. I tried to go over it in my mind, but not too hard. Sleep was coming like . . . like a silent black train. What a strange thought! But I couldn't wait to get on the train. My eyelids lowered themselves like . . . like blinds on a window. Hmm. Another strange thought. But nothing could keep from sleep tonight, not after so much action. Closer and closer came the silent black train. I got on board and—

But no. Instead, the train vanished. My eyes opened. I rose and started walking around the house, checking Bernie's room first. A few rays of moonlight flowed through a gap in the curtains, and there he was on his back, one arm thrown over his face, softly breathing. My Bernie. No tiger was getting anywhere near him. That was a promise.

I checked the office, the living room, the kitchen, Charlie's room. Charlie's mattress was bare, except for a pillow with no pillowcase. A baseball lay on the pillow. I went over and sniffed at it, not sure why. I didn't pick it up. I wasn't sure about that either.

I paced up and down the hall. Except for me and Bernie, no one had been in the house. It wasn't that. It was more like . . . I didn't know what it was like. And I'd just been doing so well with likes! And now, when it counted . . .

Whoa. It counted. Yes, I knew that. How, why, what—on all that, I had zip. But something was up.

I went to the back door, a door with a thumb-pusher knob I could press easy-peasy, meaning I had no problem opening the back door if it wasn't locked. We'd worked on that so often I could do it with my eyes closed, as humans often say. Once I'd attended—very briefly—a birthday party for one of Charlie's little buddies. The kids had played a game called Blind Man's Bluff, which seemed to prove humans couldn't do anything at all with their eyes closed. Except sleep. Hey! Was that a joke? I'd strayed out of my territory.

And none of that had anything to do with my current problem. The door was locked, locked with a sliding bolt. We'd worked on those, too, worked long and hard, with a Slim Jim after every session, successful or not—and not was the result every time. It sounded so simple. There were just two parts. First, you pawed that round end on the bolt, pawed it straight down. Then you kind of turned sideways a bit, got your paw on the round end, and gave it a push. *Just like this, big guy.* And Bernie had given the bolt a push with the palm of his hand. So simple! But not for me. Sometimes I got a bit beside myself and started messing up on the easy, pawing-the-bolt-down part. When that happened, we always took a Slim Jim break and dropped the whole thing until another day.

Why was it so hard? You just pawed the round end down like so, turned a little sideways, gave it a push, and then you were done.

Whoa! Click. Froomsh. Huh? Had I done it?

I'd done it! How do you like that? Without even hardly trying! What a life! Then came the easy-peasy part, and the next thing I knew, who was on the patio? Chet the Jet!

Anyone would have been tempted to prance around for a bit, but a strange smell in the air put a stop to that for me. Not strange, exactly, more like unexpected, plus it was a smell I didn't like—namely, vinegar. Lots and lots of vinegar, as though a big vinegar party had been happening on our patio when we weren't around. I sniffed here and there, and all but drowned by the vinegar, I could sort of pick up the scent of the partygoers, but it was all confused and jumbled. I paced back and forth, sniffed, paced some more. Then I trotted into the house and entered Bernie's bedroom.

He was still lying on his back, but no longer with an arm over his face. Now he had his arms crossed over his chest . . . as though . . . as though he was being taken on a long journey. Without me? I was already disturbed enough. I barked my low rumbly bark. Bernie's eyes opened. He started to smile. Then he gave me a closer look, and the expression on his face changed. He got up and, wearing just his boxers, followed me to the back door.

It was open, of course, just the way I'd left it. Bernie went to it, examined the bolt, checked the door on the other side.

"Hey!" he said. "You did it! Wow! Congratulations!" He rubbed the top of my head, ruffling up my fur in a way that felt great. Then he crouched down. "But practicing at night, big guy? What's up with that? Huh?"

I didn't quite follow.

"Seems a little driven, no? We don't want that, not from you. Need your sleep, Chet. But . . . but just wow." He rose. "Now how about we get some shut-eye?"

I barked my low rumbly bark.

"Chet?"

I went outside. Bernie followed. He sniffed the air. "What's that?" He sniffed some more, then turned to me. "Smell anything?"

Well, yes and no. I smelled an ocean of vinegar, no problem, but everything else—the smells I wanted to smell—were all muddled up.

Bernie sniffed again. "Remember that time the wind knocked the salad bowl over? I think I can still smell the dressing. And that was last month!" He grinned at me. "I'm getting like you."

Good grief. We are alike in many ways, but not when it comes to our noses and what they can do. What we had going on out here on the patio had nothing to do with salad. It had to do with . . . I didn't know. But something was going on.

Bernie yawned. "Come on, Chet. Let's knit up that raveled sleeve."

Now he'd lost me completely. Bernie was wearing only his boxers, as I believe I've mentioned, meaning no sleeves. I was wearing my gator skin collar, also sleeveless. Plus the only knitter we knew was Mrs. Singh, and she'd never been here and certainly never spent the night. I barked again, this time more sharply.

"Chet? Something up?"

Yes, exactly. But what? I had no idea. And no idea how I was going to get an idea. When my nose is confused, I'm confused. I paced back and forth across the patio, faster and faster, and panting started up.

"Chet?"

Bernie reached for me as I went by and tried to gently slow me down. But I didn't want to slow down. We ended up pacing side by side, with me in the lead, if that makes sense. Back and forth, up and down, back and forth. I stopped beside the fountain. Have I described it already? There's a pool, and in the middle stands the stone swan. The water trickles from the swan's mouth into the pool, making a lovely sound and cooling the patio, but we hardly ever turn it on anymore on account of evaporation, a puzzling issue that came up a while back on a case involving two hydrologists, one good and one bad, of which I remember nothing except getting paid by the three ex-wives of the good hydrologist, all of whom wore yoga pants and gold watches.

I stepped over the low tile wall and into the dry pool.

"Hot?" Bernie said. "Want to cool off, is that it?"

No. It had nothing to do with cooling off. The vinegar smell was strongest around the fountain, and in its confusion, that was where my nose wanted to be, instead of as far away as possible, which made more sense to the rest of me. That should tell you all you need to know about the power of my nose.

Meanwhile, Bernie went to the tap over in the corner of the patio and turned on the water. Well, not exactly. In fact, all he did was turn the tap. No water came trickling from the swan's mouth, and I heard none running in the pipes under the patio floor.

"Hmm," said Bernie. He fiddled with the tap, turning it off and on, off and on, getting nowhere. Then he stepped into the pool and stuck his hand into the mouth of the swan.

"Hmm."

He gave the swan's head a couple of smacks, not hard. Swans are birds, in case you didn't know. I thought, *It's okay to smack a little harder, Bernie.* But he did not. Instead, he went over to the tap and tried again.

"Hmm."

He went back to the fountain and felt around in the swan's mouth once more. I'd only had one interaction with a swan in my career—working a case up at Geronimo Lake—and that was enough. I only mention that because our stone swan was about the same size as the Geronimo Lake swan who'd scared the— well, not scared, more like unsettled me, but hardly at all and only for a moment.

"I don't under—" Bernie began and then pulled a short length of copper pipe right out of the mouth of the swan. He examined it from this angle and that and laid it aside. Then he got a good grip on the swan, one hand under its neck and the other under its tail, and tipped it carefully on its side.

Underneath where the swan had lain was a hole with a sawed-off copper pipe sticking up in the middle. Wedged around the pipe was a large sort of package in Bubble Wrap. I barked. My nose finally started working on my side.

We pulled the package out of the hole, Bernie doing most of the pulling and me encouraging him. Then we laid the package out flat, using the same sort of teamwork. There was a man in the Bubble Wrap, no longer alive, not even close. At first, I had a crazy thought: *It's Vanko!* Bernie tugged at the Bubble Wrap. It went pop, pop, pop, and then the man's face came into view, a face with a round red hole in the middle of the forehead. Not Vanko but Mickey Rottoni.

Bernie sat back on his haunches. I did the same. He glanced over at me. "Good boy," he said.

But I wasn't! I'd allowed my nose to get all screwed up on account of the vinegary smell! I should have known about this whole fountain situation the moment we came home! I'd failed!

"You're a real, real good boy."

Maybe he was right. Wasn't Bernie always right? My tail started up. I was a good, good boy.

Bernie rose and rubbed his chin. He walked to the gate, checked the lock, another bolt, but bigger and heavier than the one at the back door. Bernie opened the gate and examined it from the other side.

"No damage, Chet. That means . . ."

Whatever it meant remained unsaid. A trail leads from the gate into the canyon. We started up, climbing the hill to the big flat rock on top. When we got there, Bernie peered down at our house and especially the patio. Had I ever seen our home like this, by moonlight? How beautiful it looked! My job was to protect it, now and forever.

"How did they do it?" Bernie said. "A couple of ATVs? And maybe a ladder, to scale the walls? Somebody cased the place, no doubt about that. Any idea who that could've been?"

Nope. I knew casing the place, of course. Bernie and I had cased lots of joints, but this particular casing wasn't on us. I would have remembered, and besides . . . why . . . why would we case our own place? What a thought! So sharp! Like a knife through butter, as humans say. Wow! My mind was like a knife through butter tonight. We really were pretty good, me and Bernie.

"An easy one, huh?" he said. "And so's what's coming next."

Oh? I waited to hear, but Bernie didn't say. Instead, he said, "Gotta move fast, big guy. No way we can implicate anyone else, but I don't see how . . ." He got a faraway look in his eyes. For a moment or two, they turned the color of the moon. A somewhat scary moment, but in that moment, I also knew we couldn't be beaten.

Bernie took out his phone and made a call.

"Sylvia?" he said. "Bernie Little. Sorry to call so late."

I heard Sylvia Rottoni's voice on the other end. A harsh voice and not particularly friendly, but I was glad to hear it. Sylvia was the client, if I was remembering right. It was always nice to have a client.

"It must be important," she said. "And I don't sleep."

Whoa! That sounded pretty bad. But wouldn't it leave her more time for work? Not all clients actually ended up paying, which I knew from experience, but I felt good about Sylvia.

Twenty-seven

The old part of South Pedroia was quiet at night, no lights show-ing in the dusty windows of the brick warehouses along the nar-row streets. We stopped in front of Rottoni Transport, the sign unlit but the picture of the truck with the big grin on its face clear in the moonlight. A wide steel door in the brick wall rolled up, and we drove into a big dark space. The door rolled down beside us. Bernie cut the engine.

A light went on above us, just a single dangling bulb. We got out of the Porsche. A good thing—I was feeling mighty cramped. Trying not to use much force but having to in the end, Bernie wrestled the Bubble Wrapped–body of Mickey Rottoni out of the car, laid him on his back on the cement floor, got him all straight-ened out.

Sylvia Rottoni appeared out of the gloom. She wore her cat's-eye glasses and a robe of the kind possibly called a *kimono*. Suzie had one, as I remembered, although not tattered like Syl-via's. What else? The dolly. Sylvia was pushing a dolly, the long flat kind. She didn't say anything, didn't even look at us. Her eyes were on Mickey. She gazed down at him. Her face twisted like she was about to cry, but she got it untwisted fast, and there was no crying and not a single tear.

"Wish I didn't have to loop you in, but there was no—" Bernie began.

"Shut up," said Sylvia. She gave Bernie an angry look. "Gonna help me with this or just stand there wasting air?"

Wasting air? A new one on me. I knew wasting water, of course, from Bernie being so strongly against it. My guess he'd be pretty good about not wasting air as well, so we weren't going to have a problem with Sylvia. All the same, when she and Bernie hoisted Mickey onto the dolly, something told me not to get involved in any way, not even to give them some quiet encouragement.

Sylvia wheeled the dolly to the back of this garage or whatever it was, hard to tell in the weak light of that single hanging bulb. A white freezer stood against the wall, the shape of a coffin, only bigger. I could feel the cold inside. Sylvia opened the lid. She and Bernie lifted Mickey off the dolly and laid him in the freezer. Sylvia closed the lid, locked it with a padlock, and stuck the key in one pocket of her kimono. From the other pocket, she took out a pack of cigarettes and shook out one for Bernie and one for herself. She struck a match with her thumbnail and lit them both. Hadn't Bernie recently quit smoking? Or had he started up again? He took a drag, and I could tell he was making himself do it. By the time the next drag came along, he wasn't.

"What do I owe you?" Sylvia said.

That sounded promising, but Bernie didn't always take advantage of openings like that, and this was one of those times.

"Nothing yet," he said.

"Why not?" said Sylvia, her voice very hard. "The family hired you to find the body, and . . ." She reached out and gave the freezer lid a gentle pat-pat.

I'm always loyal to Bernie, goes without mentioning, but just this once I was on someone else's side.

"You hired us to find the body plus, quote, whoever killed him," Bernie said.

Sylvia blew out a tiny cloud, her eyes narrowing against the smoke. "Maybe I don't want to know anymore."

"Why not?"

She took another drag. A column of ash fell to the floor. She ground it under the heel of her bedroom slipper. "Mickey was a thief and a sneak, but he wasn't a killer."

"Not sure where you're going with this," Bernie said.

"No? I thought it was pretty clear that Mickey tried pulling something sneaky on somebody. But this somebody or somebodies turned out to be way more than he bargained for. Like a boy against men."

"So?" Bernie said.

"So I'm sensing influence in high places, including Valley PD. Maybe I don't want these homicidal somebodies coming after me and my family. And maybe you don't want them coming after you either."

Bernie's face went stony, a look I'd seen before, although not often. I thought Sylvia would look away, but she did not.

"This," Bernie said, pointing to the freezer, "is about tactics, not fear. But I'll think of some other place for Mickey."

Now Sylvia did look away. "No," she said, the word catching in her throat. She tried again. "No. Keep going. Get the bastards."

Back home, Bernie got the fountain back up straight, then went inside and started tidying the whole house. These tidying—what would you call them? Frenzies, maybe? These tidying frenzies hardly ever happened, and never at night.

"Lie down, Chet. Go to sleep. There's nothing for you to do right now."

I lay down. My eyes stayed open. I got up. I followed Bernie around. The house got tidier and tidier. Finally, it was tidier than I'd ever seen it. Bernie took a shower. I pushed open the bathroom door and stuck my nose through the shower curtain once or twice. Bernie sang "I Was the One," his favorite Elvis song. I did a bit of woo-wooing at the end.

He got dressed—fresh jeans off the hanger, sneaks, plus the Hawaiian shirt with the ice cream cone volcanoes, an excellent choice. He filled my water bowl. Then he got started on brewing a pot of coffee. After that, he opened the fridge, but closed it without removing anything.

"We'll have breakfast after the predawn raid," he said.

Whatever the predawn raid was, I hoped it wouldn't take long. All of a sudden, I was famished.

Somewhere across the canyon, a rooster crowed. And crowed and crowed some more. What is with them? I looked out the kitchen window. Still nighttime, but the moon was gone and the stars didn't seem as bright. Bernie sat at the kitchen table, sipping coffee and reading a book. I heard a sound, faint and powerful at the same time, of big, fast things approaching, and started toward the front door. Bernie closed the book.

Out front, I heard cars braking, car doors opening and closing, lots of footsteps on our lawn. "Shh," said Bernie, coming up behind me. "Not a sound."

On the other side of the door, a man said, "On three. One, two—"

Bernie, in no particular hurry, reached out and opened the door. Two SWAT team dudes came stumbling in, one actually falling down completely, and their battering ram crashed on the floor and rolled to a stop.

"Oops," Bernie said, coffee mug in hand. "Thought I heard a knock."

Normally, I'd have been deeply involved in the action by now, but hadn't Bernie said *Shh*? Plus I was in the mood to be a good, good boy.

Outside, we had some confusion going on. A bunch of uniformed Valley PD guys and gals, all unknown to me, were sort of shuffling around and gaping at the two SWAT teamers, now dusting themselves off and also looking confused. Then from the back, Captain Ellis stepped forward, holding some papers.

"This," he said to Bernie, "is a warrant signed by Judge Fleckman to search your entire premises."

"Fleckman?" said Bernie. "Isn't he still in rehab?"

Ellis's face, on the reddish side to begin with, reddened some more. "You have a right to read the warrant." He shoved it at Bernie.

Bernie waved it away. "No need," he said. "I know the quality of your work, Von."

A muscle jumped in the side of Ellis's face. "Then you raise no objection to the search?"

"Not in a legal sense," Bernie said.

Ellis glared at him. A faint milky light glowed in the lowest part of the sky, turning Ellis's eyes the color of milk. "How's that smart-ass mouth of yours gonna play in prison?"

"We'll never know," Bernie said. "I won't be visiting you."

From back in the crowd came a snicker. A snicker is one of the more unpleasant human sounds, but I kind of liked this one.

Ellis swung around to the PD folks. "Turn the fucking place upside down."

Bernie gave me a quick look, a look that didn't seem the least bit angry or upset. Valley PD were going to turn our place upside down and we were going to let them? Then it hit me: that was exactly what we wanted! Were we brilliant or what? Bernie stepped aside, and so did I. Chet the Jet, in the picture. You may be asking yourself why that was exactly what we wanted. I did not. May I mention that that's the difference between you and me? I'm not going near the question of which approach is better. But I think you know the answer.

I've seen a number of PD searches in my career, including the turning-the-place-upside-down kind, but this one was different from the get-go. For one thing, the actual house didn't get searched, at least not at first. Instead, everyone followed Ellis down the hall, out the back door, and onto the patio.

Bernie and I watched from the kitchen window. He sipped his coffee. I picked up a chewy I'd found on a recent walk—possibly on someone's lawn or even doorstep, the very best kind of chewy—and held it in my mouth because . . . because I could.

Out on the patio, everyone went right to the fountain, and a few of the cops began raising the swan.

"Just knock the goddamn thing down," Ellis told them.

But the cops glanced over at us and continued with what they'd been doing, lifting the swan off the base and setting it down on the patio, almost gently. Then everyone gathered around the hole where the swan had stood and peered inside. A tiny edge of the sun popped into view at that moment, spreading a clear lemony light. No one could have missed what there was to see in the hole—the sawed-off copper pipe and nothing else.

Now there was more confusion than ever on the faces of the cops. They all turned to Ellis. He ignored them, instead fastening his gaze on us, a gaze partly confused but mostly furious. Bernie, stirring his coffee with his finger, looked right through him. I chewed my chewy.

After that, our place did get searched, but pretty quickly, and only one thing got turned upside down. That was Bernie's coffee mug. It happened to be sitting on the kitchen counter as the cops were leaving, and Captain Ellis happened to knock it off as he was passing by.

Bernie swept up the pieces of the broken mug.

"Wait a minute, big guy."

He got out the vacuum and vacuumed where he'd swept.

"Okay. Good to go."

I came over and sniffed the floor. There was lots of shoe polish scent in the air, a PD sort of thing. Bernie fixed breakfast for two. Did that mean we'd already had the predawn raid? I wondered about that as I was chowing down. We weren't quite done before the phone buzzed.

"Bernie?" It was Captain Stine. "What the hell's going on?"

"Not much," Bernie said. "Chet and I are just finishing breakfast. He's having that kibble from Rover and Company he likes, plus a little flaxseed for his coat, and I'm—"

"For crissake—you know what I mean. What's going on with this guy Mickey Rottoni or whoever the hell he is? Things are in uproar down here."

"Can't help you," Bernie said.

"Not buying that for a second," said Stine. "We got Ellis telling everyone you killed Rottoni and hid the body."

"Who's his source?" Bernie said.

"He's keeping the source confidential for now," Stine said.

"I'll bet he is."

"What's that supposed to mean?"

"I suggest you find that source. As for Mickey, who was in charge of the search of the Zinc Town mine?"

"Look, I know you and Ellis have this feud, but—"

"Feud?" said Bernie.

"Stop being so goddamn—" Stine began, but Bernie clicked off and lay the phone on the table, upside down. It buzzed again, vibrating slightly. Bernie ignored it. Instead, he went for a little trip inside the house, me alongside. We collected a couple of things— the putter and the purple-covered high school yearbook—and returned to the kitchen.

"Are these clues, Chet?" Bernie said. "Or just random noise?"

I listened to the putter and the yearbook, didn't hear a peep out of either of them. They had to be clues. The day was off to a great start. Predawn raid, nice big breakfast, two silent clues. Who could ask for more?

Bernie paged through the yearbook. "Here's the rodeo team, Wynona at the side, Johnnie Lee front row center. See how happy she looks?" He showed me the picture, but I would have needed a bit more time to make sense of it. "This here must be a scene from *The Crucible*." He pointed. "Neddy? Gotta be. And this is Mavis, for sure. Even then she was . . ."

Whatever Mavis was back then stayed in Bernie's mind. He turned to another page. "The senior class photos, big guy. Hmm. Johnnie Lee got a piercing after the rodeo team photo. Here's what she had to say. 'Been a blast, buckaroos. Shout-out to Coach Wynona, the bestest! I'll always remember Pooh Bear, the prom after the prom after the prom, and the Hole in the Wall. See you when I see you. Ride 'em, babycakes!'"

Bernie looked up. "Pooh Bear?" he said. "Hole in the Wall?"

I couldn't help him. But bears had come up already in this case, during our conversation with Scott Kyle, or perhaps Kyle Scott, who was no longer answering our calls, if I remembered right. Was it possible the bears had gotten him? I knew the smell of bears very well. There was not a whiff of bear in the whole house. We were safe for now.

Bernie closed the yearbook, picked up the putter, took a practice putt or two, then putted a kibble nugget that had somehow fallen to the floor and gone unnoticed. A fallen kibble nugget unnoticed? That wasn't like me at all. I snapped it up before it stopped rolling.

"How about we pay a visit to Shaky Insterwald?" Bernie said.

Shaky Insterwald? Hadn't seen him in ages, hadn't even thought of him! What an amazing idea, straight out of the blue! But that was Bernie.

Twenty-eight

When it comes to golf, Shaky Insterwald is our go-to guy. He'd also been the go-to guy for lots of folks interested in buying beachfront property in Mexico. Some of those folks ended up hiring me and Bernie when it turned out that those beachfront properties didn't exist, and neither did the beaches, meaning we'd lugged the surfboard down there for nothing. But all that was in the past, and Shaky's days of breaking rocks in the hot sun were behind him. Now he ran Buckets and Buckets o' Balls, Cheapest Driving Range West of the Mississippi, Come Knock Yourself Out, which I believe was the full name of the place, written on the monster sign out front.

Shaky sat in the shade of an umbrella in front of the office, which looked like a shack, or possibly a tiki bar in need of repair. He had a few customers whacking balls off the farthest away tees and was enjoying a cold frosty drink, a drink that was spewing out the unmissable smell of tequila sunrise.

"Well, well, well," he said. "Come to smack some balls around? Best way to start the day."

"Maybe later," Bernie said, pulling up a rickety-looking lawn chair and sitting down. What was this? A wince in his eyes? Was he in pain? Why would that be? Our little dustup with Vanko? Ah. Was I putting things together or what? And was there some swelling on one side of his beautiful face? Perhaps, but hardly noticeable, and that wince was here and gone in a flash. We're fast healers, me and Bernie. I sat beside him.

"God almighty," Shaky said. "Is he still growing?"

"I don't think it's possible at his age," said Bernie.

"No?" said Shaky. "Check out some of the dudes in the NFL."

Whatever that was, it struck Shaky as very funny. He laughed and laughed.

Then he glanced down the tee boxes to his customers and gave me another look. "Chet's not planning to do that thing where he chases balls all over the lot, is he?"

"I think that was a onetime event," Bernie said.

Shaky nodded. "Too bad in a way. Business picked up for a week or so, folks who heard about him and wanted to see with their own eyes."

Wow! I hadn't known that! Would there be any harm in—

Bernie gave me a look, just raising one eyebrow the tiniest bit. I got the message.

Meanwhile, in the closest tee box, a thick-necked guy with skinny legs was loading up his swing.

"Christ," said Shaky. "Wish to hell I had more tee boxes."

"Why?" Bernie said. "You've got plenty of empty ones."

"I mean way down thataway." Shaky waved toward the thick-necked guy—now missing the ball completely—and beyond. "So I don't have to see all this horrific shit."

"Those are your customers," Bernie said.

"They suck. Practically everyone in the whole world who ever picked up a club shoulda put it right back down. Although not you, Bernie. You got that sweet natural draw. You could be decent—more than decent—if you gave it a chance."

Decent? More than decent? Once, I'd seen Bernie hit a golf ball. This was on a case. I don't remember the case, or why he suddenly had the client's club in his hands. I just remember the beautiful thwack and the ball vanishing into the blue.

"You're the golfer, Shaky." Bernie laid the putter on the table. "What do you make of this?"

Shaky checked the writing on the blade. "Tiger, huh? Once took a grand off him at Pebble."

"Yeah?" Bernie grinned, looking so happy.

"Son of a bitch took ten back from me the next day. I'd like to think he wasn't setting me up."

"Course not," Bernie said. "Probably you celebrated a little too much the night before."

Shaky laughed, grabbed a quick gulp of tequila sunrise,

laughed some more. "Know what I learned on the tour? You can be great at something, world-class, and still not have any fun. In golf, anyways, it's the model. The fun ones crash out. Take that guy there." He pointed to the thick-necked guy, now taking an enormous swing and topping the ball, which rolled a little way on the sunburned grass. "He's having more fun than any of the guys in the top ten." Shaky picked up a bullhorn. "Hey, number ninety-seven. Free bucket waiting for ya, courtesy of Buckets and Buckets o' Balls." The thick-necked guy gave a happy wave of his club.

Shaky picked up the putter. He was a tall, thin, stooped sort of dude who could have used a shave, a haircut—and a toenail trim, most of all. Those toenails! Wow! Also he had bad teeth. One of the easiest smells out there—didn't Senator Wray have a bit of that, now that I thought about it? But back to Shaky, bad teeth and also he did shake a bit, but when he took that putter in his hands and got into putting position, here in the shade of this crummy tiki bar or whatever it was, the shaking stopped and Shaky somehow looked kind of powerful. And his hands were huge! They wrapped around the shaft of the putter like a thick leathery snake. Whoa! A scary thought. I actually backed away a bit.

Shaky waggled the putter. The waggle is one of the best parts of golf. Once, Bernie showed Charlie how to do it. The fun we had that morning, which turned out to be a school morning, Charlie ending up late, leading to difficulties with Leda and also perhaps with Ms. Minoso, Charlie's teacher, who didn't seem to get any of Bernie's jokes when we finally arrived.

Shaky looked up. "Feels a little off," he said.

"I removed the grip," said Bernie.

"So's I noticed." Shaky waggled the putter again. "It's not that. More like something got loose inside—but what? Nothin' in there to get loose."

"No tiny screw or anything like that?" Bernie said.

"Tiny screw? In a putter shaft?" Shaky waggled the putter one more time. "Any objection to me prying off the cap, taking a gander inside?"

Gander? A kind of goose, if I wasn't mistaken? I'd learned that on a visit to a bird sanctuary, me, Bernie, and Suzie, where unfortunately . . . something unfortunate happened, ending the visit on the early side. So although I'd been following this putter conversation pretty well, I might have missed a thing or two before the moment Shaky pried off the cap at the end of the shaft with his teeth—bad smelling, yes, but still very useful, especially for a human—and turned the putter upside down and gave it a shake.

Some small papers rolled out, bound by a rubber band, and landed on the table, actually in a wet spot next to Shaky's tequila sunrise. Bernie reached for the papers, but Shaky, surprisingly quick, grabbed them first. He sort of cleaned up the wet spot with his elbow, snapped off the rubber band, unrolled the papers, and spread them on the table.

Not papers, but photos.

"Probably best if you didn't—" Bernie began.

But it was too late. Shaky was hunched over the table, peering at the photos. We all took a nice, long, long peer.

In the first photo, two people stood on a deck of a big house, overlooking a lake. Hey! I'd seen that house and that deck! And also that lake, both of them only by night, true, but I recognized them. I'm a pro, don't forget. The two people had their arms around each other and were kissing. I recognized them, too: Mavis Verlander and Senator Wray.

In the next photo, Mavis and the senator were on a bed and their clothes were on the floor. Over the head of the bed hung a big painting of a woman. I recognized her, too, from our little get-together at Billy Baez's horse ranch, where I'd met her and her horse. The horse's name was Capitol Hill, if I remembered right, and hers was Caroline Wray. She looked happier in the painting than she had at Billy's. Somehow that bothered me.

"Don't know the gal, but she's a knockout," Shaky said. "The old coot looks familiar."

"Uh-huh," Bernie said.

The last photo showed Mavis and Wray again, still without clothes, although now standing up. She had her back to him, but had turned her head to look his way. They were both laughing. Some sort of square thing was stuck to her butt.

Shaky squinted at it. "That a bumper sticker? What's it say?"

"'Wray's OK,'" said Bernie, his voice low and kind of hard.

"Thought I recognized the bastard."

"You know him?" Bernie said.

"Nah."

"Am I hearing a little extra spin in that nah?"

"Nah," Shaky said. Then he laughed. "How come your hearing's so frickin' good, Bernie?"

Whoa! Had something suddenly happened to Bernie's ears? I gave them a close look. They seemed unchanged, nicely shaped and of useful size, but I knew for a fact that Bernie's hearing wasn't frickin' good or anywhere close.

"Don't know him personally," Shaky was saying. "Buddy of mine plays with him." He gestured at the photos. "Is this important? Can you tell me what's going on?"

"Yes," said Bernie. "And no. Who's this buddy of yours?"

"Assistant pro over at Belhaven Springs. Gets looped into a foursome with Wray once in a while. He cheats."

"At golf?"

Shaky took another glance at the photos. "That, too."

"Cheats how?"

"Most basic way—on the scorecard. Anyone calls him on it, he's always like, *Nope, it was a four. Drive a little left over by the pond, five iron back of the bunker, chipped to eight feet, lipped it in*. A story with details, just leaving out that the chip left him a thirty footer and he two putted. The little lie and the big lie all mixed together, you see what I mean."

Bernie smiled. "Very much so."

"You take every edge you can," Shaky said. "That's the game. But screwing with the score? That's changing history." He drained his tequila sunrise. "And then what's the point of living right?"

Bernie rose. With one hand, he picked up the putter and the photos. With the other, he took some money from his pocket and tried to hand it to Shaky. Shaky shrank away.

"No way I take your money. Wouldn't've gotten back on track, hadn't been for you."

"I'll book some lessons after this case," Bernie said.

"Hey, that'll be fun!" Shaky said. "Meantime, I'm guessing I ain't seen no photos nohow."

"Yo," said Bernie.

Twenty-nine

"Blackmail," Bernie said. "I'd like to think I had that feeling, but I didn't."

Blackmail? How interesting! We'd worked a number of blackmail cases, although none recently, our recent jobs having been mostly about divorce. Blackmail cases are much better than divorce cases, but stolen property cases are my favorite, especially the one involving the hijacked eighteen-wheeler hauling a full load of biscuits from Rover and Company. We'd recovered each and every box! And returned a good number of them!

"The Mickey Rottonis of the world never realize they're out of their league until it's too late," Bernie said.

We stopped at a red light. A cat in the rear window of a pickup gave me a look I didn't appreciate, not one little bit. A soft growl rose up and joined all the traffic sounds.

Bernie glanced over at me. "Rough on Mickey, I know, big guy. Maybe even worse, that horrible realization is their very last thought."

What was that? Totally missed by me. The light turned green. The pickup made a turn. We kept going straight. The growling died away. I realized I'd had a momentary drop right out of the picture. To get back in, I kind of pawed Bernie's shoulder, but in the nicest way. Around then, we happened to veer into the next lane and possibly the one next to that. When the honking died down, Bernie said, "Thirsty? Let's take a quick break."

I wasn't the least bit thirsty! I simply wanted back in the picture! But Bernie's the best wheelman in the Valley, so this little driving blip had to mean *he* needed a quick break. And there I was, back in the picture. We communicate, me and Bernie, end of story, probably the reason this case—blackmail, was it?—was going so well.

We sat outside a small and quite fancy café we'd never been to. Bernie had iced tea. I had wonderfully icy water in a huge tin bowl. The waiter said nice things about me. What a find this place was!

Bernie was looking through the high school yearbook again. "Got to confront the question of whether it was a setup, big guy. Was Mavis in on the blackmail? Just don't see it. Why did Mickey beat up Johnnie Lee? Had to be when . . ."

I sipped more of the lovely water, waited to hear Bernie's guess, an amazing one for sure, but it never came.

"We know Mavis and Wray met when Johnnie Lee took her to the holiday party. Then what? Mavis tells Johnnie Lee what's going on? She tells Mickey? Or he simply finds out? Then he needs some details about the affair, the wheres and whens? Johnnie Lee won't cooperate? He beats her up? She gets the restraining order? He gets himself a camera with a long lens and makes his play anyway, maybe with incomplete information?"

Wow! What a lot of great questions!

"Then came the blowback. Johnnie Lee got our name from Wynona, but we scared Mavis off, totally by accident, as it turned out. That's the past. But what's happening now? And what could happen?" His finger went tap, tap on a yearbook page. He took out his phone.

"Wynona? Bernie Little here. Any chance you've heard from Johnnie Lee or Mavis?"

"I have not."

"Has anyone else been asking about them?"

"Yes."

"In person?"

"Very much so."

"Who was it?"

"A foreigner of some kind. I never quite got his name."

"What kind of foreigner?"

"Russian, maybe."

"A real big guy or an actually huge guy?"

"A really big guy. The actually huge guy stood by the car."

"What did he want to know?"

"Basically if I knew where to find the girls, as they called them. Apparently, they'd applied for entertainment jobs on a cruise ship, and these guys wanted to hire them."

"Did you tell them anything?"

"Didn't you say not to?"

"True, but—"

"And do I look like some sort of hick who'd fall for bullshit like that?"

"You do not."

"Then there's your answer," Wynona said. "And they also asked about Neddy."

"Did he apply for a cruise ship job, too?"

"Supposedly. And it would be believable in his case. But I kept my lips zipped."

"Thanks," Bernie said. "One more thing—does the Hole in the Wall mean anything to you?"

"Sure," Wynona said. "Once upon a time, it was a cool teenage hangout—for the kids fit enough to make the climb. But then they found some artifacts up there, so the trail's been closed off for years."

"What trail?" said Bernie.

Wynona started in on something that sounded complicated. Bernie flipped open what Leda used to call his *ratty little notebook*—although no rat had ever been near it, trust me—and started making notes. Maybe I would have taken a swing at following it, but I got distracted by some very well-dressed ladies coming out of the café door. They all headed for cars parked along the street, except for the very last one, who saw us, paused, and stepped back inside. I came very close to recognizing her, despite the fact she wore big sunglasses and a fancy sort of cowboy hat that kept her face in shadow. Pretty good on my part.

Meanwhile, Bernie had said goodbye to Wynona and was putting his phone away when it buzzed again.

"What the hell is going on?" It was Captain Stine, sounding not his best.

"We're on a little hydration break," Bernie said. "And you?"

"And me? And me? I just got back from hours and hours of digging up that goddamn mine in Zinc Town—that's how I am. Redigging it up, to be accurate."

"You were digging personally?"

"Yes, you son of a bitch, plus a whole team working double overtime and blowing up the budget from now till the end of time."

"Did you find Mickey Rottoni?" Bernie said.

Stine was quiet for what seemed like a long time. Then he said, "What do you think?"

Bernie reached out and scratched between my ears, very brief but perfect, and out of the blue. "I don't know what to think," he said.

I sure did: Bernie was the best!

"The answer," said Stine, "in case you don't know, which I doubt, is no. But would it surprise you to learn we found another body in there?"

"If Ellis was in charge, yeah," Bernie said.

"Ellis? Ellis is suspended as of ten minutes ago. A heavy lift, by the way. He's got a lot of backers on the twelfth floor. But even those assholes can see that whatever went down at Zinc Town's a disgrace."

"How did Ellis take it?"

"He doesn't know yet. Or maybe he does, unofficially. We're looking for him."

Bernie sipped his iced tea.

"I'm waiting," Stine said.

"For what?"

"For you to ask about this other body."

"I don't like to pry," Bernie said. He clicked off and put the phone down. It buzzed again right away. He took another sip of iced tea and turned to me. "Did we get hold of the levers of power, big guy? Just for a minute or two?"

Poor Bernie. All he had hold of was a glass of iced tea, couldn't have been clearer. I had hold of nothing, although that might change, half a biscotti lying under the table within easy reach. But maybe we'd get hold of the levers of power one day, whatever they were.

Bernie drummed his fingers on the table. I loved seeing that! Now all I had to do was wait for something amazing.

"Cruise ship," he said or possibly muttered or even mumbled. "She's right. Could appeal. So how would you get in touch with . . . doesn't he have an agent? Some funny name, kind of—?"

Bernie cut himself off before he could get to the amazing part. The woman wearing the sunglasses and cowboy hat had come outside and was walking toward our table. Caroline Wray. I'd almost known!

She stood before us, taller than I remembered. Bernie's legs tensed like he was about to rise, but in the end he did not.

"Ah, our private investigator, if memory serves," she said. "Are you investigating me? Or is your presence here only a coincidence?"

"Kismet," Bernie said, losing me completely.

Although perhaps not Caroline. "More the opposite," she said. She pulled up a chair and sat down, taking off her sunglasses but leaving the cowboy hat on so her eyes were in shadow. When we'd surfed in San Diego, we'd kept going until after the sun went down. The color of the ocean then was the same as Caroline's eyes now.

"What is it you want?" she said.

"In what context?" said Bernie.

"In the context of you dropping whatever you're doing—or think you're doing—and going on a long vacation."

"Like to Kauai?"

"Kauai has its charms, but I don't really care. How much? What's the number? Men do so love to have a number."

"I have no number," Bernie said.

"You prefer an initial offer?" Caroline said. "You're the haggling type?"

"What I want," Bernie said, "is Mavis Verlander, safe and sound."

"A very pretty young woman, I hear. It's possible I met her once, but unfortunately—very unfortunately—I don't recall. You're not the first to want her, and you won't be the last. Girls like her go round and round until the music stops. Round and round and round."

"Is it too late?" Bernie said. "Is that what you're telling me?"

"In general, when that question is asked, the answer is yes," Caroline said. "But be more specific."

Bernie's voice got hard. "Can you still stop all this?"

"I?"

"And if not you, the senator?"

"Griffin?" Caroline started laughing. What a laugh she had! So rich and musical and confident! Some women don't have confident laughs. They put a hand over their mouths. Men never do. What was that all about? No time to figure it out now. Caroline didn't cover her mouth. Her teeth were big and white, her tongue nice and pink. Was it the happiest laugh I'd ever heard? Not close.

"Oh, dear." She took a silk handkerchief from her little gold purse and dabbed at the corner of her eye.

"What are you telling me?" Bernie said.

Caroline stuffed the handkerchief back in the purse and snapped it shut. "You may think you know what you're doing— Bernie, is it?—but trust me. You do not." She rose, walked over to a car, and drove away in no particular hurry. And not just any car but a Porsche, unless I was very mistaken, brand new and shiny, and quite similar to the color ours had been several paint jobs ago.

The waitress came with the check. Bernie was reaching into his pocket when he suddenly went still. "Mad Dog Creative," he said. "How could I forget a name like that?"

"Excuse me?" said the waitress.

"MDC," said a woman on the other end of the line.

"I'd like to speak to the agent who reps Neddy Freleng, the comic."

"Moment."

Silence. Then another voice, this time a man's. "Mr. Frood's office."

Bernie repeated the whole thing about Neddy Freleng.

"Moment."

Silence. Another man came on. "Wyatt Frood," he said.

"You rep Neddy Freleng?"

"Correct."

"My name's Lou Mayer. I'm with the Upper Valley Regional High School Association in Arizona. Ran into a couple of cruise ship entertainment scouts and they told me about Mr. Freleng. I'd like to find out if he'd be interested in visiting some of our classrooms next year."

"What's it pay?"

"Nothing monetary. But our speakers can claim a charitable donation. And the kids always make a nice gift or two."

"Neddy was supposed to—" Mr. Frood backed up, tried again. "Did the cruise ship scouts say they'd already met with Neddy?"

"Not that I remember. I'd like to meet him, too."

"I can give you his office number."

"Out there in LA?"

"No. His office where you are." Mr. Frood told Bernie the number.

"And the address?" Bernie said. "I need to mail a brochure."

"Mail," said Mr. Frood, almost like he'd never heard of it. I was very familiar with mail, and mail deliverers most of all. "Here you go—14362D West Horizon Road."

"Thanks," said Bernie. Mr. Frood was already gone.

The Valley goes on and on in all directions. You have to get used to that if you want to be happy here. And I'm very happy here. Being a good napper in the car is a big help.

"Wakie, wakie."

I opened my eyes. We have lots and lots of strip malls in these parts, from the very fanciest to the very crummiest. This one was

in the very crummiest group, or possibly below, a squat, crum-
bling adobe building with a broken taped-up window or two, no
parked cars, no people. We walked from door to door, all of them
plastered with notices and padlocked.

"A, B, C—D must be around the back," Bernie said.

We circled around to the back. It was a lot like the front, except here we had some trash lying around.

"F, E, D."

We stopped in front of D, the only unpadlocked door in the
whole place. A glass door, but with a blind hanging on the other
side so we couldn't see in. That didn't keep me from smelling in,
if you understand what I mean.

Bernie did. He didn't bother knocking, just tried the door,
and when it didn't open, he picked up a rock and shattered the
glass, first telling me to step back, of course, just one of our many
techniques at the Little Detective Agency, all adding up to make
it what it is.

We swept the blind aside and stepped in. A very crummy office and very small. There was barely room for the two guys already there, never mind us. The desk was the bricks-and-board
type, and the chairs were plastic lawn chairs. Neddy was slumped
in one of the lawn chairs. He wore a white T-shirt that was mostly
red in front, and had a gun in his hand, not held tight, but his fingers had stiffened around it. More like loose and stiff at the same
time, not a very professional look.

The other guy lay twisted and facedown across the slanting
desk board, his feet among the bricks, most of them scattered
around. He had a gun in his hand, too, his grip on it much better
than Neddy's, with none of that looseness. Bernie flipped him
over, not gently.

It was Ellis. He wasn't in his gold-braided uniform, instead
wore a blue button-down and jeans. The blue button-down was
all red in front, just like Neddy's T-shirt.

"Any chance Crime Scene will get this right?" Bernie said.

I didn't understand the question.

He turned to me. "Smell Olek, Chet?"

I got that one! What a great question! And the answer was yes, I sure did. Who could miss that borschty aroma?

Bernie rose. "I don't know many Russian words, but one is *bespredel*." He gestured with his chin at the scene in Neddy's office. "Now I'm pretty sure they have it in Ukrainian, too." Bernie took one last look at Ellis and . . . and spoke to him. "Did you die thinking you were still in charge?"

I'd never seen Bernie speak to a dead person before, and hoped this was a one-and-done situation. He got the blind back in place. We went out and closed the door.

Thirty

Up and up we climbed on a trail that twisted through a green and silvery forest, the trees smelling nuttier the higher we got, the feel of the air growing lovelier and lovelier. We came to a clearing with a stream flowing on the other side, not a muddy little trickle but bubbling water on the move. The next thing I knew, I was standing in the middle of it, the water almost up to my shoulders. I gave it a taste. Ah! Delicious, some of the best water I'd ever sampled. Were we in New Mexico? I thought so. Not a very nice place in the matter of speeding tickets, but I had no complaints about their water. I lapped up some more.

Bernie sat on the bank, dipping his bare feet in the stream. He opened the backpack, took out his water bottle and his notebook, the one no rat had ever been near. He studied the notebook and drank water. I studied him. He looked a bit worried. Did we have anything to worry about? Not that I could think of. For one thing, the .38 Special was in that backpack, as well as a tuna sandwich for Bernie and a Slim Jim or two for me. Can you lose with a combo like that? We never had. Tuna sandwich, Slim Jims, .38 Special. Remember that and you'll come up roses. Just watch out for the thorny parts, which can mean a trip to the vet.

Bernie gazed over my head, past the stream, the hills rising on the other side, all the way to some red-gold cliffs in the distance, cliffs with spiky rock towers at the top.

"The Hole in the Wall's somewhere up there, big guy." He closed the notebook, got everything put away, crossed the stream with the backpack slung over one shoulder and his shoes in his hand. My Bernie! But he looked more worried than ever. "Let's see if we can pick up the pace."

I was off like a shot.

"Smell Olek, Chet?"

I did not. We were climbing a steep hill on one of those trails that was not always visible. Fine with me. No Olek smell, no human smell at all other than Bernie's, always a comforting one to have nearby. Also we had scents of elk, snake, fox, bear, bighorn sheep, wild turkey, coyote, on and on. What a highly entertaining hike from the nose's point of view!

We reached the top of the hill, which turned out to be the last hill on the hike. Ahead, a rocky plain extended all the way to the base of the red cliff. The cliff wasn't totally straight up and down until almost the very top. I thought I could make out a trail switchbacking up the not-totally-straight-up-and-down part, but I wasn't sure. Above the end of the trail, if that's what it was, I saw a black hole in the face of the cliff.

Our own trail led across the plain, but a sign was posted on the very last tree in the forest. Bernie read it: "'Trail closed. Do not proceed under penalty of law. By order of the USDA Forest Service.'" We kept going. Bernie gave me a glance, a certain kind of glance that means, *Anything up, big guy?* Was this about Olek again? There was no Olek scent in the air. There might have been a whiff or two of other human scent, but it was a bit confusing at the moment because of a vinegary smell streaming in on the breeze. Up ahead, the sun, getting lower in the sky, dipped below the top of the cliff and put us in shadow.

Sometimes in our part of the world you can see where you're headed—in this case, the tall red cliff with the black hole in its face—but it won't come any closer, even might try to move farther away. That was what we had happening now, me and Bernie. He began to jog. I trotted along beside him. How worried he was, and what a hurry we were in! I suddenly thought of Gail. Bernie sped up a bit. I trotted along beside him.

The sky was purple with orange streaks, and the shadow of the cliff was almost as dark as night when we finally reached it. Bernie gazed up at the cliff face, not straight up and down until you came to a ledge quite a way below the black hole. From here, I could see something I hadn't been able to before—a rope ladder dangling down and down from the mouth of the black hole to the ledge below.

We started up the steep zigzagging path, me first, but when I glanced back and saw Bernie had to go down to all fours on the toughest parts, I moved behind him, just in case. Bernie on all fours is not at his best. He was dusty and sweaty when we reached the ledge, and there was a line or two on his face that I'd never seen before.

It was as close to silent on this ledge as the world ever gets. A little green lizard with a yellow head ducked under a rock partway down the switchback trail, and I heard the scramble of its tiny, hard feet. But other than that, we were soundless. Bernie gave me another of those searching looks. The air began to smell of vinegar. There were other scents, too, but with vinegar around, they just wouldn't line up for me. Bernie took the .38 Special from the backpack and stuck it in his pocket. He lay the backpack beside me, crouched down, rubbed the top of my head. "Sit," he said. "Stay. Guard the backpack for me."

I sat. I stayed. I guarded the backpack. Bernie gave me the silent signal—finger across his lips—walked over to the rope ladder, got a grip with his hands, and started up. We'd done lots of ladder work, me and Bernie, and I was not bad on them, not too bad at all, but we hadn't gotten to rope ladders. This one swayed and wobbled as Bernie climbed. That didn't slow him down in the slightest. Higher and higher he went at the same steady pace, hands and feet, arms and legs, his whole body in beautiful motion. He reached the lip of the back hole, pulled himself up, gave me a quick glance—even a quick little wave—and disappeared inside.

After that, nothing. Well, perhaps a faint thump or footstep. I rose. Still staying, of course, as Bernie had suggested. I thought about the faint thump or footstep. I edged over toward the rope ladder, still staying on the ledge, meaning my obedience was beyond question. From above came not a sound, no thump, no footstep. I gazed up at the black hole and placed one paw on the first rung of the rope ladder. It swung away from me. I tried again, and again, and was about to try once more, when a figure appeared up above, on the lip of the black hole. A very small figure, but one I knew. It was Griffie.

I barked, not loudly, a bark partly surprised, partly annoyed, and partly just hi. Then I remembered the silent sign and barked again, much more softly. You wouldn't have heard it, but perhaps Griffie did. He backed away, out of sight.

I got a paw—a front paw—on a rung of the rope ladder, not the lowest as before, but the next one up. That was more or less an accident, but a good one, because one of my back paws got involved with that lowest rung and the next thing I knew, I was sort of on my way up! This was nothing like the wooden ladders of my experience, but definitely doable, as long as I—

A figure appeared on the lip of the black hole. Not Griffie, not at all a very small figure, but a very large one. It was Olek. Olek! I hadn't sniffed a trace of him—hadn't sniffed a trace of Griffie, either, whose smell was much stronger. There was no time to think about any of that. Hateful looks are usually hot, in my experience, but Olek's was cold. He drew a gun from a shoulder holster he was wearing, leaned out over the lip, and fired.

The bullet went by my head, oh so close, the whizzing sound and the bang of the gun happening at the same time. I leaped off the ladder, or maybe fell, stuck my landing, and sprang right off the ledge. Bang! Bang! Bullets tore up the steep slope beyond me even before I landed on it. I hit the ground, not caring whether I was on the switchback trail—trails seldom making much of a difference to me—and darted behind a big round rock that looked like it might start rolling down at any moment.

No more gunshots. But was Olek still watching for me? I took a quick glance. No sign of Olek. The rope ladder no longer hung down, at least not all the way. A rung or two dangled from the lip.

I stayed where I was, hearing nothing. The vinegary smell began to fade away. Up above, purple changed to black, and the stars began popping into view. A faint yellow glow flickered at the mouth of the black hole, but no one came in sight. I moved out from behind the rock and was waiting for an idea, even a bad one, when a familiar smell cut through the night air. From the other direction, meaning the back side of this mountain, came Griffie.

I looked down at him. He looked up at me. I looked down at him some more. He wandered off, past the big round rock and out of sight. I gazed at the flickering yellow light at the mouth of the black hole.

Griffie returned. I looked down at him. He looked up at me. He wandered off, past the big round rock and out of sight. This time, I followed him for no particular reason.

A starry night, the stars shining in Griffie's eyes whenever he turned back to look at me, which was more than once. He headed down, then up, but mostly around the mountain, and so did I, Griffie for reasons of his own and me not because Griffie was doing it. Don't think that for a moment.

This was not an easy hike, very steep at times, some shifting scree along the way, and a surprising number of small round cactuses, very spiny. Griffie had no trouble with any of it, so neither did I. After what seemed like a long time, we stood at the very top. I went to the front edge and peered out from between two rocky towers. Not far below lay the lip of the black hole, with the coiled-up rope ladder, and below that, the ledge with our backpack, still lying there.

Griffie was not interested in the view. He stood close to the center of this flat little mountaintop, his attention on a hole in the ground. This was a man-size hole of a type I knew well from our explorations—mine and Bernie's—of old desert mines. Griffie popped down the hole. I stood at the edge. Lots of smells rose up from the hole. One was Bernie's. I popped down myself.

Bernie always brings a flashlight on our tunneling expeditions, but I don't really need the light myself. This particular tunnel would have been pretty easy even without having Griffie to follow. And I wasn't actually following him. He just happened to be ahead of me. We went mostly down but turned sideways at the end, the only tricky part. These bends can get pretty narrow, and sometimes you get stuck, which I did now. The tricky part is not being able to move and the feeling of no air to breathe. But then you hear a voice in your head—namely, Bernie's—saying, *We're good, big guy, just wriggle a bit.* You wriggle and presto! You're free.

We came to the end of the tunnel, me and Griffie. The end of the tunnel seemed to be fairly high up the wall of a sort of cave. The cave was lit by a camping lantern on the floor—we had one just like it—and by the light of the lantern, I saw Bernie! He lay on his back, asleep on the hard-packed dirt floor, his chest slowly rising and falling. Seated on the floor over to one side, hands bound behind their backs, were two women I knew—Mavis and Johnnie Lee. Mavis's face had no color in it at all. Johnnie Lee looked a little better but not much.

Olek sat on the other side of the lantern. Between sips from a vodka bottle—the same magical kind he'd given us—he was building a bomb. I was familiar with bombs because Bernie had spent a lot of time studying bombs, and I spent a lot of time studying Bernie. We'd even built a couple for practice, Bernie handling the actual building.

Mavis started to cry. "Why are you doing this if Mickey's dead? I'll never tell anyone anything, I promise."

"Shut your mouth," Olek said.

Mavis shut her mouth. That was when Griffie decided to leap—well, more of a glide, like he knew how to fly—down to the cave floor. He pitter-pattered over to Mavis, crawled up, and sat on her shoulder.

Olek glanced at the cave entrance. "Where the hell were you, my pretty little souvenir? Come to *tato*."

Griffie didn't move.

Olek patted the floor. "Come!"

Griffie stayed on Mavis's shoulder. Did his presence there give Mavis the courage to open her mouth again? I had no idea, but that was what she did. Johnnie Lee saw what was happening and gave her head a quick little shake. Mavis didn't see, or else she ignored her.

"Please," she said. "I'm begging you." She sobbed. "We're so young. How will you live with your conscience if—"

"Come!" Olek shouted. "Come!"

Griffie did not come.

"You don't obey?" Olek said. He whipped the gun from his shoulder holster, aimed at Griffie, and shot him right off Mavis's shoulder. Well, almost. Just before Olek pulled the trigger, Mavis screamed a terrible scream and the gun barrel wavered the tiniest bit. The sounds of the shot and the scream and the ricochet of the bullet off the rock wall echoed and echoed. Griffie leaped into the shadows.

Bernie moaned and sat up. There was dried blood in his hair, but not a whole lot.

"Now look what you've done," Olek said. He rose, fished plastic cuffs from his pocket, and moved toward Bernie. I sprang out of the tunnel and soared through the air, striking Olek with all my strength and power. He fell and—

But not quite. It was mostly a stagger. I bit his arm with everything I had, our faces so close. Did he hate me? Oh yes, and I hated him just the same. I shook my head back and forth, trying to rip that arm right off him, trying to throw him to the ground, but none of that happened. Instead, Olek raised his other arm. He still had the gun. Olek pointed it right at my face and—

And that was when Bernie tackled him, so hard he swept Olek right out of my grasp. They landed on the ground, crushing a metal canister, from which rose a huge invisible vinegary cloud. Bernie and Olek rolled over and over, ending up near the lantern with Olek on top. He drew back his huge fist and grinned a horrid grin at Bernie. Taking the time to do that was a mistake. Bernie grabbed the lantern and swung it against the side of Olek's head.

The horrid grin froze on Olek's face. Bernie hit him again, much harder. Olek toppled over. The lantern went out, and we had total darkness in the cave.

I heard Bernie rise. "You okay, Chet?"

I was fine. Maybe not quite back to fine and dandy, but fine.

I heard Bernie go over to Mavis and help her to her feet. I heard Johnnie Lee coming the other way. She stopped nearby. I heard her stomp on something, very hard.

"Griffie? Griffie?"

There was a lot of calling for Griffie—more than necessary, in my opinion—but Griffie did not appear. The rest of us hiked out of the forest by starlight, and toward the end, we had moonlight, too. I was first, Bernie last, Mavis and Johnnie Lee in the middle. Mavis cried a lot.

"It's all my fault! None of this would have happened except for me."

"You're being ridiculous," Johnnie Lee told her. "Like he's some wallflower? The asshole's old enough to be your father—grandfather, even."

"That's what I mean! I'm just a stupid no-good whore."

Bernie spoke up, although not loudly. "You're none of those things. And here's how we'll handle this. No one's going to find out from us. I'm talking about your involvement, Mavis. If they find out, they find out, but it won't be from us, and it won't be easy to prove, not without those pictures, which I'll send you today. My advice is to destroy them."

Mavis touched Bernie. "I should have trusted you."

"Well," said Bernie. "Um."

We walked on. After a while, Johnnie Lee said, "So he ends up getting away with it?"

"Who?" said Bernie.

"Wray," Johnnie Lee said.

"Depends what you mean by getting away with it," Bernie said. "And I'm not so sure he was the one in charge."

There was a lot of silent walking after that. Then Johnnie Lee said, "The bumper-sticker-on-the-butt pic should be on the cover of every poli sci textbook in the country."

Bernie laughed. Mavis laughed, too, although it quickly led to tears. And back again.

"I turn out to be the funny one," Johnnie Lee said.

But maybe she was wrong about that, Griffie ending up as the funny one after all. There was certainly a lot of delighted laughter when he popped up out of nowhere and glided onto Mavis's shoulder. On Mavis's shoulder, yes, but giving Bernie one of those adoring looks—completely unacceptable from a certain point of view.

"Should I keep him?" she said.

"Why not?" said Johnnie Lee. "The bastard gave him to you."

"And he seems pretty happy where he is," Bernie said.

So Griffie would be living with Mavis from here on in? I felt a quiet and quite relaxing moment of—what would you call it? Relief? Something like that.

Suzie called. "Your name is coming up."

"Yeah?" said Bernie.

"Supposedly, you were up on stage with Senator Wray the other day."

"Kind of weird."

"So I hear," said Suzie. "From multiple sources. The retiring Senator Wray, as it turns out. He won't be running after all."

"No?" Bernie said.

"Allegedly for health reasons. What do you think of that?"

"Well, he is getting on, and—"

"Bernie, please. It's crap. What's going on?"

"I didn't even know he's retiring until you just told me."

"There's also talk that he and Caroline are splitting," Suzie said. "And that she might run herself. Any thoughts on that?"

"Um, she's a formidable person," Bernie said.

"Can I quote you?"

"I don't see why not, but—"

"Bernie! For god's sake! What's going on?"

"Can't say."

"Can't or won't?" Suzie said.

"Yeah," said Bernie.

"What about the Ukrainian thing? I told you Jacques and I are working on that. Do you think it's worth pursuing? Is there a McGregor angle?"

"Try a guy named Scott Kyle, in that order."

"What else?" Suzie said.

There was a long silence. Then Bernie said, "For you, anything, Suzie, but not this."

We had some other calls, all sent direct to voicemail, one before lunch from the chief of Valley PD, one after lunch from the new chief of Valley PD, and one from Les Erlanger.

"Bernie Little? Les Erlanger, here. I'm running for Senate, as I'm pretty sure you know, heh heh, and I'd love to take you to lunch anytime at your convenience."

Bernie gave me a long look after he listened to that. "Heh heh," he said.

A diamond ring that looked familiar arrived by messenger. We sold it to Mr. and Mrs. Singh and for some reason failed to pocket the money. I believe it ended up at the South Pedroia shelter. Rick Torres sent a case of the bourbon with the roses on the label that Bernie likes, plus a squeaky chewy for me, unfortunately misplaced by Bernie.

We took Charlie to Buckets and Buckets o' Balls, Cheapest Driving Range West of the Mississippi, Come Knock Yourself Out for his very first golf lesson.

"Hold the club like so," said Shaky Insterwald. "Feet this way.

Club head back to right here. Load up your power. Feel your power loading up?"

Charlie nodded a vigorous nod.

"How's your eyes?" Shaky said. "Work pretty good?"

"I think so," said Charlie.

"See the dimples on the ball?"

"Yeah."

"I'm gonna make a red mark on a dimple." Shaky bent down with a red marker. "With them pretty good eyes of yours, you're gonna watch that dimple and you're not gonna look up until I say so. Got it?"

Charlie nodded another vigorous nod.

"Now load up, feel the power, and knock that son of a—son of a gun to kingdom come."

Charlie swung. Crack. The ball took off.

"'Kay," Shaky said. "Look up."

Charlie looked up.

"There's your ball," said Shaky.

He pointed. The ball was surprisingly far away, still rising, straight and true. A lovely look appeared on Charlie's face, an even lovelier one on Bernie's.

We went for a nice walk with Weatherly along the bank of the Arroyo Seco, although we could have walked right in it, the Arroyo Seco being dry, as usual. She'd been reinstated and smiled a lot, also gave Bernie more than one kiss on the cheek. After a while, her face got more serious.

"I've been looking into the Gail Blandina case a little more," she said.

"Oh?"

"Officially unsolved."

"That's my understanding," Bernie said.

"There were a number of potential suspects in the early part of the investigation, but none panned out," Weatherly said. "One was called Melvin Ellis. He didn't have much of a record—just the one conviction for animal cruelty. The last name caught my eye. Turned out to be a distant cousin of our Ellis. They hadn't kept up with each other but had lived in the same house as children."

Bernie nodded and said nothing.

"I tried to track him down," Weatherly said. "Got nowhere. Like he disappeared off the face of the earth."

Bernie nodded and did more of saying nothing. Weatherly gave him a close look, then shook her head and took his hand.

Meanwhile, I came upon what looked like a brand-new tennis ball, all fluffy the way I like it, just lying there on the path. I grabbed it and brought it to Bernie. He hurled it far down the arroyo.

I took off after it. And what was this? Trixie taking off after it, too? Did I mention that Trixie, now coneless but supposedly still taking it easy, had tagged along on our walk?

Now comes something you're not going to believe, so please stop right here.

Trixie got to that tennis ball first! Some might almost say she beat me to it! I knew you wouldn't believe me.

ACKNOWLEDGMENTS

Many thanks to my very talented editor, Kristin Sevick; to Linda Quinton at Forge for her support of this series; to my agents, Molly Friedrich and Lucy Carson; and most of all to the loyal— even passionate—readers of the Chet and Bernie novels: they're the wind at my back.

Turn the page for a sneak peek
at the next Chet & Bernie mystery

BARK TO THE FUTURE

Available Summer 2022

One

"Let's see what this baby can do," Bernie said.

And there you have it. Bernie's brilliance, lighting up the whole oil-stained yard at Nixon's Championship Autobody. *Let's see what this baby can do.* Can you imagine anyone else saying that? I sure can't. I wouldn't even try, and who knows Bernie better than me? Sometimes humans talk to themselves, as you may or may not know. Humans have a lot going on in their heads. Too much? I couldn't tell you. But I wouldn't trade places. Let's leave it at that. The point is that when they're talking to themselves they're trying to dig down through all the too-muchness and get to what's at the bottom, digging, as it happens, being one of my very best things. Maybe we'll get to that later. For now, the takeaway is that Bernie talks to himself in front of me. So I know what's at the bottom of Bernie, way down deep, case closed. Closing cases is what we do, by the way, me and Bernie. We're partners in the Little Detective Agency—Little on account of that's Bernie's last name. Call me Chet, pure and simple. Our cases usually get closed by me grabbing the perp by the pant leg. Although there were no perps around right now and we weren't even working a case, my teeth got a funny feeling.

Nixon Panero, owner of the shop and our good buddy, patted the hood of our new Porsche. We've had others—maybe more than I can count, since things get iffy when I try to go past two—but never one this old. Could I even remember them all? Perhaps not, although I have a very clear picture of the last one in my mind, upside down and soaring through snowy treetops, the windows all blasted out and me and Bernie also in midair, although slightly closer to the ground. I'd miss that Porsche—especially the martini glass decals on the fenders—but this one, with an interesting black and white pattern, as though a normal PD squad car was rippling its muscles, if that makes any sense, looked none too shabby. In fact, and in a strange dreamlike way, a thing of beauty. And to top it off, my seat—the shotgun seat, goes without mentioning—couldn't have been more comfortable, the leather soft and firm at the same time, and possibly quite tasty. A no-no, and I forgot that whole idea at once.

"One last thing," Nixon said.

Bernie, hands on the wheel, ready to go, glanced up at him.

"All parts guaranteed original and authentic," Nixon said. "Excepting certain aspects of the engine."

"No problem," Bernie said. "You're the expert."

"Thanks, Bernie. But what I'm saying is in horsepower terms authentic might be stretching it the teensiest bit. So my advice would be to take it on the easy side at first."

"Sure thing," Bernie said, sliding his foot over to the gas pedal.

"On account of what we've got here," Nixon began, "is kind of a—"

Beast? Was that what Nixon said? I couldn't be sure, because at that moment Bernie's foot—he was wearing flip-flops, one new-looking, the other old and worn—touched the pedal, just the lightest touch to my way of thinking, but enough to get our new engine excited in no uncertain terms. It roared a tremendous roar and this new dreamlike ride of ours shot out of Nixon's yard and into the street. I felt like my head was getting left behind, meaning that shooting out doesn't really do the job here. Was it possible we were actually off the ground? I believed we were.

"Woo-eee!" Bernie cried as he brought us safely down, all tires on the pavement. "Woo-eee, baby!"

As for me, I got my head and body properly organized, sat up straight and howled at the moon, although it was daytime and cloudy to boot. We had a beast on our side. No one could touch us now, although the truth was no one ever had before. I felt tip-top, or even better.

"My god," said Bernie, as we came off a two-laner that had taken us deep into the desert and far from the Valley, where we live, and merged onto a freeway, the tops of the downtown towers visible in the distance, their lower parts lost in the brassy haze. "Can you believe what just happened?" We slowed down to what seemed like nothing, although we were zooming past everyone else. Bernie patted the dash and glanced my way. "Rough beast, big guy, its hour come round at last." That one zipped right by me, but Bernie laughed so it must have been funny. "Did we hit one forty? Next time I'll snap a picture of the speedometer. You'll have to take the wheel."

No problem. That had actually happened once, if very briefly, down Mexico way, where Bernie and I had had to leave a nice little cantina in somewhat of a hurry, following a misunderstanding between Bernie, a very friendly lady, and a late-arriving gentleman who turned out to be her husband and also the head of the local cartel. Bottom line: Bernie could count on me.

Not long after that we were winding slowly down the ramp at the Rio Vista Bridge, close to home. There's always a backup on the ramp, and at the bottom a few leathery-skinned men holding paper cups or sometimes cardboard signs are waiting. Today there was only one, a real skinny barefoot guy, wearing frayed cargo shorts and nothing else, his shoulders the boniest I'd ever seen. He was mostly bald, but had a ponytail happening at the back, a gray ponytail with yellow-stained ends, the same yellow you see on the fingertips of smokers. Also—and maybe the first thing I noticed—a small but jagged scar across the bridge of his nose. A cigarette was hanging from the side of his mouth but its tiny fire had gone out. Traffic came to a stop when we were right beside him. He looked down at us, his eyes watery blue. I was pretty sure I hadn't seen him before, and certain I'd never smelled him. My nose is never wrong on things like that. In this case it wasn't even a close call. Had I ever picked up a human scent so . . . how would you put it? Complex? Rich? Over the top? You pick. As for me, I was starting to like this dude a lot. Meanwhile Bernie dug out a few bills from the cup holder and handed them over.

Except not quite. Yes, Bernie held out the money, but the dude made no move to grab it. Instead he shook his head and said, "Can't take your money, Bernie."

"Excuse me?" Bernie said.

The dude took the cigarette out of his mouth, plucked a little twist of something from between two chipped and yellowed teeth, and said it again.

Bernie gave him a close look. "Do I know you?" he said.

"Guess not," said the dude. He glanced down at the money, still in Bernie's outstretched hand, and his lips curled in a sort of sneer, like that money was way beneath him. "But I'll take a light," he said.

Bernie stuck the money back in the cup holder, fumbled around inside, found a book of matches and held them out. The guy took the matches, broke one off, but he couldn't get it lit, his hands suddenly very shaky. In front us traffic started moving. From behind came honking, not easy on my ears. Bernie pulled off the ramp, getting us mostly onto the narrow dirt strip next to the bridge supports. He opened the door, put one foot on the ground and looked back at me.

"Better stay, Chet."

Too late. Meanwhile the traffic from behind was on the move, perhaps still slightly blocked by us, but hardly at all. A truck driver leaned out of his window, an unpleasant expression on his face. He opened his mouth to say something, saw me, and changed his mind.

"Here," said Bernie, holding out his hand.

"Here what?" said the dude.

"The matches."

The dude handed over the matches. Bernie lit one, cupped the flame. The dude leaned in, got his cigarette going. For a moment, his face—so weathered, wrinkled, with little blotches here and there—was almost touching Bernie's hand, so perfect. The dude straightened, took a deep drag, let it out slow, smoke streaming from his nostrils.

"Waiting for me to say thanks?" said the dude.

"No," said Bernie.

"Then get back in your super-duper car." He glanced over at me, turned away, then gave me another look. "The both of you."

"In a hurry to get rid of us?" Bernie said.

The dude was silent for what seemed like a long time. Then came a bit of a surprise. He smiled. Not a big smile, and lots of teeth were missing and the tip of his tongue was yellow-brown, but he no longer looked quite so messed up.

"You haven't changed," he said. "Always those goddamn questions."

"For example?"

The dude thought for a moment or two. Then he stiffened and shouted at Bernie, a shout with a sort of whispery, ragged edge, so not particularly loud, but real angry. "You makin' fun of me, Bernie? That's another question you just asked. Think I'm nothin' but . . . but . . ." Whatever it was, he couldn't come up with it.

"Sorry," Bernie said, "I didn't—"

The dude's eyes narrowed down to two watery slits. "You was always an asshole but not mean. What the hell happened?"

"Look," Bernie said, "I—"

"Aw, the hell with it," the dude said, his anger vanishing all at once. He waved his hand—fingers bent, nails thick and yellow—in a throwaway gesture. "You stood up for me. I don't forget things like that. Well, I do. I forget . . . you name it." He laughed a croaky laugh that got croakier until he finally spat out a brownish gob. It landed at the base of one of the bridge supports. I moved in that direction. At the same time, the dude took a very deep drag, blew out a thick smoke ball, peered through it at Bernie, then wagged his finger. "But I sure as shit remember that time with Raker."

"Coach Raker?" Bernie said.

"Who the hell else are we jawin' about?" said the dude. "He was gonna bench me for showin' up late to the game against Central Tech and you said hey Coach bench me I forgot to pick him up on the way to school. Which wasn't even true. No way you don't remember that. You were on the mound and don't deny it. Two outs, bottom of the ninth, bases loaded, up one zip, and some dude hits a scorcher in the gap and who runs it down?" The dude tapped his skinny chest. "Game over. Took us to the state, uh, whatever it is."

Bernie has wonderful eyebrows, with a language all their own. Now they were saying a whole bunch, but amazement was a big part of it.

"Championship," he said softly.

"Yeah, state championship, what I said," said the dude. "Next year you guys won it but I was . . . was . . . like movin' on."

"Rocket?" Bernie said. "Rocket Saluka?"

The dude—Rocket Saluka, if I was following things right—nodded a slow, serious kind of nod, and stood very straight before us, there in the bridge shadows, his shoulders back, his scrawny bare chest rising and falling. He and Bernie had played on the same team? Had I gotten that right? Baseball, for sure, bottom of the ninth and bases loaded being baseball lingo, but how was it possible? Rocket was an old man.

Traffic on the ramp was now mostly stop and not much go, meaning folks had plenty of time to check us out. Rocket didn't seem to notice them, and neither did Bernie. He and Rocket were just standing there, Rocket smoking his cigarette, Bernie watching him. At last Bernie said, "I could use a burger."

Rocket nodded another slow, serious nod.

"How about you?" Bernie said.

Rocket took one last drag and tossed the butt away. Bernie ground it under his heel. I took a good close-range sniff of Rocket's brownish gob, lying in the dirt. Was actual tasting necessary? I was leaning in that direction when Bernie made the little *chkk-chkk* sound that meant we were out of there. Burgers or brownish gobs? Burgers! Burgers for sure! But that was Bernie, always the smartest human in the room. Just follow him—especially from in front, like I do—and you can't go wrong.

There are many Burger Heavens in the Valley—just one of the reasons it's the best place on earth—but our favorite is the one between Mama's Bowlerama and Mama's Kitchen, Bath and Fine Art, mostly because Mama owns it, too, and Bernie's a big fan of Mama, has told me more than once that she's what puts America over the top. Perhaps a bit confusing—I had a notion that Bernie and I were Americans and that was pretty much it—but it didn't matter. Mama's burgers were the best I'd ever tasted. I was enjoying one now just the way I liked it at a picnic table on one side of the Burger Heaven parking lot, on a paper plate, no bun, no nothing, and over in a jiff. Bernie sat on one side of the table, dipping fries into a ketchup cup. Rocket sat on the other side. He'd polished off his first burger real fast, taken a little more time with the second, and was now working his way through the next one, the number for what comes after two escaping me at the moment. Except for ordering, no one had said a thing. Now and then, Mama glanced our way from the kitchen window of the hut, her huge gold hoop earrings the brightest sight in view.

Rocket burped, sat back, searched the pockets of his cargo shorts, pulled out a switchblade knife, not an uncommon sight in my line of work, but it seemed to surprise him. He shoved the knife back in his pocket. The top of the handle, rounded off with a green-eyed human skull decoration, peeped out from inside his pocket.

"What you got there?" Bernie said.

"MVP," said Rocket.

"Most valuable player?"

"Close, real close," Rocket said. "Most valuable possession."

"What makes it valuable?" Bernie said.

Rocket shoved the knife deeper in his pocket, the green-eyed skull now disappearing from view. "Let's keep that between the two of us, me and me," he said. "Keep on keepin' it thataway." His hand was still in his pocket, rummaging around. It emerged with a bent cigarette. "Smoke?"

"Sure," said Bernie, meaning he was about to take one of those breaks from giving up smoking.

Now would be when most folks would be expecting Rocket to produce another cigarette, but that didn't happen. Instead he broke the bent one in two and handed half to Bernie.

"Thanks," said Bernie, striking a match.

They smoked in silence for a while, Rocket taking quick glances at Bernie, Bernie looking nowhere special. I got the feeling something might be going on in Bernie's mind, but whatever it was he was in no hurry. I was about to settle down under the table for a little shut-eye when the Burger Heaven back door opened and Mama stepped out with a package in her hand. She came over to the table. Rocket didn't seem to notice her until she was right there. Then he looked startled.

"What the hell?" he said. Rocket's hand went right to his cargo shorts pocket, the one with the flip knife inside.

ABOUT THE AUTHOR

Lannan O'Brien

SPENCER QUINN is the pen name of Peter Abrahams, an Edgar Award winner and the author of the *New York Times* and *USA Today* bestselling Chet and Bernie mystery series, as well as the #1 *New York Times* bestselling Bowser and Birdie series for middle-grade readers. He lives on Cape Cod with his wife, Diana, and dog, Pearl.

spencequinn.com
chetthedog.com
Facebook.com/ChetTheDog
Twitter: @ChetTheDog